UNDER THE Northern Lights

UNDER THE Northern Lights

LINDSEY BROOKES

HARPETH ROAD
PRESS
Nashville

HARPETH ROAD PRESS

Published by Harpeth Road Press (USA)
PO Box 158184
Nashville, TN 37215

POD: 978-1-963483-37-6
eBook: 978-1-963483-36-9
Library of Congress Control Number: 2025942352

Under the Northern Lights: A Charming, Touching Romance

Cover Design by Vanessa Mendozzi
Cover Images © Shutterstock

Harpeth Road Press, August 2025

CHAPTER ONE

"I always save the best for last," Billy, the private tour guide Aurora Daniels had hired through Duck, Duck, Goose Tours out of Juneau, announced with a smile as they worked their way down the hillside's muddy, rain-dampened path.

The best.

Excitement coursed through Aurora. She lived for these moments. For the chance to shoot nature's glory in all its forms through the lens of her camera. If only it weren't raining. It wasn't heavy rain thankfully. More of an inconvenient drizzle.

Billy had been taking her that morning, as per her request, to fishing spots along the river that were off the beaten path to get shots for *World Adventures Magazine.* Aurora had been contacted by the esteemed adventure travel magazine because she specialized in nature photography. Using Aurora's photographs for an article the magazine planned to publish in an upcoming issue would introduce their readers to lesser-known river fishing destinations in the southern parts of Alaska.

The opportunity to work for her dream magazine was even more exciting than all of the awards and accolades she'd received over the years for her photographs. Especially when it came with the very real possibility of being offered a permanent position with the magazine. *If* she delivered exactly what they were looking for.

"It's right down there through those trees," Billy said.

"I can hear it," Aurora acknowledged with a nod.

"I can't imagine the river view being better than the last fishing spot we went to," Aurora said as she eyed the opening at the base of the woods where the hillside appeared to spill out onto an expanse of wet grass. The river was close, its gurgling flow growing louder.

"Just wait," her guide, whom Aurora guessed to be somewhere in his early sixties, said as he grabbed onto one tree trunk after another on either side of the trail, slowing his descent. Age had not made him less sure-footed.

Aurora did the same, following him down the steep hillside at what felt like a snail's pace. It wasn't as if she'd never done this sort of thing before. She had; it was part of being a professional nature photographer. Whether that required climbing mountains or hiking down into valleys, she was all in. Just as she was now, despite the rain. Because there was nothing she wanted more than to get that perfect shot.

Her eagerness to see the pristine Alaskan river, to capture its flow in photographs, had her wishing she could race ahead of Billy. "You don't have to go slow on my account," she said. "I'm pretty nimble on my feet." No sooner had the statement passed her lips than Aurora's boots slipped out from under her. She landed on her backside with a squeal, her backpack somewhat cushioning her fall. Momentum carried her down the hill past her guide, whose expression was one of alarm.

"Miss Daniels!" Billy cried out as she slid down the muddied path.

"I'm good!" Aurora called back as she shot through the opening at the edge of the trees. She kept a protective grip on the camera bag strapped beneath her oversized poncho until her wild ride finally came to an end. Sitting up, she gasped as she took in the grandeur of the nearby river.

"Miss Daniels!" Billy hurried to reach her. "Are you hurt?" he asked with a worried frown, his bushy eyebrows knitting tightly together.

She gave an embarrassed laugh. "Hurt, no. Embarrassed, yes. Nimble? Apparently not as much as I thought myself to be."

Some of the panic eased from his weathered face. "Here," he said, offering her a hand, "let me help you up."

As she got to her feet, Aurora glanced once more at the river. "Another twenty feet or so and I might have been taking a very cold swim today." She laughed. Fortunately, she hadn't. Her cameras were weatherproof, not waterproof.

"You sure know how to age an old man," Billy said with a shake of his graying head.

Reaching up, she quickly worked several damp tendrils of hair back into the ponytail holder they had escaped from. Then she brushed the muddy debris from the back of her jeans as best she could.

"Oh dear," Aurora said as she discovered one side of her rain poncho had ripped apart at the seam during her slide down the hillside.

"No worries. I've got you covered," Billy said. Reaching into his backpack, he pulled out a bright yellow duck poncho with the tour company's name imprinted across the back. One that matched his own. "We always have spares on hand in case our guests need a rain poncho during their tour."

"Thank you," she said as he handed it over to her. "I'll pay you for it when we get back to the SUV."

"Consider it a souvenir," he replied with a smile.

She was grateful for the replacement poncho, duckbill hood or not. It would help to keep her camera bag dry. She switched out of her ripped poncho and into the new one. Then Aurora took a long moment to focus on her surroundings. She used to dream about traveling to Alaska. It was where her parents first met and fell in love. It was also where Aurora and her ex were supposed to spend their honeymoon that very month. But she'd realized, thankfully before it was too late, that they were trying too hard for the romantic, spend the rest of your life together kind of love. Theirs was more of a deep friendship with no real promise of becoming what her parents shared together. After she voiced her concerns and he'd had a few moments to mentally digest them, Ben agreed, and the engagement was over.

Aurora's decision to accept the assignment for the magazine hadn't been as easy as it would have been before her breakup. A part of her feared that being in Alaska might be too painful a reminder of what she'd given up. A safe, comfortable marriage to her good friend. Surely, she and Ben wouldn't have been the first couple ever to marry without those butterflies-when-I-see-you stirrings. However, Aurora wanted more in her marriage. Deserved more. And so did Ben.

Aurora pulled her camera out from beneath the poncho, her gaze fixed on the river. "This spot is picture perfect. If only the drizzle would clear up."

"Do you want to head back up to the Jeep to wait and see if this weather eases up some?"

Aurora shook her head. "I have too much riding on these pictures to let a little inclement weather, or an unexpected slide down a muddy hillside, keep me from accomplishing what I came here to do." She glanced in Billy's direction. "But there's no reason for you to stay down here in this rain. I'm sure I can find my way back up to the Jeep when I'm done."

"I'm Alaskan born," he said. "We're used to the rain. Go on and get your pictures," he added, motioning in the direction of the rushing water beyond the grassy bank. "I'm going to step away and let you do your job."

"Thank you." She smiled back. "I'll try not to lose track of the time." Easy to do when one is caught up in the beauty of nature.

"I'll give a whistle when it's getting close to leaving time. And remember what I told you at our first stop. If you happen to see a bear or moose while you're standing out here by the water—"

"Keep my distance," she finished for him with an acknowledging nod. "I will." Emilia McBain, a.k.a. Emmy, being her very best friend, had already stressed to Aurora before she'd flown to Alaska that while moose are quite huggable in stuffed animal form, they were not anywhere near as cuddly in real life. Especially during mating season, which, according to the internet, they were currently in.

After her guide walked away, Aurora turned and began snapping a few test shots. The lens she'd chosen did well in low lighting and could be safely used in damp conditions.

Stepping forward, she made her way along the river's edge. Aurora focused on taking pictures she believed would stir a fisherman's interest and lure him, pun intended, to

Alaska. Because that's what *World Adventures Magazine* was looking for.

It wasn't until the rain started coming down harder that Aurora was forced to put her camera away. The oversized duck head hood of the poncho Billy had given her had helped to keep the camera dry while she'd been shooting, but the wind had begun to stir, the occasional gusts sending the light rain sideways. She was still careful despite having a waterproof casing over her prized possession.

A loud whistle had Aurora glancing back in the direction from which she'd started. She was surprised to find that she had wandered farther down the riverbank than she'd intended to.

Billy, who gave her the "you don't want to miss your flight" signal, had backed himself up beneath the cover of the trees. His bright yellow duck hood, with its droopy orange bill, was pulled down low over his face to block out the shifting rain as he stood patiently waiting for her to take her pictures.

She returned a quick wave to let her guide know she had heard his whistle as she started back. Fussy weather or not, her day had been a success. The hike back up the wooded hillside with her tour guide was far less eventful, and thankfully so. Her backside wasn't up for another go at being a human bobsled.

"Thank you," she said as Billy hurried past to open the Jeep's passenger door for her. Aurora set her backpack inside and then ducked into the passenger side. Once she'd buckled herself in, she pulled her cell phone from the front pocket of her backpack and checked to see if she had any missed messages. No signal. Aurora pressed the power button, putting her phone to sleep.

"Sorry you spent more than half of your tour in the

rain," Billy apologized as he buckled in and started the engine.

"It worked out okay," she assured him. "I'm sorry you had to stand out there for as long as you did. I completely lost track of time."

"Easy to do when you're someone who appreciates the outdoors," he acknowledged. "And I can tell you do."

She nodded. "This," she said, motioning to the grandeur around them, "truly is my element."

Smiling, he shifted the Jeep into Drive. "If you ever consider living somewhere else, you would make a great Alaskan."

Aurora laughed softly. "I would have to put a little work into my wet hillside descents, but thank you for the compliment."

They had only driven about a mile and a half back on the winding, mostly narrow road to town when Billy slammed his booted foot on the brake. His arm shot out at the same time, instinctively trying to keep Aurora from being thrust forward, despite her already being secured by the seatbelt.

"Hold on," Billy said, his voice calm, though the vehicle fishtailed to and fro on the rain-slicked road.

When the Jeep finally came to a stop, Aurora sank back against her seat in relief. Ahead of them, a waterfall of water, mud, and loose rocks spilled out onto the road and down the mountainside.

"You okay?" the older man asked worriedly as he glanced her way.

Aurora nodded, realizing how close they'd come to being under that sudden deluge. Maybe her having lost track of time back at the river hadn't been such a bad thing after all. "Well, that certainly added a little more excitement to the day."

"Bad timing for a mudslide," Billy replied with a troubled frown as he took in nature's untimely temper tantrum.

Aurora followed his gaze to the still-oozing mess not even ten feet in front of them. "Do we drive through it?" she asked, knowing that driving through flood waters was a no-no, but this was mostly mud and a few rocks they could probably carefully navigate around.

His expression didn't look the least bit reassuring. He gave a firm shake of his head. "Too risky. It's not the worst mudslide I've ever seen. Road's fairly clear. But there's a chance a few trees might still come down with the rainwater running down the hillside." Putting the Jeep into Reverse, he backed safely away from the mess on the road. "We're going to have to wait it out."

"Wait?" Aurora repeated. "For how long?"

"Until I know it's safe to pass through. Don't you worry. We've still got plenty of time," he assured her, his gaze fixed on the road ahead.

"And if the rain picks up?"

As if reading her panicked thoughts, Billy glanced her way. "I'll get you to the airport. Don't you worry."

He'd said it with such determination, Aurora couldn't help but smile. Billy was an Alaskan tour guide for a reason. He understood the area, its beauty and its dangers. She just hoped he wasn't wishful thinking. She knew all about how that usually turned out.

"You really should reconsider my client's more than generous offer," warned Clive Wagner, the intermediary

Spark Capital Management sent with their offer to buy his family's retreat. "If not for your sake, then for the rest of your family, who stand to lose everything if your fishing retreat business goes under. Word around has it that such a time could be near."

Gage Weston gritted his teeth, trying to tamp down his growing irritation. Clive had been relentless in his determination to meet and discuss his client's previous offer to buy Gage's family's property and the business that came with it. The private equity firm Clive represented wanted to come in and build a high-end resort. The reason smaller private fishing retreats in the area were going under. Swallowed up by the bigger, wealthier conglomerate fish.

No, Gage thought angrily as he dug deeper into his store of determination. His family's business was not going to go under. Not if he had anything to do with it. He had agreed to that afternoon's meeting for one reason only—to put an end to the realtor's pursuit once and for all.

Thankfully, the lunch hour had passed, leaving the small port diner empty, except for two elderly local women who frequented Glady's Glacier Grill, where the menu's playful catchphrase was: *Good eats found here, don't Juneau?*

Mrs. Hodgkins and Mrs. Gilroy were chatting away at a two-seater table near the front entrance. They were finishing up their slices of Glady's freshly baked apple pie between sips of hot tea. From where he and Clive were seated across the room in front of a small gaslit fireplace, Gage doubted the women had overheard much of the conversation he and the persistent intermediary had been having.

Redirecting his focus back to the man sent to broker a deal, Gage said evenly, "I'm not sure where you're getting your information from, but Living the Good Life Fishing Retreat is staying in my family where it belongs. It's not for sale. Never has been. Never will be." Leaning forward, he pushed the offer back across the table to Clive and then went back to eating the open-faced pot roast sandwich he had ordered before the other man had joined him.

Clive shoved the paper back into his dark brown leather briefcase. "I had thought you might see things differently now, considering your father's continuing health issues."

Gage's gaze snapped up, pinning the realtor in place. His dad's recovery from the stroke he had a little over ten months earlier was not going to be used as a bargaining chip by Clive Wagner or anyone. "My father is on the road to a full recovery. Until then, all decisions regarding the lodge have been turned over to me. We're *not* selling."

Clive stood up from the table, briefcase clutched at his side.

Gage stood as well.

Extending his hand, Clive said with a sigh, "If you change your mind, you know how to reach me."

Something Gage would not be doing. With a nod of acknowledgment, he extended his hand to the other man in a firm handshake, then stood watching as Clive, along with his client's generous offer, walked out of the diner.

Lowering himself back into his seat, Gage dragged a hand through his dark brown hair with a sigh. Then he picked up his fork and stabbed at the lukewarm pot roast with its now soggy bread base. Not that it mattered. His appetite had left with Clive's not-so-subtle reminder of the issues Gage's family business was facing.

The end of the main fishing season was nearing and that would mean less money coming in. That's how it normally was during the off-season. But the rest of the year always made up for it. However, they had seen a decline in bookings thanks to the opening of the Reel and Relax Resort, a nearby resort offering its guests not only fishing excursions, but spa amenities as well. One of several that had been built along the coastline and on two other remote Alaskan islands in the past four years.

While Gage and his family had made the difficult decision to limit their bookings in the months after his father returned from the hospital, the deluxe resort chain had drawn in several of Gage's regulars. Selling out would be easy, but Gage wasn't looking for easy. He was looking for a way to save his family's legacy.

His gaze shifted to the two elderly women across the room as they stood. Mrs. Gilroy bent to place a tip on the table between the two teacups, and then the two friends pulled on their rain jackets, zipping them up tight.

"Be safe on your flight home, dear," Mrs. Hodgkins called over to him.

"Verna, it's Gage," Mrs. Gilroy said as they tugged the hoods of their jackets up over their beauty-salon-perfected heads. "That young man doesn't need anyone telling him to be careful. No one pilots a plane better than he does."

That brought a much-needed grin to Gage's face. Almost everyone in this part of Juneau knew Gage and his family. Both his father and mother had grown up here, and Gage's family had made plenty of trips into town to pick things up for the retreat over the years.

"You two ladies be careful walking out in that rain. The ground might be slick."

"It's barely more than a drizzle now," Mrs. Hodgkins assured him. "But you're a dear for thinking of us." With a wave, the two women slipped out into the still-slightly-inclement weather.

"Care for a refill?"

Gage turned to find Glady Walters, a close friend of his mother's and longtime owner of Glady's Glacier Grill, smiling down at him, coffeepot in hand.

He nudged his empty cup closer to the edge of the table to make pouring easier for her. "One more for the road, I suppose."

"In your case, I think that would be one more for the air."

Gage chuckled. "True."

Her expression grew serious. "I hope that man finally got the message," she said with a shake of her head as she refilled the cup.

Gage's brow lifted.

"It's a small diner," she admitted with a shrug. "When it's all but empty during the mid-afternoon lull, conversations tend to carry in here."

Which was why he'd chosen that time of day to have his talk with the private equity group's go-between. The fewer people around to overhear their conversation, the better. He wasn't concerned about Glady overhearing. She and his mother had probably already discussed at least some of the lodge's situation. But at the reminder of how easily words carried in the near-empty room, Gage cast a glance in the direction the two older women had been sitting.

"No need to worry about Mrs. Gilroy or Mrs. Hodgkins," Glady assured him. "Those two talk as loudly as they do because they're both hard of hearing."

"That's good to know," he said, relief moving through him. Then, realizing what he'd said, quickly added, "Not that they have hearing issues. I would never think of that as being a good thing."

She laughed softly. "I knew what you meant." Glady

walked over to return the coffeepot to its warmer plate. "Not that my opinion matters, but I'm glad you're not selling out. Too much commercialization in these parts would take away the true charm of Juneau and its surrounding islands."

Before Gage could respond, the door to the diner whipped open, sending the damp chill of the rainy afternoon whirling into the cozy eating area. A misshapen figure draped in a bright yellow, rain-drenched poncho came sloshing in, stopping just far enough inside to close the door behind them. The drooping hood, which resembled a duck's head, effectively covered the newly arrived restaurant patron's face. One thing he did know was that whoever they were, they had clearly been out with one of Juneau's local tour guides. That poncho was a dead giveaway. Whoever it was under the oversized poncho couldn't be more than an inch or two over five feet.

Gage was just about to turn away when a slender, very feminine hand shoved free of the winged sleeves and reached up to push back the wet, duck-beaked hood. Tendrils of damp brown hair were plastered to her cherry-stained cheeks, while determined raindrops clung to the woman's long lashes.

She glanced down, and then, with a gasp and a fretful scan of the room, took a step back to where the oversized, all-weather THANK YOU FOR COMING mat lay just inside the doorway.

Glady, obviously seeing the woman's troubled expression, hurried over to her. "Honey, is everything alright?"

The woman, who looked to be somewhere in her late twenties, nodded in response, sending a spray of raindrops downward. She looked at the wet floor with a grimace. "I'm so sorry about the mess I'm making. I was in such a hurry to get in out of the rain that I didn't even stop to think about bringing it in with me."

"This is Juneau," Glady said, not the least bit concerned. "September tends to be a rainy season. I promise you're not the first to trudge in from foul weather, and you won't be the last."

"If you'll give me a mop, I'll clean it up," the woman offered, fretting her lower lip.

Glady waved the suggestion away. "Now push your suitcase up against the wall and then peel yourself out of that poncho. You can hang it on one of those wooden pegs by the door. When you're done, have a seat at a table close to the fireplace so you can dry off. In the meantime, I'll go get some hot tea to warm you up." She hesitated. "That is, unless you'd prefer coffee."

"Tea would be wonderful," the woman answered. "Thank you."

"Get yourself settled in. I'll be back in a few," Glady told her before scurrying back to the kitchen.

Gage watched as the woman peeled the oversized rain poncho off, surprised to see a camera bag resting against the side of the insulated parka she wore, its black nylon strap draped over her shoulder and across the coat. What looked to be a very full backpack was strapped securely to her back. That explained the Hunchback of Notre Dame appearance she'd first had when she'd come into the diner.

So, he concluded, definitely a tourist. One who clearly enjoys taking a lot of pictures. She was pretty, her petite form practically swallowed up by the coat and camera bag that weighed her down. She glanced his way and offered up a halfhearted smile. Halfhearted or not, her smile packed quite a punch. Gage felt as though he'd just been trampled by a herd of moose.

CHAPTER TWO

"Wet one out there," Gage said as if the rain-drenched woman wasn't already fully aware of that. Giving himself a mental head slap, he added, "Can I lend you a hand with your bags so you can take off your jacket too?"

The woman looked down as if she'd forgotten they were there and then back up at him. "That's nice of you to offer, but there's no need. I'm used to hauling my bags and carry-on around with me when I travel."

Definitely a serious picture-taker.

"Can I at least help you with your coat?"

She eased her travel-battered carry-on up against the wall where it would be out of the way. "I'm too chilled to take my jacket off right now, but I will need to remove my backpack before sitting down," she said as she struggled to work the straps down over her shoulders while balancing the camera bag dangling at her side.

Gage shot up from his seat and hurried over to where she still stood by the door. "Here, let me help you with that," he said as she pulled her arm free of the first strap.

Lifting the pack off her back, he waited as she twisted slightly, moved the camera bag out of the way, and then slipped her other arm free of the remaining strap as he held it.

"There you go," he said.

Turning to face him, she reached for her bag. Then, looking up at him with a grateful smile, she said, "Thank you."

"My pleasure," he replied, his gaze drawn to those perfectly aligned pearly whites and the naturally full, pink lips that framed them.

"Umm . . . my bag," the woman prompted.

Gage blinked, and then forced his gaze away from her mouth only to have it detour to her thickly lashed, chocolate-brown eyes. Giving himself a mental kick in the backside, he looked down at the strap still held firmly in his grasp at his side. Inches above which, her much smaller hand awaited the bag's release.

"Sorry, I was . . . uh, just making sure you had a good grip on it before I let go. The bag's pretty heavy."

"I've got it," she assured him with a grin.

Releasing his hold on the bag, Gage offered up a quick smile. "All yours." Then he turned and made his way back to his table, trying to gather his scattered thoughts. He wasn't even sure what had caused them to be that way. Maybe he'd better refrain from drinking any more coffee, even if that meant wasting the cup Glady had just poured for him.

Attempting to block out all thoughts of the woman standing across the room hanging up her poncho, Gage forced himself to redirect his focus to his own issues. Mainly, keeping his family's fishing retreat from going belly-up in these ever-changing times.

The kitchen door swung open.

"Here's a selection of teas for you to choose from," Glady announced as she returned to the dining area. Crossing the room, she set the basket of assorted tea bags down onto the vacant table next to Gage's. "Come on and have a seat over here before you catch yourself a chill. You can warm yourself up by the hearth while you drink your tea. The water is heating on the stove as we speak."

"Thank you." The woman hesitated, glancing down at her feet and then back up at Glady with a troubled expression. "I should probably take my hiking boots off first. They're pretty damp from the rain, not to mention a little muddy. I'd hate to track water and mud across your floor."

"That's what mops are for," Glady said. "Now leave those boots on and bring yourself on over here by this cozy fire before you catch your death."

"Thank you."

Gage fought a grin as he watched the woman practically tiptoe across the room in the direction of the table Glady had insisted she take. One a mere three feet or so away from his own.

She lowered the hefty backpack onto the floor next to one of the table's legs and then settled herself, cameras and all, into the chair facing the fireplace. Facing him.

If only he'd chosen to sit where Clive Wagner had been sitting instead. Then the pretty newcomer wouldn't be right in the line of his far-too-curious vision. Gage watched as she pulled her cell phone from her coat pocket and began tapping at the screen as if searching for something.

Gage glanced away, not wanting to be caught staring. A moment later, she placed a call. His gaze did a slow, casual sweep of the room, trying to look at anything but the woman seated in his direct line of vision. Even that hadn't kept him from noticing that her focus had been on the lace tablecloth before her, a slight frown pulling at the perfect contour of her full lips.

"Hi, it's Aurora," she began with a worried frown and then went on to tell whoever was on the other end of the call that she had missed her flight and would let them know once she had booked another flight home.

Wanting to give her a little more privacy, Gage shifted his chair slightly and then extended his flattened hands toward the heat rising from the flames inside the fireplace. Out of sight was not out of mind, or, in this case, out of hearing. As Glady had pointed out, voices carried in the near-empty diner, and the woman's conversation didn't have to travel far to reach his ears.

She told someone by the name of Emmy that she had gotten caught in a mudslide during her tour and that was how she'd ended up missing her flight back to Seattle. She stressed to the other woman that she was uninjured and would call her once she had flight info to give her. The call ended with the beautiful, bedraggled traveler telling Emmy not to worry, she hadn't hugged a single moose.

Hugged a moose? It took everything in Gage not to look her way.

"Here you go," Glady said as she emerged from the diner's kitchen. She made a beeline to the woman's table, steaming cup of hot water centered on a saucer in hand.

"Oh, thank you," the woman said as Glady placed the teacup and saucer down onto the table in front of her. Reaching out, she began sifting through the basket of flavored tea bags until she found one to her liking.

"If there's anything else I can get you, you just let me know," the older woman offered.

"This tea is exactly what I needed to help chase the chill away while I try to reach the airline," she replied. "I should have been boarding my flight back to Seattle as we speak, but I was unexpectedly delayed by a mudslide during a tour I booked and missed my flight."

"Oh no. I'm so sorry to hear that," Glady empathized as she moved about the room, wiping empty tables with a damp rag. "Even if your visit here hasn't gone quite as you had planned it to, we're—and I'm speaking on behalf of the town—more than happy to have you here with us a little longer. Welcome to Juneau, Alaska. I'm Glady, owner of this lovely little establishment."

"It's so very nice to meet you, Glady," the woman answered with an easy smile. "I'm Aurora. Aurora Daniels."

Appropriately named, Gage already decided. Just like the aurora borealis drew one's gaze to its beauty, so did this young woman's naturally pretty face. Gage winced inwardly. When had he begun to think so poetically? That was more his brother Reed's thing.

Gage wrangled his errant gaze back to the coffee cup that sat on the vinyl lace tablecloth before him. *Focus on your own problems*, he mentally scolded himself. The woman was in a safe, dry place, and her missed flight could be rebooked.

"A mudslide's not the best way to end a tour," he heard the always-friendly diner owner say.

"No, it's not," Aurora replied and then went on to explain, "I was on a private tour with—"

"Duck, Duck, Goose Tours," Glady finished for her.

Aurora looked her way in surprise. "How did you know?"

The older woman laughed softly. "The poncho you

wore in was a dead giveaway. Especially with Duck, Duck, Goose Tours printed in bold, black letters on the back of it."

"Of course." Aurora giggled softly. "That would make it pretty obvious. I slipped in the mud while coming down the hillside and tore my poncho. The tour operator was kind enough to give me one of the company's."

"Oh dear," Glady gasped, a look of concern crossing her face.

Gage couldn't help himself. He looked in the women's direction, zeroing in on the pretty newcomer. "You aren't hurt, are you?"

She met his worried gaze and shook her head. "No. Thankfully, all of my limbs are still intact."

"That's good," he replied, relief sweeping through him.

"Why on earth did Billy have you out traipsing about rain-slicked hillsides?" Glady asked, clearly disapproving.

"I knew there was a possibility of rain today," the woman answered honestly. "But that wasn't going to keep me from doing what I'd come to Juneau for. So getting caught in the rain was all my fault. Not his," she added in the older man's defense, something Gage admired. Some travelers in her predicament might have tried to throw the local tour operator under the proverbial tour bus.

"Rain comes and goes in September," he said.

"Mostly comes," Glady chimed in with a nod as she straightened her ruffle-trimmed apron.

"I hope you were able to enjoy at least some of your Duck, Duck, Goose tour, despite all the unplanned excitement you've had today."

"I did," she replied. "Billy took me around to some of Juneau's off-the-beaten-path prime fishing streams."

"All this beauty to see," Glady said with a sweep of her arm, "and that old man takes you to fishing spots?"

Aurora laughed softly. "I hired him to take me to those places so I could get pictures. It was a great day, despite the rain, an untimely mudslide, and a missed flight."

This time it was Gage letting out a chuckle. "I'd sure like to know what you consider a bad day."

"Cup half full," she replied with a pretty smile.

Glady groaned in empathetic commiseration. "I bet Billy felt just awful about you missing your flight."

"He did," Aurora acknowledged with a nod. "He even offered to refund my money, but I assured him it wasn't his fault. The tour was well worth the cost. I was able to get a lot of what I think will be really good pictures for a job assignment I came here on."

"Well, I hope you did too. So how did you end up at Glady's Glacier Grill?" Glady asked. "The airport for Juneau is in the other direction."

"When we realized I wasn't making my flight, I asked Billy where he would recommend to get something warm to drink while I work on rescheduling my travel plans. He suggested your place and was kind enough to drop me off right out front on his way back to the company's tour office. I just hope he doesn't get in trouble for running late getting back."

"I think his job's safe," Glady replied. "Billy owns Duck, Duck, Goose Tours."

"He does?" Aurora said, thickly lashed doe eyes widening. "He never mentioned that."

"I'm not surprised," Glady said. "Billy's not a boaster. But he's very good at what he does. People have traveled to Juneau from all over the world just to have Billy take them out on private tours."

"I believe that," Aurora replied. "He seems to know all the perfect places to go."

Gage found himself more and more drawn into the conversation going on next to him. Her response to Glady explained the size of the camera bag she had with her. It was part of whatever her job was.

Glady nodded toward Aurora's cup. "I should let you be so you can enjoy your tea."

"I don't mind the company," Aurora replied. "I really appreciate the warm welcome you've given me." She glanced toward the entrance. "Especially after I made such a mess at your front door."

Glady waved that statement away. "You have more pressing issues to worry about at the moment. Like making calls to those who will be worried about you not making your flight."

"I already let my friend Emmy know what happened. Now I just need to book another flight back to Seattle."

"There is a vast expanse of untamed land around here. Your husband isn't with you?" Glady said speculatively, casting a glance in Gage's direction. As if her question and Aurora's impending response were supposed to mean something to him.

The woman paused for several long moments as if Glady's question had struck a nerve, then shook her head. "I don't have one."

"Forgive me for asking," the diner owner replied apologetically. "What on earth is wrong with young men these days, not snapping up a pretty little thing like you?"

Aurora laughed. "Thank you, but I can't place all the blame on them. I'm not looking for just any kind of love. I'm looking for the all-encompassing love my parents found and don't want to settle for anything less."

"Well, good for you, standing your ground. One of these

days the stars will align just right, and you'll find that love you're searching for."

"I hope you're right," she replied with an earnest smile. "In the meantime, what I'm in search of is a place to stay for the night. I know it's busy season, so my options are probably greatly limited. Would you, by any chance, have any suggestions?"

"As a matter of fact," Glady said, pinning Gage with her gaze, "I do. Let me introduce you to the handsome young man seated at the table next to yours. Gage," she called out, giving him no choice but to look in their direction, "this is Aurora Daniels. Aurora, meet Gage Weston."

He wasn't sure "young" was a category he still fit into, considering he'd turned thirty-two on his last birthday. But he supposed to Glady he was still the young boy she'd known since he was born.

"It's nice to meet you, Aurora," Gage said with a polite nod and a friendly smile.

"Same here," Aurora replied as their gazes met and held.

"As I'm sure you're already aware, *Miss* Daniels missed her flight back to Seattle. Do you think you might have room for her at your resort?"

"You have a resort?" she asked, hope lighting her eyes.

"It's a family-owned fishing retreat on Conley Island, a short flight from Juneau."

"Maybe she could fly with you back to the island." Glady looked at Aurora. "Gage here is a pilot. Even has his own plane."

Aurora looked his way, brown eyes wide. "You own a plane?"

"It's a floatplane," he explained. "We use it to shuttle

guests to and from Juneau to Conley Island, where my family's fishing retreat is. Ten passenger max capacity."

Hope flickered to life in her eyes. "Would you happen to have a room available for tonight?"

"There should be a room open in the main lodge and a cabin or two open in the outer lodging areas."

"A cabin sounds wonderful."

"They're not fancy," he warned.

"Nonsense," Glady said. "I've seen them, and they are as cute as a button."

He put up his hands. "Any and all decorating credit goes to my mom and my sister."

"And we'd have to fly to get there?" Aurora asked, sounding beyond excited by the idea of it.

"You should know up-front that a floatplane isn't like a roomy jet airliner," he said. "It's a lot tighter quarters. And you're going to feel a lot more movement when you're in the air. You don't get motion sickness, do you?"

She shook her head. "No. I've flown in small planes, even in helicopters. As long as you're an experienced and licensed pilot, I'm good."

"He's more than experienced," Glady said with a bright smile. "Gage is one of the best bush pilots in these parts, flying into remote areas where other types of transportation can't get to as long as there's water for him to land his plane on."

Gage wanted to roll his eyes. Glady made him sound like some sort of superhero, which he was far from being. If he were, his taking over the running of his family's lodge would have been the answer to everything. It hadn't been.

The sound of a phone ringing on the other side of the partially open kitchen door drew Glady's gaze in that direction. She cast a hurried glance at Gage and her stranded patron, and offered up an apologetic smile. "If you two will excuse me, I need to grab that." Without waiting for a reply, she spun about and hurried back to the kitchen, her long, white apron strings swinging to and fro behind her as she went.

"Thank you for coming to my rescue in this unexpected situation," Aurora said with a sweet smile.

Gage shifted his attention back to the woman, finding her expression desperately hopeful. Similar to the one his father had been wearing when he'd handed the running of the family fishing resort over to Gage. Like he had every faith that Gage could step in and make things right.

Not one to let his father down, Gage had done his best to bring in more business. Even though they'd experienced a small uptick in bookings, he'd be lying if he didn't admit, if only to himself, that there were times it felt as though he were fighting a losing battle. Longtime clients were being lured away, little by little, to those newer fishing retreats that offered not only an Alaskan fishing experience, but all the bells and whistles of high-end resort living.

"I don't want to be an imposition. I can hire a boat to take me to your family's retreat if you have a cabin I could rent for the night."

Her words pulled Gage from his warring thoughts and back to the predicament Glady's overly enthusiastic boasting had gotten him into. Living the Good Life Fishing Retreat was very well-kept, but not the kind of resort women Aurora's age expected to stay at. His polite refusal trailed off as he took in the sight of her sitting there. Cheeks still a deep pink from the chill outside. Damp strands of shoulder-length hair hanging limply around her face where the rain had worked its way under the loose edge of the duck poncho's hood. And those eyes. Big brown eyes, rimmed in long, thick lashes, looking up at him with such hope it tugged hard at his heartstrings.

Gage knew at that moment that he was going to be the hero she was hoping for, because for him not to be that hero meant turning away someone in need. Something he would never do. With a resigned nod, he said, "No need. I'll take you."

Relief washed the worry away from her pretty face. Then those full pink lips drew upward. "Are you sure? I'll pay you for flying me there."

He couldn't help but chuckle. "I'm sure. And I'm not about to charge you when I was flying back to the island anyway."

She smiled up at him. "Thank you."

"I couldn't very well leave you stranded here in Juneau. Just let me know your rescheduled flight time when you have one," he said. "I'll make sure to have you back to town in time to get to the airport."

"As soon as I book it, I will. I have to admit that I'm tempted to stay longer. Juneau is amazing," she said with an almost wistful smile. "I absolutely love the raw, untouched land that makes up so much of this area."

She's saying that now, Gage thought to himself, memories of his ex's opinions of Alaska shoving their way to the surface. Tuck this newcomer away for a few days in the wilds of Alaska, and she'd be singing another tune. Just as Jess had done after she'd moved to Conley Island from Anchorage, where she'd lived the life of luxury beneath her wealthy parents' roof, to be closer to Gage. She'd wanted to work at the lodge alongside him and his family.

The isolation Aurora Daniels found so alluring would no doubt become unbearable for her, too, were she to spend any real length of time there. It took a certain kind of woman to take on the harsher elements that were a part of his world.

"Oh, and did I mention how in awe I am of Alaska's snow-covered mountain peaks? And the varied array of wildlife?"

"Don't forget the rain," he teased as his gaze took in the bits of mud clinging to the damp denim of her jeans from the knees down. At least she'd worn sensible hiking boots for that day's outing.

"Even the rain," she answered with a nod. "Despite it having been the sole cause of my not getting as many river shots today as I had hoped. As long as I managed to get even three or four good shots, it will have been worth it. Besides, I have other river pictures that I got before flying into Juneau."

"You're looking specifically for rivers to photograph?"

She met his questioning gaze. "Yes. They're for a magazine I've been wanting to get my work into for what feels like forever. This is my big chance. All I have to do is stay focused and get those incredible shots."

She'd definitely piqued his interest with this unexpected tidbit of information.

"So, you're a professional photographer?"

"I am. A professional wildlife photographer, actually."

"Most of our guests come to our resort with the intention of going out on one of the lodge's fishing boats into deeper waters," he explained. "But we do have a few guests who prefer to remain on land to fish as Conley Island boasts several rivers that are more than abundant with salmon and trout."

"It does?" she said with unrestrained excitement as she moved to sit at his table in the chair opposite without prompting of any sort. "Tell me more about Conley Island."

"It's a little more rustic than what you're probably used to," he warned. It was definitely a far cry from life in Seattle. Not that his family didn't do their best to see to their guests' needs. "The main lodge, where my family stays and guests eat and socialize, is skirted by a dozen studio and one-bedroom cabins. It's fairly remote. Guests can only get to the island by floatplane or by boat."

Why was she still smiling? Gage sighed as he went on. "Living the Good Life Fishing Retreat is located in a fairly remote area. No stores for shopping or fancy restaurants for dining out. Just a small gift area at the lodge next to the front desk. Sit-down, family-style meals are served for breakfast, lunch, and dinner to any guests who choose to eat at the main lodge. Oh, and it can get black as pitch when night settles in."

"That sounds perfectly wonderful," she said with a soft sigh.

His dark brows lifted. "It does?"

"Very much so," she replied. "Visiting your island will give me the chance, however briefly, to experience even more of what Alaska has to offer. I'm so excited to stay in one of your cabins with the wilderness wrapped around me."

"That same wilderness will be 'wrapped' around you every time you walk from your cabin to the main lodge. It's not unheard of to have a bear, or two, pass through. Even elk, males in particular, tend to be more aggressive in the fall. So if you'd prefer to stay at the main lodge, I'll see if we have any rooms ready when we get to the island."

"I appreciate the offer and the warning, but I'm good with a cabin. Let me know what I'll owe you for tonight."

"No charge," Gage heard himself say and immediately wanted to kick himself in the backside. Offering free lodging, even for one night, was no way to get his family's business turned right-side up again.

"I insist," she replied determinedly.

Take the offer, his head screamed. But compassion effectively shoved common sense aside. He was not about to take advantage of someone who was down on their luck. That would make him no better than Clive Wagner.

"Look," Gage said with a sigh, "the cabin is sitting there empty, which means we weren't going to make anything off of it tonight anyway."

"If you're sure," she said hesitantly.

"I'm sure," he replied.

Her gaze drifted down to the plate in front of him where a now-cold chunk of pot roast and a lump of cold mashed potatoes sat. "I'm so sorry. I've been sitting here talking away and keeping you from finishing up your meal." She pushed away from the table.

"You don't have to leave."

"You might starve if I stay there asking you a million questions," she told him as she returned to the other table.

Part of him wanted to insist she join him again and ask any questions she might have. But he refrained. If he didn't finish his now-cold meal, Glady would be wondering if her cooking that afternoon wasn't up to par. Besides, he needed a bit of space to let his head clear. To process how it was he'd gotten so distracted from the reason he'd come to town in the first place.

"If it's not raining tomorrow morning," Gage told her as he picked up his fork, "and if your flight doesn't go out early in the day, I'd be happy to take you to a couple of picturesque river spots on the island. That is, if you're interested."

"There's no 'if' about it," she replied, her eyes alight with excitement. "I would love that."

You would have thought he'd just given her a rainbow, complete with a pot of gold beneath, from the way Aurora's face lit up. Her reaction made him feel like the superhero Glady had tried to make him out to be. Almost ridiculously so. And he kind of liked it.

CHAPTER THREE

"Here she is," Gage announced with a smile as they started toward his pride and joy. The floatplane was secured to the dock a good ten or so feet ahead of them.

Aurora lifted the overhang of the duck hood to get a better look. "It's bigger than I expected," she noted as she eyed the long floats on either side, which were bobbing gently in the water next to the dock it had been secured to.

"It being a ten-seater makes for far fewer trips when transporting guests to and from Conley Island."

"It's really pretty."

He knew she was referring to the strip of snowcapped mountains with a bald eagle soaring majestically above. "My brother dabbles in artistic painting in his spare time. Mostly to my plane and the retreat's two fishing boats. But you might catch him on occasion painting on an actual canvas."

"Well, he's very good at it," she admitted. "He and Emmy would get along great."

"Emmy?"

Her gaze shifted to the tall, very attractive pilot walking

next to her. "My best friend. She makes a living as an artist and recently opened her own art gallery in Seattle."

"Sounds like they would have a few things in common," he agreed. "So you're here for river pictures, right?"

"Yes."

"Well, you might be able to grab a few shots from the plane if you keep your eyes peeled."

"That would be wonderful!"

"Let's get you onboard. You're welcome to sit up front next to me during the flight. Or, if you're not comfortable getting an up close and personal view of Alaska from the air, you can take one of the backseats and close your eyes."

"The front works for me," she said, looking forward to the unplanned flight.

"Then the front it is," he replied with a nod. "I'll have you board via the rear passenger entry door. It's a more accessible opening with wider steps. Once onboard, you can make your way up to the front passenger seat."

She smiled up at him. "Sounds like a plan."

"I'll load your bags first," he began as he moved to take the handle of her wheeled carry-on from her grasp. "They'll be safe in my plane."

"Be careful. The zipper is broken," she warned.

Aurora had insisted on pulling it to the plane on her own. Now he understood why. The zipper around the top of the carry-on had pulled apart, wide enough that several pieces of clothing were protruding through the opening and were clearly wet. And the rain had, no doubt, soaked down into the clothes inside the bag.

"You should have said something. I would have carried it instead of you wheeling it up and down over sidewalks and across the road and risking that zipper giving way altogether."

"You're doing enough for me already. The last thing I wanted was to burden you any more than I already am."

"It's not a burden if I offered to help you," he told her. A dark brow lifted as his gaze zeroed in on the broken zipper. "Now I know why you opted not to change into something dry before we left the diner. Everything in that bag is probably at least a little bit wet."

"That would be my guess too," she said with a frown as she stared down at her wheeled carry-on.

"Would you like to make a stop in town and pick up something dry to change into before we fly out? I'd offer to give you a dry sweatshirt from my family's minuscule gift shop, but I wouldn't want you catching a chill on the way there."

"It's okay," she replied. "I'm alright."

He didn't miss the slight shiver that ran through her. Not surprising. The rain left a bit of chill in the air. Combine that with damp pants and hair and you were going to be uncomfortable.

"I insist," he countered. "It's only a short walk back to town where you can pick up something dry to wear. And from the look of things, I'd say the rain will have passed through by the time we fly out if we take this little detour."

"Is it better not to fly in a floatplane in the rain?" she asked.

He chuckled. "I'm not concerned about this light rain. I was thinking more about your being able to get better pictures while we're up in the air if it's not raining."

"I hadn't thought about that. I suppose I should at least try and find something in one of those shops we passed. I'd hate to get into your nice plane with dried mud on the back of my jeans."

"I think you'd be more comfortable. But be forewarned,"

he told her, "your shopping options will be limited to our local gift shops. The retail clothing stores here in the port area of Juneau tend to close earlier in the day, starting mid to late September." Gage held out his hand. "Hand me the rest of your bags. I'll lock them in the plane and then walk back with you."

"I can find my way."

"Considering how your day's been going so far, I think I should probably insist on accompanying you," he offered with a grin.

She laughed. "I appreciate you watching out for me." Aurora handed her backpack and prized camera bag over to him. Surprisingly, she trusted him to make sure her things were safe. "That bag rarely leaves my side," she confessed. "At least, during working hours. But then one never knows when the perfect photo op might come about."

"I understand," he said as he collected her things.

Aurora stood watching as he made his way up into the floatplane to store her belongings. The man certainly was agile.

When he came back out, he smiled and said, "Everything's tucked safely away. Ready to go?"

"Ready."

He joined her on the rain-dampened dock.

Aurora spun about to start back in the direction of town. As she did so, her boot slipped on the wet wood, arms flailing beneath the yellow poncho as she attempted to catch her balance. Her efforts proved futile and just when she prepared to go down, strong arms wrapped around her, thankfully stopping her imminent fall.

"You good?" he asked.

"I'm good," she replied, and then he released his supportive hold on her. Aurora attempted to glance up behind her, but her view of Gage was completely blocked by the oversized beak of the rain slicker's hood. It had dropped down over her panicked face during her futile windmilling, but at least it hid the blush that burned her cheeks. "Apparently, it's a good thing you insisted on accompanying me."

A grinning Gage pushed the hood back from her face. "First of all, I'm glad you didn't fall. But I have to admit that it was quite entertaining watching your efforts to remain upright before I got to you."

She laughed. "I'm sure it was a sight to behold."

"Kind of like a duck determined to take flight but never getting liftoff."

"Talk about embarrassing," she said with an abashed smile as she looked up into those humor-flecked blue eyes. Between Gage's tilted grin and that strong jaw framed by a shadow of dark whiskers, the man was beyond attractive in a rugged, outdoorsman kind of way.

Aurora's stomach quivered unexpectedly. What was wrong with her, reacting to this man like that? She promptly collected herself, needing to focus on something other than her rescuer's far too handsome face. So she busied herself with straightening the bright yellow rain poncho. "I promise I'm not usually this accident-prone, or unlucky, for that matter. Today has definitely been an exception."

"You're definitely working hard to put the term 'lucky duck' to rest," he said as he gave the hood of her duck poncho a playful tug.

Laughing, Aurora fell into step beside him as they started for the port's shopping area. Glancing around, she took in the towering mountain range behind the well-kept storefronts with their old-time facades. Gift shops, sunglass shops, jewelry shops, and tour offices lined the busy street.

A few restaurants with local favorites like salmon and clam chowder sat next to the port where the cruise ships docked. Ornate double-lamp streetlights lined the main street across from the tourist shops. Baskets of colorful flowers hung from the lamps, adding to the town's charm.

"Look," Gage said as he stopped to point out an eagle perched atop one of the towering pines that were part of Juneau's natural backdrop.

Aurora let out a gasp. "It looks so majestic sitting there."

He nodded. Then he pulled his cell phone from his jeans pocket and snapped a quick picture. "I'll forward it to you when we get to the island."

"Juneau is such a quaint little town," she said as they continued. "I could've sworn I'd read that it was much more populated."

"You read right," he told her. "Juneau has a population of over thirty thousand."

"Oh, wow." She glanced around, trying to imagine that many people in such a small area.

"Don't let this part of town deceive you," he told her. "Juneau is spread out pretty far with homes and businesses lining the outer edge of this entire mountainous area."

"It's easy to see why so many people want to live here," she said, taking it all in. "It's so breathtaking."

"I'm pretty fond of the place," he agreed. They stopped in front of one of the many gift shops, and Gage made a sweeping gesture with his arm. "Your new wardrobe awaits."

She glanced up, reading aloud the carved wooden sign that hung above the shop's door. "ANNIE'S ALASKAN TREASURES."

"They carry just about everything in there and then some."

She smiled up at him as Gage reached out for the door's pull handle. "So, do you hit up the tourist shops here in town often?"

Gage chuckled as he swung the door open. "Only when I'm in the mood for some locally made chocolate-covered caramels." He motioned her inside. "Or need a gift for that one special lady in my life."

She glanced his way as she passed him, suddenly feeling both guilty and awkward for having admired his handsome features. She should have known a man as attractive as him would have a special someone in his life. "So, you're married?" she heard herself say. Oh, why did she have to sound so disappointed by the thought?

"Far from," he replied as he followed her into the store. "I'm too busy running the retreat to focus on a relationship of any sort. I was referring to my mother."

She'd gone from something akin to disappointment to an unexpected burst of inner joy at learning that Gage wasn't in any sort of permanently committed relationship. That little bubble of joy promptly burst a second later as he admitted that work left him no time for anything more. And why Gage Weston's personal life even mattered, she had no idea. She didn't know him. Would never get to know him. Not with her leaving for Seattle in less than twenty-four hours. Realizing how silly the direction of her thoughts was going, Aurora gave herself another mental head shake.

"I'm sorry your clothing options are limited to more touristy selections," Gage apologized as he followed her through the store.

"Well, I am a tourist," she told him, casting a smile back at him over her shoulder. "It's not like I'll be needing anything fancy for my overnight stay here."

"You might feel that way now," he said with a chuckle

as his gaze moved about the store. "Wait until you see what your options are."

The store was mostly empty of customers now that all but one of the cruise ships had departed. Aurora spied a circular rack of sweatshirts in both pink and pastel tie-dye camo. She moved in that direction with Gage right on her heels.

Lifting the sleeve of one of the camo-design sweatshirts that hung on the circular rack, she looked back at Gage. "What do you think? Pink camo or should I go with the multicolor one? Neither color is really me, but my options really are limited."

His mouth quirked as he eyed the choices before him. "If you're going for straight-up fashion, I think you'd look good in either color. If you're going with a camo print to try and blend in with your surroundings, neither pink nor rainbow-colored is going to do the job. A Mossy Oak-style print would be your best option for that."

"You think?" she asked as she studied her selection.

"But it only comes in men's sizes, which will probably swallow you right up. How about over there?" he asked, nodding toward a circular display stand that had a selection of solid color hoodies.

"Oh, options," she said happily. She stepped over to the nearby rack and began sifting through the hooded fleece tops until she found her size. She lifted its hanger from the rack and then turned to face him. "Better?" she asked, holding it up in front of her.

"I think I'm in love," he said with a grin. His gaze lifted from the hoodie to her face and what had to be very wide, shocked eyes looking up at him.

His words had definitely thrown Aurora for a loop. A really big loop. "Excuse me?" she stuttered as her mind sought to come up with the words he'd actually spoken as opposed to what she thought she'd heard. Because there was no way Gage Weston could like the sweatshirt or her, to the point of professing love for either of them.

He nodded toward the sweatshirt's front. "Apparently, *you're* in love with Juneau."

She followed his gaze downward, seeing the hot pink embroidery centered on the front of the navy-blue hoodie. Looking at it upside down made it hard to read exactly what it said, so Aurora held the sweatshirt away from her. A soft snort escaped her lips as she took in the **I think I'm in love** embroidered in an arch directly above an orca breaching the water, with a tree-covered mountain behind it. A few scattered clouds and a floatplane flying over in the distance completed the design. Below the stitched graphic, only in an upturned arch and smaller wording, were the words . . . **With Juneau, Alaska**.

Aurora giggled. "So very true," she admitted. Juneau was one of those love-at-first-sight kind of towns. It was hard to mind being stranded there. Especially when she was in the company of a very attractive bush pilot who had come to her rescue. Wait until her sister Jade and, of course, Emmy heard all about this travel adventure she'd unexpectedly found herself on.

"It's perfect," she decided. "And I'll have a keepsake to remember my visit to Juneau. Look, you're even on here." She pointed to the tiny, embroidered floatplane.

He gave a husky chuckle. "I guess I am. So other than a sweatshirt with me on it, what else do you need?"

"I'll need something to sleep in." Draping the sweatshirt, hanger and all, over her forearm, Aurora stepped over to a nearby shelving unit filled with neatly folded T-shirts and matching sweatpants and began sifting through the different designs.

Gage leaned in to look over her shoulder. "Do they have any that say—*I got drenched in Juneau?*"

"They might," she replied with a grin as she continued her search, "but I'm not going to stand here wasting any more time by being choosy. A T-shirt is a T-shirt. I don't really care what's on the front of it." After all, she'd only be wearing it to sleep in. She'd rinse her socks and underwear out in the cabin before going to bed and then hang them up with her jeans to dry for the night. Hopefully, she would be able to brush most of the mud from the back of her pant legs once it dried. She hung a baby-blue T-shirt over the sweat-shirt that rested on her arm and then moved over to the sweatpants.

"Here," Gage offered, as the hanger kept catching on things and the T-shirt kept sliding off every time she bent over to sift through for her size, "let me hold those for you while you shop."

"Thank you," she replied with a grateful smile as she handed the sweatshirt and T-shirt over to him. "It looks like these sweatpants only come in men's sizes. I'm looking for a small."

"I think you'd be more of an extra small. Probably not a size they carry many of," Gage noted.

Obviously not, she thought with a frown. "I'll have to make do with what I can get. Beggars can't be choosers and all that."

Gage looked at her apologetically. "Sorry."

Didn't it just figure? "It's not your fault." Reaching out, Aurora snagged a pair of size small, navy-colored sweat-pants from the shelf. Then she turned to Gage. "I think I'm ready."

With a nod, he led her back toward the front of the store.

"Gage, wait," Aurora called out, pausing briefly at a clearance rack with several fun pairs of red boxer shorts with tiny moose all over them. Upon closer inspection, she was delighted to discover they came with a pair of matching moose socks. She quickly, and thankfully, found her size and then turned to find Gage, grinning down at her selections.

One dark brow lifted. "Moose boxers?"

"I'm buying them for the socks," she said. Although she'd probably use the boxers as sleep shorts in warmer weather. "I thought I might need them for sleeping in the cabin tonight. Then I'll wear them tomorrow when you take me back to Juneau."

"The cabins are heated, but it's probably not the same kind of warmth you're used to, so socks for sleeping in are a good idea. Anything else you need?"

"I'm all set. Ready to check out."

He led her over to one of the registers where another customer was in the process of checking out. Once there was room on the counter, Gage set Aurora's purchases down on it.

Aurora followed suit, placing the boxers with socks set next to them. While they waited, Aurora perused the display stand just before the checkout counter. Spying a wicker basket filled with souvenir lip balms, she plucked one up to add to her other purchases.

"Did you find everything you needed?" the young woman behind the checkout counter asked as she reached for Aurora's purchases to begin ringing them through.

"Actually," Aurora said, spying a selection of specialty caramels next to the register, "I'll have one of these as well."

The display tag said they were locally made, so she hoped they were the same ones Gage had mentioned having a thing for. Handing them over to the cashier, she flashed a smile back at Gage. "For your mother. A small token of gratitude for her son having come to my rescue."

"You don't have to do that," Gage told her. "I'm happy to help out."

"Hello, Gage," the young woman behind the counter greeted with an eye-fluttering smile.

"Sheila," he replied with a friendly nod.

"Long time no see," she practically cooed.

"The retreat keeps me pretty busy."

The cashier's gaze shifted to Aurora, which prompted Gage to make introductions. "Sheila, this is Aurora Daniels. She was out with Billy and missed her flight."

She gave Aurora a once-over. "I thought I recognized that duck poncho."

"My rain poncho had a few issues during my tour today," Aurora explained. "Billy was kind enough to give me one of his."

"I'd say it's the least Billy could do after getting you back late and causing you to miss your flight." She shook her head. "I swear, put that man in the woods and he loses all track of time."

"It wasn't his fault," Aurora said in the older man's defense as she'd done earlier. She certainly didn't want people to think poorly of his abilities as a tour operator for something that was out of his control.

The cashier's eyes lowered to the decorative men's moose boxers and then up to Gage.

"They're not for me," he was quick to clarify, drawing both Aurora and the cashier's gaze his way. "Not that I'm averse to boxers. I'm just not a cutesy boxer kind of guy."

The more he said, the higher the color climbed up his cheeks.

Aurora laughed. "They're for me. I'm buying them for the socks."

"The socks are great," Sheila said, turning back to Aurora. "I bought two different sets of these for myself. One like yours, and the other has little black bear cubs all over them. The socks will definitely keep your feet warm."

Aurora smiled. "That's good to know."

"Will you be staying in Juneau long?"

"It depends on when I can catch a flight out," Aurora told her. "The more I see of Juneau, the longer I want to stay here."

"Understandable." Sheila placed the folded stack of clothes into a plastic bag with the store's name on it. Then she slid the bag across the counter to Aurora. "That'll be sixty-three dollars and ninety-five cents."

After Aurora made her purchase, Gage reached for the bag. "Sheila, do you mind if she uses the restroom to change out of her wet clothes and into some of the clothes she bought here?"

"No, not at all," she replied and then pointed to the rear left side of the store. "It's right back there."

"Thank you," Aurora said.

"I'll wait for you outside," Gage said.

"I won't be long," she promised with a grateful smile.

Aurora changed as quickly as she could. The sweatpants were too long and had to be rolled up, but that was the story of her life. When you were somewhat vertically challenged, pants usually had to be rolled or altered. Today, it was rolled.

When she stepped out onto the covered entrance area

where Gage waited, Aurora's gaze lifted to the lightening sky just beyond the roof's overhang. "You were right."

"About?" Gage asked.

"We shopped long enough for the rain to end."

He grinned. "When you fly as often as I do, you get to know the weather patterns."

"Afternoon, Gage," an elderly man greeted as he and his dog, a beautiful light-haired golden retriever on a bright yellow leash, came toward them up the sidewalk.

"Out for your daily walk, I see," Gage replied.

The older man stopped, giving Gage a chance to give the dog a quick scruff behind the neck. "My Bailey girl here is determined to keep me young," the man said as the dog ate up the attention Gage was giving her.

"She's doing a fine job of it," Gage said.

"Looks like you found someone to help keep you young too."

Aurora returned his kind smile. "Only for a day," she said. "I'll have a flight to catch tomorrow if everything works out."

"Aurora Daniels," Gage said, "this is Mr. Wilson and his faithful companion, Bailey. They live in the apartment above the diner."

"It's so nice to meet you," she said. "You must have the best view of the water and the ships coming in and out."

"We do," Mr. Wilson replied.

Aurora knelt next to the dog. "Aren't you pretty?" Like Gage, she scratched the dog behind its soft, floppy ears. The dog tipped its head into her outstretched hand in a show of both acceptance and affection.

"Pity she's got to leave," the older man said and then, leaning in toward Gage, added, "she's a breath of sunshine on a dismal fall day. Bailey here agrees. Don't you, girl?"

As if on cue, the dog straightened and gave two short barks and then sat there, looking as if she were smiling up at Aurora.

Aurora laughed softly. "Thank you both. That's the sweetest thing anyone's ever said to me."

"Then you're spending time with the wrong 'anyones,'" Mr. Wilson said with a wink aimed in Gage's direction. "Okay, Bailey, time for us to move on. These two have places to be, and so do we."

"See you next time, girl," Gage said, reaching out to give the tail-wagging pup one last ear-scratching. Then he straightened and nodded to her owner, who nodded back as he gathered up his sweet dog's leash and started off down the sidewalk.

Aurora watched as they moved away in the opposite direction she and Gage were going to be heading.

"He's right, you know," Gage said.

She looked his way.

"About your spending time around the wrong people if a seventy-two-year-old man and his dog managed to give you the sweetest compliment you've ever received."

Her head snapped back around. "He's seventy-two?"

Gage nodded with a smile. "Doesn't look a day over sixty. He lost his wife about five or six years ago. Sold his house and moved into the apartment above the diner."

"How heartbreaking. I'm sure being around so many people helps to keep his loneliness at bay," Aurora said with a nod.

"Mom thinks Glady is sweet on Mr. Wilson and that he might feel the same way, but neither of them has ever done anything about it."

"Maybe someday," Aurora said hopefully.

Gage nodded. "Maybe so."

Turning, they started back in the direction of the docks. Aurora's focus shifted to the man walking beside her. Gage Weston was tall, an inch or two over six feet if she had to make a guess. He definitely towered over her own five-feet-two-inch stature. He was lean with broad shoulders and muscular arms, which she'd not missed in the restaurant when he'd helped her with her backpack. What she had really picked up about Gage during their brief time spent together was that he was thoughtful and kind. And, to make him even more likable, he had a soft spot for dogs. She had always loved dogs.

Aurora risked a glance Gage's way only to be on the receiving end of one of his disarming grins. Her heart gave a little flutter. She had to believe his smile had that kind of effect on most women he crossed paths with. It was one she longed to capture with her camera. And people were rarely the subject of her photographs. Her passion was capturing nature. But Gage, in his open khaki jacket, flannel shirt, and slightly faded denim jeans, especially if he were out in the woods, could very well tempt her to capture him in the wild.

CHAPTER FOUR

Gage glanced over at his pretty passenger who had barely spoken a word since takeoff minutes before. Her wide-eyed gaze shifted between the floatplane's front window and the one next to her. Her camera, secured by a slender strap around her neck, was held in both hands, ready for that perfect shot. Aurora's distraction as she captured pictures of the passing landscape gave him the opportunity to really study her.

She had removed the bright yellow duck poncho when they'd boarded the floatplane and had draped it over the seat behind her. Then, after taking a moment to fluff out her shoulder-length, wavy hair, she'd slipped on a fawn-colored knit hat that she'd pulled from one of the outer pockets on her backpack.

Gage had never been so aware of a woman's hair before. The setting sun's golden glow coming in through the windows touched on the still-dry strands that had been protected from the falling rain by her poncho's hood. They weren't the dark brown he'd first thought her hair to be. It was lighter with honey-colored strands mixing in with the slightly darker hue.

"I can't take my eyes off this incredible view," Aurora said in awe as she brought her camera up for another shot.

He knew the feeling. Only it wasn't Alaska that had captured his attention during that flight to Conley Island.

The floatplane dipped, eliciting a startled gasp from Aurora.

"Nothing to worry about. Just an air pocket," he calmly explained in an effort to soothe her concern.

"I know," she replied with a nod. "I gasped because I missed a really great shot of a mountain goat I saw standing on an outcropping."

He chuckled. Of course she wasn't scared by a little midair dip. She'd already survived an unexpected slide down a muddied hillside and then had narrowly missed being swept up in a mudslide.

"Sorry about that," he said.

"It wasn't your fault," she replied, her gaze remaining fixed on the world outside.

"You'll have another opportunity to get some good shots tomorrow when we head back to Juneau."

"As long as the weather cooperates."

"It will," he said assuredly.

She looked his way with a smile that had his stomach flipping. Not in the "I'm not feeling so good" kind of way, but in a way he hadn't felt for a very long time. If ever. Not even with his almost fiancée. It was a sensation he wasn't prepared for, especially since this unexpected stirring was caused by a woman he knew nothing about.

Gage had learned the hard way, two years earlier, that his emotions couldn't always be trusted to guide him in the right direction. Because when it came to Jess, his ex-girlfriend and almost fiancée, his heart had definitely led him astray. Thankfully, Aurora Daniels, with her pretty smile and passion for all things nature-related, would be flying back to Seattle soon. She was definitely a distraction he didn't need. Not right now. His focus needed to be fixed solely on turning things around for his family's business.

"I forgot," she said. "You're not only a pilot and a businessman, you're a weather forecaster as well. Is there anything you can't do?"

"Hula hoop."

Her perfectly shaped brows sprang upward, making it clear that his answer had taken her completely by surprise.

Gage chuckled. "I kid you not. My sister spent hours when we were growing up perfecting the art of keeping that thing going around and around. Every time my brother Reed and I tried to master that particular skill, the hoop would drop to the ground like it was coated in oil and filled with cement."

She laughed, a soft, lilting sound. "I would have so loved to have been there to see that."

"Be thankful you never had the opportunity," he told her with a grin. "I promise you it wasn't a pretty sight. Reed and I looked like a couple of marionettes whose strings had broken where they should have been attached to our hips."

"Oh, the image that stirs in my mind," she replied.

His gaze returned to the expanse of water they were flying over. One lined by jagged mountains covered in pines and rocky outcrops. "How about you?" he asked, determined to steer the conversation away from his hula-hooping shame.

"What about me?"

He glanced her way. "Other than a passion for taking

pictures, made clear by the professional-looking camera bag you carry, what are some of the things that call out to you?"

"Adventure," she replied without hesitation. "Traveling. A starlit sky—something that is rarely visible from the balcony of my apartment near downtown Seattle. And dogs."

"Which you can't have where you're living currently?" he asked.

"No, but my sister has a dog. An Australian shepherd named Mac. So I get to fill my need for canine affection whenever I leave the city to go to Jade's house."

"Jade?"

"My younger sister," she replied. "She and her husband, David, got married last February. They decided to expand their family about five months ago, adopting Mac from a nearby animal rescue. So I guess you could say I'm officially an aunt."

He chuckled. "I guess you are. Have you always lived in Seattle?"

Lifting her camera, she snapped another picture of something that caught her eye down below. "No. I grew up in Oregon. My parents and Jade still live there. But our family sort of began in Alaska."

"Sort of?" he asked, his interest definitely piqued.

"My parents met while working here as wildlife biologists. I grew up hearing all about Alaska's unforgettable untamed beauty." She looked over at him with a smile. "You know, it's possible they visited Conley Island at some point during their time here. They worked and traveled all over Alaska."

"Wouldn't that be a small world," he acknowledged, returning her smile before shifting his gaze back to the flight path ahead. "What did your parents like most about Alaska?"

It took a moment for her to answer, that brief hesitation causing Gage to glance her way. "The Northern Lights," she answered. "They still talk about coming back to visit someday. At one point, they considered retiring to Alaska, but then Jade got married. Mom and Dad know that grandchildren won't be far behind their new grandfurbaby."

He nodded. "My mom and dad would hate the thought of being away from their grandchildren too. But they understand that Reed and Julia will end up wherever their hearts lead them to be."

"Not yours?"

"My heart is here," he answered, his attention returning to the familiar landscape that was part of Conley Island. "So I can understand your parents' desire to return to Alaska."

"I can too." Twisting slightly, Aurora went back to admiring the view below.

Shifting his full focus to the controls in front of him, he said, "Secure your camera. We're going to be landing."

She did so without question. "Your family's island is much larger than I expected it to be."

"We don't own the island," he clarified as he prepared for their landing. "But we do own a good chunk of the land on this side of Conley Island."

"It's beautiful," she said, the words coming out as a sigh as the plane descended.

"Your timing is perfect. The fall leaves still have a brilliance to them. Another week into September and you wouldn't be seeing this."

"I love capturing the subtle and not-so-subtle differences found in the changing of seasons."

"Something tells me a tree is never just a tree to you," he said with a grin as he eased the plane down, the floats gliding smoothly across the surface of the water.

"Never," she said as she watched the passing scenery drift by.

Gage carefully maneuvered the floatplane up alongside the dock. "And here we are."

"You're really good at this," Aurora said with a sweet smile.

"Years of practice," he told her as he cut the engine. "My dad began flying long before Reed and Julia and I came along. So I began learning at an early age."

He pointed past her out the passenger window to the two figures moving in hurried strides toward the dock. Reed and Hank, a longtime employee at Living the Good Life Fishing Retreat, moved to secure the floatplane to the extended dock. Gage reached down to unfasten his seatbelt while Aurora did the same.

"The one in the red stocking cap is my brother, Reed," he told her. "The older gentleman behind him is Hank. He's been working here since my dad first opened the lodge."

"You didn't even have to point your brother out," Aurora told him as she watched the two men work to secure the plane to the dock. "He looks just like a younger version of you, minus the incredibly perfect beard shadow."

"He takes more time than me to shave." As her words sank in, he looked at Aurora, dark brows lifting. "Perfect, huh?"

She glanced his way. "As if you don't know that it's the slightly unshaven, five o'clock shadow kind of beard that heroes have on the covers of romance novels."

"Can't say that I do know that. The only reading material you'll find on the coffee table in the great room at the lodge are fishing magazines and outdoorsy books," he replied. Truth was, he wasn't looking to grow a beard, but shaving every day proved to be an annoyance. So he'd shave and then wait a few days to do so again. He had more important things to do than stand in front of the bathroom mirror every morning, working at a clean-shaven face. *Perfect, huh?* Maybe he'd wait until *after* he'd taken Aurora back to Juneau to rid himself of his apparently book-cover-worthy whiskers.

The door next to Gage swung open, and Reed's face appeared. "Just making sure everything's alright," he said. "You never take this long to leave the plane." His gaze drifted past Gage to Aurora, and his lips lifted into a welcoming smile. "Well, hello."

"Hello," she replied, returning his smile.

"Reed," Gage said, "this is Aurora Daniels. She'll be staying as a guest in one of the cabins tonight. Aurora, my *baby* brother, Reed." He wasn't certain why he'd felt the need to add *baby* to his introduction of his brother, but that's how it came out.

"Who is only two years younger than Gage's ancient old age of thirty-two," his brother promptly pointed out.

"Thirty-two?" she said with a glance in Gage's direction. "That is getting up there a bit."

His brother chuckled, focusing on Aurora. "You and I are going to get along just fine. With that being said, I'd like to be the first to welcome you to Living the Good Life Fishing Retreat."

Gage didn't miss the fact that his brother had greeted their guest with far more enthusiasm than he normally met visitors with.

"Thank you," Aurora replied. "I look forward to my stay here. Even if only for a night."

Reed looked at Gage. "You never mentioned we were expecting another guest, or I would have dressed for the occasion."

Gage looked at Aurora. "Meaning his favorite red flannel shirt instead of the REEL MEN FISH sweatshirt he's wearing. Which, I might add, happens to be one of our bestsellers at the lodge's gift shop."

"*Catchy*," Aurora replied with a giggle.

"She's good," Reed acknowledged with a responding chuckle.

"And in your brother's defense," she said, "he didn't know he would be bringing another guest back with him. I missed my flight out of Juneau, and your brother came to my rescue." She looked at Gage with a grateful smile.

"A regular hero, that brother of mine," Reed remarked, his grin widening.

With a perfect beard, Gage mentally tossed out with an inner smirk. Then he shook the silly thought away. "Would you mind opening the rear passenger door and helping Aurora down? I'm going to grab her things, and I'll meet you on the dock."

"Of course," Reed said and backed down the ladder, closing Gage's door.

"After you," Gage said, motioning toward the rear section of the plane.

She stood and slipped between the two front seats to the back where his brother had just opened the larger door. Then she grabbed for her camera bag and her backpack, slinging them on before exiting the plane.

"I'll be right behind you," Gage told her as Reed helped her down the steps. Turning, he reached for the duck poncho, folding it up. Then he grabbed for her carry-on and the bag of purchases she'd made back in Juneau and made his way out of the plane.

Aurora and Reed were waiting for him at the edge of the dock where she'd disembarked from the floatplane.

"I can get those," she said.

"I've got them," Gage told her as he placed the neatly folded, now dry, poncho into the large plastic bag that held her purchases. "You take care of your camera bag."

Reed glanced down at the bags hanging just below her waist on both sides. "Serious picture-taker."

"I suppose you could say that," Aurora replied. "I'm a professional photographer."

Reed tipped his perfectly sculpted chin upward in a pose. "If you ever need a model . . ."

Gage gave him a playful shove. "She's already on a job. You'll have to stick to selfies."

Hank, who had finished checking to make sure the plane was secured to the dock, stepped over to join the group. "All good," he told Gage.

Gage nodded. "Thanks, Hank."

The man's curious gaze slid to Aurora. "Well, if this isn't a pleasant surprise. I didn't realize we were expecting another guest."

"We weren't," Reed said. "Gage came to her rescue after she missed her flight."

"Hank," Gage said, "this is Aurora Daniels. Aurora, Hank Mills."

"Welcome to Conley Island," he greeted with a wide, welcoming smile.

"Thank you," she replied.

"Hank's our go-to man here," Reed explained. "He helps captain one of our two fishing boats whenever groups go out, and he can fix anything and everything around here that needs fixing."

Hank gave a hearty chuckle. "Keep talking up my many professional attributes, and I might just have to ask for a hefty raise." He glanced in Aurora's direction. "Let it be known that I've taught these two everything I know, so they're every bit as capable as I am."

"If Gage captains a boat even half as good as he flies that plane, then you've taught him well," Aurora said.

"Reed's more skilled behind a ship's wheel," Gage admitted. "My specialty is flying."

"He does both well," his brother countered. "But let's not waste time talking about Gage's skillsets. We have a guest to get settled in."

They made their way up the wooden plank walkway.

"We were beginning to wonder if you were going to be back in time for dinner," Hank said.

"My meeting with Clive ran over, and then Aurora showed up in a bit of a fluster."

"And your brother offered to help me. Since I was a little wet from the rain, we stopped in town so I could pick up a few things before leaving Juneau," Aurora explained.

"Do you like salmon?" Reed asked.

"I do."

"Good. I'll tell Mom to add one more place setting at the dinner table this evening," he replied.

"Oh, no," Aurora said, "I don't want to intrude on your family's dinner plans."

"You have to eat," Gage said. "And it's not intruding. Our family and our guests share meals at the lodge. Although a few of our guests bring their own groceries and choose to cook in their cabins."

Reed raised an arm, casting a glance at the watch

peeking out from under the cuff of his denim sleeve. "It's a few minutes before four. Unless something unforeseen happens in the kitchen, and it could," he added with a grin, "dinner will be served at five thirty." He looked at Gage. "Julia's helping."

"Oh, boy," Gage replied with a husky chuckle.

"Oh, boy?" Aurora pressed as she walked beside him.

A grin tugged at his mouth. "My sister can catch fish with the best of them, even clean them herself, but put her in the kitchen with one . . ."

"Let's just say she gives new meaning to the term 'blackened,'" Reed finished for him, making a face.

Hank shook his head, tsking. "Don't listen to these two. They're just jealous that their baby sister can fish circles around them."

"There might be a bit of truth in that," Gage conceded with a nod.

"I've got work to do," Hank announced. He looked at Aurora. "If we don't cross paths before you leave tomorrow, it's been nice meeting you."

"Same here," she replied.

Recalling her clearance rack purchase, Gage said, "I'm putting Aurora in the Sleepy Moose cabin."

"Good choice," Reed said. "I've got to go fix a loose handrail across the way. I'll see you two at dinner."

"The Sleepy Moose?" Aurora inquired after Reed had walked away.

"Continuing the moose theme you started earlier," he said with a grin. "Come on, I'll show you to your cabin."

They moved down the wide, well-worn trail that led to a semicircle of one-bedroom cabins that bookended one side of the main lodge. The larger cabins slept up to four comfortably. Tucked among the trees on the opposite side of the lodge were an equal number of studio cabins, also surrounded by woods.

He watched as Aurora did a slow visual sweep of the cabins.

"I know they look rustic," Gage said. "But inside they're a bit more modernized. They've got both running water and electricity. And there's Wi-Fi. Your sign-in password is BIGFISH. If you forget, it's on a small, framed magnet on the fridge."

"That's awesome. I wasn't sure if I would have cell service out here or not."

"It's decent until the weather isn't. Then it's a bit spotty."

Running water and electricity were a plus, but Aurora had gone without before during her many travels. But having Wi-Fi was so appreciated. Not only could she stay in contact with her friends and family, but she could also work when time allowed.

"I don't mind rustic," she assured him as she breathed in the crisp, clean air with hints of pine and light floral under-tones she couldn't quite put a name to. While the trail they'd taken there had been only sparsely wooded, no doubt having been cleared out to make travel to and from the main lodge easier for guests staying in the surrounding cabins, a thicket of trees stood just beyond the cabins.

As they moved farther into the wide, half-moon-shaped clearing, Aurora got a better glimpse of her accommodation for that night. The cozy little log cabins were spread far enough apart to give guests a sense of privacy, yet not so distant that it might feel uncomfortably remote. Each one was tucked back into the denser woods.

Gage came to a stop in front of one of the cabins. "Wel-come to the Sleepy Moose. Not only does it go with your socks, it's located nearest to the trail leading back to the main lodge."

Aurora laughed. "It's perfect." She took in the small wooden deck that lined the front of the cabin. Beyond it, a dark green door stood beside a wide, curtained window, its trim done in the same dark evergreen color. Beside the door was a sign with the profile of a moose over the words THE SLEEPY MOOSE. She reached up to run her fingers over the sign. "This is so cute."

"Figured you like it better than the Lazy Salmon, which is the next cabin over."

"I like the cabins having cutesy names."

"You have Julia to thank for that," Gage said as he stepped over to adjust the pile of logs at the far side of the porch. "We were looking for ways to add character to the cabins, and my sister came up with the idea of giving the cabins names rather than assigning them numbers."

"Well, I love it."

Gage crossed back over to the door. "I would've offered you one of the cabins across the way, so you'd have other people staying around you, but there aren't any available," he said as he reached out to punch a code into a keypad above the doorknob. "We have a group staying with us right now as part of the lodge's fishing retreat package."

"Don't give it another thought," she told him. "Peace and solitude of any sort will be more than welcome."

Gage turned the knob and opened the cabin door. "Give me a sec to turn some lights on and open the curtains. They're room darkening and definitely live up to their name."

Aurora waited just outside the doorway. "This cabin is beyond perfect. I love the feeling of being immersed in nature."

"Not what I would have expected to hear from a city girl," he told her as the fading sunlight filtered into the cabin window through the surrounding trees.

Aurora laughed. "I might live in Seattle, but I have traveled extensively. Believe me when I tell you that this 'city girl' has spent more than a few nights sleeping on the ground in tents. Some of those having no bottoms to them."

"Now that's impressive. I've never camped without a base attached to my tent. Come on in," he said, motioning her inside. "I won't think any less of you, however, if you happen to change your mind about staying out here alone. The offer still stands for the vacant guest room over at the main lodge. If it's not ready, it won't take long to get it so."

"I'll keep that in mind," Aurora told him as she stepped into the charming little cabin. Gage had done so much for her already. In fact, he'd given far more attention to her needs in the few short hours she had known him than Ben had during the entire time they were together.

"You can hang your jacket on the hook by the door."

Gage had placed her carry-on against the cabin wall next to the door. Her purchases sat on top of a small table in the far corner of the room where the cabin's kitchenette was located.

Aurora slid the backpack from her shoulders and set it down next to her carry-on. Then she pulled off her camera bag, setting it on the floor by her feet.

"We're not expecting any more rain for a couple of days," Gage told her.

"That's good," she replied as she removed her jacket and hung it on the hook. Then, gathering up her camera bag, she moved farther into the room. She did a quick sweep of her surroundings. The kitchen area consisted of a bistro-style table for two, a sink, microwave, mini fridge, and a few cupboards, no doubt for those who were staying longer and had brought some additional food with them for cooking during their stay.

"There are bottles of water in the mini fridge," he said. "And a selection of individually packaged snacks and breakfast bars in the cupboard above it if you happen to get hungry between meals at the main lodge. There's also a flashlight in the stand next to the bed in case you need it." He glanced around. "There is a guest laundry room at the lodge. The machines are free to use if you have need of them." He paused. "I hope I didn't leave anything out. Julia and Mom usually handle check-ins and info dumps."

She smiled. "I can't think of anything else I'd need to know, so you've done your job."

He returned her smile. "If you have any questions or concerns during your stay, don't hesitate to let us know."

Aurora gave an appreciative nod as her eyes slowly swept the room. Instead of the bunk beds she'd been prepared to find, the cabin offered a full-size bed. She took in the red and black buffalo plaid quilt, noting that it looked to be homemade. Alternating squares of pine trees and moose intermingled with the checkered squares, the design matching the pillow shams. A moose, standing majestic and strong, made up the base of the antique sculpted bronze lamp next to the bed. Across the room, an unlit woodstove sat tucked in the corner near the front window. The room, with all its Alaskan charm, was so inviting. It made her wish she would be staying for more than one night.

She turned to Gage. "I have a question."

His dark brows lifted. "That was fast."

She laughed. "I want to know how I'm supposed to experience what it's truly like to be out in the wilds of Alaska when this place is like a mini Alaskan all-inclusive?"

Gage brought a hand to his chin, as if in contemplation. "I suppose we could remove all the snacks from your cabin . . ."

"On second thought," Aurora said, taking an intentional sidestep to block his view of the goody cupboard, "who needs to rough it when they're inside? I think I'll just save that experience for when I'm outdoors."

Gage's eyes glinted with humor. "Sounds like a plan. I guess I should go and let you get settled in. I'll be back to show you to the main house for dinner."

Aurora touched her now only slightly damp, wavy hair. "I'm not so sure my joining in is a very good idea. I haven't seen my reflection in a mirror, but I'm pretty sure I look a mess after the day I've had. I probably should just skip dinner at the lodge this evening and dine on snacks instead."

"You really don't look the worse for wear," he assured her. "In fact, you're one of the few women I've ever met who could come out of the kind of day you've had and still look like you've just finished shooting a shampoo commercial."

Her laughter came out in an unexpected snort, making Aurora cover her mouth in embarrassment. "Sorry, I've just never received a compliment quite like that one."

His mouth pulled up to one side. "I can't say that I've ever given one quite like that before. But I meant what I said. You look great."

She certainly didn't want his mother going out of her way for her. "Gage, I've already imposed enough on your family, coming here without any notice or a reservation."

"Your being here isn't an imposition," he assured her. "We had a cabin available. And I'll warn you right now, Mom loves having guests to dote on. So, your presence will make her all the happier. What do you say? Join us for dinner?"

She smiled up at him. "I certainly don't want to put your mother through any unnecessary inconvenience because I missed dinner. But I really do need to grab a quick shower before heading up to the main lodge."

"I've got a few things I need to see to. Why don't I swing by and walk you to dinner, say in about an hour?"

That was more than enough time for her to make herself presentable. She was a no-fuss kind of gal. One had to be when their career revolved around taking photographs of things nature-related. Because that meant dealing with the elements that came with it. Rain and snow. Sweltering heat and frigid cold. Even seat-drop slides down muddy hillsides.

Aurora nodded. "That works for me."

"Okay. I'll let you get settled in," Gage said as he opened the cabin door.

"Do you think your family would mind if I brought one of my cameras along with me?" she called after him as he turned to leave. "I'd really like to get some shots of the lodge and its surroundings after dinner. And, depending on the timing of all that, grab a few sunset pictures too."

Sunset had always been Aurora's favorite time of day. Especially when it came to taking pictures of those ever-changing hues of yellow, red, and orange. And watching as the blues and purples came into play across the evening sky as the sun faded slowly away below the distant horizon. Her *Sunsets of the World* photograph collection featured some of her very best works.

"They won't mind at all," he assured her, bringing Aurora back from her drifting thoughts. "Just be prepared to be asked all about photography by my sister. To the point of possibly missing your flight again tomorrow. Julia takes the pictures for the retreat's website along with any brochures we create for the business."

Aurora laughed. "Thank you for the warning, but totally not necessary. I'm more than happy to answer any questions she might have. And missing my flight again to stay here on this beautiful Alaskan island wouldn't be that much of a hardship to endure. I promise."

"You say that now," he replied with an almost sobering expression. Then Gage stepped out onto the cabin's cozy front porch. "See you in an hour."

Aurora watched as he closed the door behind him, wondering if Gage had taken her playful response about staying on longer for something other than the teasing banter she'd meant it to be. Not that staying in a place like Conley Island would ever be a hardship in her world.

CHAPTER FIVE

Aurora pulled her cell phone from her backpack and called the number to reschedule her flight. "Latest possible," she told the representative who had availability on a flight leaving Juneau at 7:55 p.m. the following day. That way she could still explore a bit more of the island, or of Juneau if Gage needed to fly her back earlier in the day. Whatever worked best for him.

Laying her phone on the table, she walked over to her slightly mangled carry-on. Lifting its handle, she wheeled it carefully over to the full-size bed with its rustic pine log headboard. Careful to keep the wheels just over the edge of the mattress so as not to get any dirt on it, she set the compact suitcase atop the buffalo plaid quilt. She struggled with the broken zipper but finally managed to open it the rest of the way. Sifting through her somewhat damp clothes, she gathered up her shower items and then walked over to look through the bag holding her purchases from town. Her choices were limited. At least until her clothes dried, which she intended to lay out around the room before leaving for dinner.

She was just about to head into the bathroom when her cell phone rang. Pausing what she was doing, she hurried over to grab it. She brought the phone to her ear. "Hello?"

"Are you at the airport?" her best friend asked on the other end of the line.

"No. I'm on Conley Island and will be staying here tonight."

"Conley Island?"

"It's a short flight here from Juneau. I had a very kind man offer me one of his family's cabins for the night."

"Aurora," Emmy gasped. "That kind man might not be as kind as you think. At least I know you're alive," her best friend grumbled on the other end of the line.

"He is," Aurora retorted with a grin. "So stop worrying."

"Hey, I watch all those cop shows. I know how convincing those kidnappers can be when they prey on beautiful young women."

"No one is preying on anyone here," Aurora replied. "But thank you for the compliment."

"You're welcome. So let me get your text straight. You missed your flight and then met a guy in a diner who offered to fly you off into the wild blue yonder. You then accepted, without so much as a background check on this Alaskan version of Captain Kirk who flies a plane instead of a really cool spaceship."

Aurora couldn't help but laugh, despite appreciating her friend's concern. "His name is Gage. And no, I did not run a background check. Glady, the owner of the diner we were in, suggested I stay at his family's retreat. I highly doubt a woman who's created a longtime eatery in Juneau is going to risk it all to send her customers off with serial killers."

"Ha!" Emmy replied. "That shows how much you know

about criminals. The accomplice is there to throw people off the trail."

"Emmy, I'm an experienced traveler. I'm here on Conley Island of my own free will. Oh, and still breathing, in case you missed that fact," Aurora countered. "Seriously, I do appreciate your concern, but Gage Weston is really charming. The retreat is very real. I'm actually standing in one of their very adorable guest cabins."

"Okay. So, you're still breathing. Tell me all about this Alaskan Captain Kirk."

Aurora rolled her eyes. "He pilots a floatplane, not a spaceship. His family has owned this part of the island since before Gage was born. He has one younger brother named Reed, who I met when we arrived at the docks, and a younger sister named Julia, who I will be meeting at dinner this evening. Speaking of which, I hate to rush you off, but I need to shower before heading up to the main lodge for dinner at five thirty. Can I call you later?"

"How about tomorrow?" Emmy replied. "I have a speed dating event I'm leaving for in about thirty minutes."

"You just got home."

"You'll never find Mr. Right if you don't put yourself out there."

Aurora nodded in silent agreement. "I can't believe you signed up for another one after the last disastrous one you and I went to."

"Hey, we were newbies. This time around, I know not to ask the man I'm getting to know if he's ever had his face painted without first explaining that I'm an artist who does a lot of work with paints and canvas."

"And if the man assumes something incorrectly," Aurora added, "like that you do face paintings at birthday parties and such, you will not be immediately offended." And dump a glass of water over the attendee's head.

"I learn from my mistakes," Emmy told her. "Have you?"

"Ben wasn't a mistake. Thinking we should get married was." Aurora glanced at her fit watch. "Emmy, I hate to rush you off, but I have less than an hour to get showered and be ready to go by the time Gage comes back to get me for dinner."

"Hmm . . . sounds like a date. Is your pilot cute?"

Aurora rolled her eyes. "He's not *my* pilot. But Gage is ruggedly handsome and thoughtful. He doesn't want me getting lost on my way to the main lodge, so he's going to walk me there. Nothing more. Besides, I'm not looking for a relationship right now. You know that."

"Sometimes relationships find you," her friend replied. "Enjoy your meal, and stay in touch so I know that you're okay."

"I will," Aurora replied. "Talk to you soon." Disconnecting the call, she tossed the phone onto her bed and then headed for the shower, Gage's smiling face shoving its way into her thoughts.

The cabin door swung open. Aurora stood there, her hair clean and wavy as it spilled over the tops of her shoulders. A hint of mascara accented her already thick lashes. Gage couldn't help but grin when his gaze came to her dinner attire. Oversized sweatpants rolled up at the cuffs, and the sweatshirt she'd bought with the tiny floatplane embroidered on it.

"Hi."

She smiled. "Hi."

"Too early?" he asked.

"Nope. Your timing is perfect. Let me grab my coat and my camera bag, and we can go."

He moved to sit on the porch rocker while he waited.

Moments later, the door swung open again, and Aurora stepped out to join him. "All set."

Gage pushed up out of the rocker and joined her as they stepped down off the porch and onto the path that ran in front of the cabins. One way leading to the docks and the other up to the main lodge.

"I was able to reschedule my flight for tomorrow. It leaves a few minutes before eight o'clock in the evening. You can fly me back to Juneau at whatever time works best for your schedule. I can find things to do there if we need to go earlier in the day, or I can spend time here taking pictures of the island until it's time to leave for Juneau."

"We probably need to leave here about three to make sure you arrive for your flight on time. Good news is the weather is supposed to be decent tomorrow."

"That works for me."

"It's still light out now," Gage said as they traversed the path, "but coming back after sunset this path can be a little dark, despite the path lights we've run along the walkway. We keep the lighting dim on purpose, allowing just enough to guide guests along, but not so much that it washes out the night sky above."

"I'll bet the stars are pretty amazing out here at night," Aurora said as her gaze lifted upward. "Even through the treetops."

He nodded. "They are. But there are places to see them without anything blocking the view. Like on the deck behind the main lodge. Or from the docks. And from late

August through late April, there's a chance you could see the Northern Lights coloring the night sky."

"I hear they're breathtaking."

Walking nearly shoulder to shoulder with her along the narrow path had almost the same effect as far as Gage was concerned. Especially with the faint scent of vanilla and cherries teasing his nose and his senses. "Pictures don't even come close to doing the Northern Lights justice," he told her as they moved away from the cabins. "No offense to your photography skills."

"None taken," she replied with a grin. "My parents say the same thing."

"Oh, that's right. Your parents lived and worked in Alaska for a while."

"They did. Mom and Dad got to see the Northern Lights on several occasions and say they never failed to take their breath away. I hope to see them myself someday."

"They are pretty amazing," he agreed with a nod. "Unfortunately, we're not expecting a geomagnetic storm tonight. Just a cloudy night sky. You'll want to be careful going back to your cabin this evening. There are a lot of trip hazards in the dark. Roots, rocks, etcetera."

"Noted," she told him as they continued onward up the winding path. "I'll even use the flashlight on my phone to help light my way back."

"I didn't mean to imply we'd be sending you back to your cabin on your own after dinner." What if she got lost? Or ran into a bear? Or a coyote? "Reed can walk you back. That is, when you're through taking pictures." Better his brother do it than him. Aurora made him feel things he hadn't felt for a very long time. Not since he'd first started dating his ex, and look how that relationship had turned out. Emotions were better off left uninvested. "Bears are actively foraging for their winter hibernation. That means you can see them during daylight hours and at night. If you happen to cross paths with one, my brother will know how to handle the situation. Reed can even take along a flashlight from the house to help light the way."

"When you put it that way . . . "

Gage smiled down at her and then looked away as he caught sight of the lodge in front of them. "Well, here we are," he announced as they left the wooded trail and moved into the open, landscaped area that fronted the main lodge.

"This is so much bigger than I expected it to be," Aurora said in surprise as they approached the lodge's wide front porch. The cedar log siding fit perfectly with the surroundings. Stone-wrapped pillars lined the oversized porch.

"I have a big family," Gage replied as they made their way up the steps. "And don't forget we have guest rooms in there as well."

Aurora paused to glance around the welcoming porch. Off to one side sat a row of six oversized rocking chairs that had been crafted from tree branches. Between each was a polished tree stump large enough to hold a couple cups of coffee and maybe a cell phone or two. A long, beige and black braided rug ran the length of the porch in front of them. To her other side, a carved wooden sign hung above a row of wooden pegs. It read: WELCOME TO LIVING THE GOOD LIFE FISHING RETREAT. Rain suits hung from the pegs with tall rubber boots placed neatly on the floor beneath.

"Most people bring their own rain gear, but we keep spare gear on hand in case they didn't know to bring it or forgot it when they were packing. Weather here can be quite unpredictable. Even in the summer months. Sunny one moment, windy and raining the next. So rain gear is essential on fishing trips and handy for venturing about on rainy days."

Aurora pulled her camera from its bag and snapped a picture of the porch.

The door opened, and a young woman with long dark hair, just a hint lighter than Gage's, came out in a flurry of smiles. "You must be Aurora!"

"I am," Aurora replied with a smile as she hurried to return her camera to the bag at her hips.

"My sister, Julia," Gage offered up with a chuckle.

"It's so nice to meet you, Julia." She guessed Gage's sister to be close to her in age.

"Same," she replied. "We're so glad to have you here at the retreat. Reed said you're a professional photographer."

"I am," Aurora answered again with a glance in Gage's direction.

"Have you ever—"

"How about we allow Aurora to get inside before bombarding her with all those questions I know are whirling about in your head?"

"Oh, I'm so sorry." Julia jumped aside. "Come on in."

Laughing softly, Aurora stepped past her into the main lodge. If she thought she'd been taken by the outside, she was even more charmed by the inside. The room was open concept with a small check-in counter to the right. Next to it was a rack of long-sleeved T-shirts in various colors and sizes. Across the back of the shirts was the retreat's logo, a bent fishing pole with the fishing line disappearing into rippling water, mountains in the background. Below the almost lifelike drawing was the retreat's name and location.

"Reed did the artwork for our shirts," Julia said as she stepped up beside Aurora.

"About ten years ago," another male voice joined in.

Aurora turned to find Gage's younger brother had joined them. "Hello again."

"Glad you could join us," he replied. "And I should be clear that the shirts are new. The drawing, however, I did ten years ago for my dad for Father's Day. Mom loved it so much it became our business logo. I promise I've gotten better since then."

"He has," Gage agreed.

"I don't see anything wrong with this drawing, but I did see the artwork you did on Gage's floatplane, and it's beautiful."

Reed's chest puffed out ever so slightly.

"Nobody told me our guest had arrived."

Aurora looked past Reed to see a tall, slender woman with salt-and-pepper hair. More pepper than salt. Gage had clearly inherited his mother's big, bright, toothy smile.

"We just got here," Gage said in his own defense. "Mom, this is Aurora Daniels. Aurora, this is our mother, Constance Weston."

"It's so nice to meet you, Mrs. Weston."

"Constance," his mother insisted. "And it's a pleasure to have you here. Reed tells us you're a famous photographer."

Aurora looked at Gage's younger brother, who shrugged with an innocent smile. "I'm not sure famous is a word I would use to describe myself. But I have won several awards." Her gaze traveled about the room. "Your place is so inviting." Its open concept with the floor-to-ceiling fireplace and windows made the lodge feel warm and homey.

Gage's mother smiled. "Thank you. We want our guests to feel at home here."

Movement at the back of the room drew Aurora's attention that way. A man, not quite as tall as Gage and Reed, and with less bulk, came in, his gait slightly off as he moved toward them. A slow smile spread across his face, lines etching the outer corners of his eyes. The same marks Gage and Reed had when they grinned but with deeper lines etched into them. He had to be their father.

"Hello. Welcome to Living the Good Life F-Fishing Retreat," the man offered in greeting as he moved to stand next to Gage's mother.

Aurora returned his smile. "Hello, and thank you for the warm welcome."

"Dad," Gage said, "I'd like to introduce you to Aurora. Aurora, my dad."

"Jim Weston," Gage's father said in introduction.

"It's nice to meet you," Aurora replied.

His father looked to Gage, his graying brows lifting upward. "Your mother didn't tell me you were bringing s-someone special home to meet us."

"What?" Gage replied in confusion.

His mother looked up at her husband and then at her youngest son. "Reed, you didn't tell me your brother was bringing someone 'special' when you told me to expect another guest that your brother had just flown in for dinner."

Reed shrugged. "I just repeated what I was told."

"Gage!" Julia gasped with a clap of her hands. "I'm so happy for you!"

"Now everyone hold on," Gage said with a frown.

"I should've realized she wasn't just another guest," Constance said, smiling at Aurora. "We've never had a woman come stay at the retreat by herself before. And you're wearing a floatplane sweatshirt."

"He does look happier," Jim noted with a nod.

Aurora's eyes widened as the misinformation train picked up speed.

"Whoa!" Gage bellowed, throwing up his hands.

Everyone looked his way, the excited chatter in the room finally ceasing.

"Aurora is not special," he told them and then groaned at how his words had come out. He looked Aurora's way with an apologetic glance as he clarified, "To me." Then his gaze shifted to his family. "She was in need of a place to stay, and we had availability. She's our *guest*."

Aurora could have sworn she saw the entire room deflate at Gage's announcement.

"Sorry about that," Jim apologized. "Gage usually doesn't introduce m-me to our guests. My wife or Julia normally do that when the guests arrive for check-in. And you are wearing a f-floatplane sweatshirt, so I assumed . . ."

"We should have known Gage wouldn't bring anyone home with him," Julia said, clearly disappointed that they'd been wrong about Aurora's connection with Gage. "Not since—"

"Well, I'm starving," Reed blurted out, cutting his younger sister off.

Gage shifted uneasily. "Same."

Sensing Gage's discomfort with the direction her introduction had taken, Aurora explained, "Like we told Reed when we arrived, Gage came to my rescue in Juneau after I missed my flight back to Seattle and found myself a bit stranded in the rain. My things got wet, and clothing options in town were limited, so we stopped by a gift shop before flying to Conley Island. That's why I'm not dressed nicer for dinner."

His mother immediately waved her words away. "First of all, we're so sorry for any discomfort we caused by thinking you and Gage were together. And second, you look adorable. Our guests dress however makes them comfortable. We don't have a dress code here."

"Other than you have to wear clothes," Reed chimed in.

His mother gave him a disapproving glance, then focused once again on Aurora. "Most of our guests arrive by floatplane. It would be perfect to wear about as winter sets in. I might just need to have Reed draw us up a design for sweatshirts with a floatplane on them and the name of our lodge to add to our cozy little lodge boutique."

"A.k.a., corner area by the check-in," Reed said, garnering another glance from his mother.

"Children," she said with a dramatic huff of feigned frustration, "you think you raised them right . . ."

Her husband chuckled. "R-Reed loves to tease his mother," he said, his words again taking a bit of effort to get out.

"And Mom can give as good as she gets," Julia said. "She's just refraining because you're here."

"True," Reed and Gage echoed at the same time.

Aurora laughed. "You all remind me so much of my family."

"We'll take that as a compliment," Constance replied. "And while you're here, consider yourself a part of ours. We want our guests to feel right at home during their stay here."

"Thus the lodge's motto," her husband said, pointing to a large wooden sign above the stone fireplace. Carved out of the plank and painted in a dark umber brown were the words, OUR FAMILY IS YOUR FAMILY.

"I'm so thankful your family had a vacant cabin I could stay in for the night."

"Well, we're happy to have you staying here with us," Gage's father replied with a smile, his arm curled lovingly around his wife's waist. "I hope you'll be joining us for dinner."

"She is," Gage's mother told him. "And maybe we'll even be able to coax her into staying and joining us for game night."

"Game night?" Aurora replied, her interest piqued.

"It's where any guest who wants to participate—and my family—spend time playing games. Sometimes by the fireplace. Sometimes right here at the table. Depending on what game we're playing."

"I'll warn you right now," Reed said, "everyone starts out playing with high hopes of winning only to have my big brother here crush those hopes to smithereens."

"It's true," Julia agreed with a nod. "Gage rarely loses at any of the games he joins in."

"I don't always win," Gage countered. "I just get really lucky."

"Don't let him fool you," Jim said. "My son is good with anything that involves memory recall and numbers."

"How about we try not to scare Aurora away from game night before she even accepts your invite to join in?" Gage suggested with a shake of his head.

"Oh, I'm not scared," she told him. "I love to play games. My family and I used to have our own game night when Jade and I lived at home."

"No one would blame you if you're not feeling up to it," he replied. "You've had a bit of a hectic day. It's okay if you'd rather go back to your cabin and rest up after dinner."

Aurora's brows lifted. "Hmm . . . sure sounds to me like someone is doing his best to get me to bow out of tonight's competition."

Gage appeared surprised by her accusation. "Who? Me?" he said, jabbing a finger in his broad chest.

"Sure sounded like it to me," Reed egged on.

"I'm in," Aurora announced.

"I thought you were hoping to get some pictures before the sun sets this evening."

Reed chuckled. "Are you actually worried Aurora's game-playing abilities will knock you off your winner pedestal?"

Gage frowned. "It has nothing to do with winning or losing. I don't want her to miss taking the pictures she was hoping to get because she got hooked into playing games with us."

"Easy fix," Julia said. "We can play after she takes her pictures." She looked at Aurora. "If you're still up for it by then."

Gage's mother nodded. "Absolutely. There is no set time for game night. Do what you need to do. If you change your mind afterward, we'll understand."

"Maybe I could join you when you go out to get those pictures," Julia said hopefully. "I'd love to see a professional photographer in action."

Aurora smiled at his sister. "I would love the company."

Aurora had taken pictures from the plane, but she'd mostly been turned away from him. Gage found himself wondering what she was like when she was free to move about, immersed in her element. Would she be focused and serious? Would she be smiling? Happy to be doing what she loved?

Gage fought a troubled frown. None of those things should matter to him. Aurora would be gone as quickly as she'd arrived, and he'd be back to life as usual. Besides, everyone knew what happened to the curious cat. But there was also the saying, live and learn. "I'll go too," he announced, his decision made.

Reed chuckled. "Since when are you interested in photography?"

Since their pretty little guest blew into the café in an oversized duck poncho. "Someone needs to be there to keep an eye out for Little John."

"Little John?" Aurora asked, her head tipped inquiringly to one side.

"He's Conley Island's most renowned brown bear," Gage's dad explained.

"Don't let the name fool you," Reed added. "Little John is a full-grown grizzly. We just named him that because all three of us siblings loved reading about, and watching, *Robin Hood* when we were growing up."

Aurora's expression settled into one of concern. "So he's really big?"

Laughing softly, Gage's mom shook her head. "Not as big as some get. He's only come around here every so often, but the boys run him off. Just be sure not to leave any food outside of your cabin, or he might be tempted to pay you a visit."

"Him or one of his friends," Reed said with a grin.

Gage could see the concern building on Aurora's face. If they kept filling her in on all the dangers of the island, she'd be making a night swim back to Juneau.

"You'll be safe with Gage along," he heard his father say.

Aurora nodded as she looked Gage's way. "I have no doubt."

"So it's settled," Julia decided. "We eat. Then we go get some pictures. Afterward, we'll come back here and play some games."

"When you kids head off on your photographic adventure, I'll get a fire going," Reed offered.

"And I'll get the g-games out and set them on the ccoffee table," Jim said. "Aurora chooses who g-goes first." He looked her way. "A perk of b-being a guest here."

"I suppose I should have asked how Gage responds to losing before I fully committed to joining family game night."

Gage arched an affronted brow as he fought to keep the grin from his face. "I can't really answer that because I never lose."

"Well, you know what they say," Aurora replied. "Never say never."

Gage's dad hooted and then glanced down at his wife. "Looks like our son m-might have met his match in this young lady. I'm l-looking forward to watching our eldest son get his g-game confidence knocked down a notch or two."

"Same." Reed chuckled.

"If we play teams, I get Aurora," Julia called out.

"We might be drawing straws for that privilege," Reed said.

Constance clapped her hands together. "Game night is going to be so much fun tonight! I love a little friendly competition. Now everyone go ahead and take a seat at the table. Julia and I will start bringing the food out."

"Can I help with anything?" Aurora offered.

"Thank you for offering, honey," Constance said. "But we are used to feeding a table full of guests. We have a system all worked out. You just relax and enjoy your stay here."

Jim released his loving hold on his wife and stepped aside so she could make her way past him to the kitchen.

On her way, she looked at Gage. "Go on over and find your seats. We'll just be a couple of minutes."

When his mother and Julia disappeared into the

kitchen, Aurora asked, "Would you mind very much if I took a few quick pictures of this room?"

Gage looked around. "It's not the wildlife you're used to photographing, but feel free to snap away."

"It makes me think of the outdoors," Aurora told him as she glanced about the room appreciatively. "It's designed so perfectly," she went on as she pulled out her camera and snapped several pictures. "From the half log walls to the log beams spanning this big, open room beneath the vaulted ceiling. The floor-to-ceiling windows and the slender, lit pines tucked away in different areas of the room give the feel of standing out in the woods as the sun is setting."

"Hmm," Reed muttered as he looked around. "Never quite looked at this room in that way."

"That's because all you think about when you're in here is eating," Gage said with a grin.

"Fact," his brother replied with an even wider grin.

Laughing at their playful banter, Aurora returned her camera to its bag.

"Mom and Dad came up with the idea for the fishing lodge when they were first married," Reed explained as they made their way over to the dining table. "They designed it as well."

"Actually," his father interjected, "this l-lodge was much smaller to begin with. When the fishing retreat began seeing a steady fl-flow of guests in its first few years, we decided to expand the lodge during off-season."

"We built this great room on and added several of the larger cabins to accommodate groups or families," Gage said.

"It's perfect," Aurora said, making Gage's father's chest puff up ever so slightly. The effort he put into getting some of his words out combined with his slightly off-balanced gait made her wonder if he'd suffered a stroke like Emmy's father had.

"Glad you like it," Gage said as he walked beside her.

"I feel bad not helping your mother and sister bring the food out," Aurora leaned over to whisper to Gage as they neared the table.

"Don't," he said. "I'm sure they appreciated you offering to help, but they have a routine for dinner they like to stick to. And tonight is easy. They're only serving dinner to one guest. They're used to serving a whole table filled with hungry fishermen."

"The other guests aren't coming?"

He shook his head. "Not this evening."

"Their group is having hot dogs over the fire down by their cabins," Reed said.

"I haven't had a hot dog cooked over a fire since Jade and I were little. My family liked to camp."

"So you really aren't a stranger to the outdoors," Gage noted in surprise.

"Not completely," she replied. "As a wildlife photographer, I spend a lot of time outside."

"And here I thought you were just a city girl with a really nice camera," he told her with a playful grin.

"Like an onion," she replied, "you have to peel back the layers."

"Duly noted." *If only there were more time.* Gage found himself wanting to know more about this beautiful woman who seemed to appreciate even the little things in life. Like lit artificial pines. He hadn't even realized how many filled the room until Aurora had made mention of them.

Aurora gasped softly, drawing Gage from his thoughts.

Her gaze was fixed on the elk antler chandelier that hung suspended over the long, twelve-seater dining table.

"I promise that no elk were harmed in the making of this chandelier," he said. "They shed their horns naturally."

"I know," she replied.

"You do?" he said in surprise.

She laughed. "I've learned a thing or two about the wildlife I photograph. I just hadn't realized how grand this chandelier was until I was standing almost beneath it. It's amazing."

"Reed made it," Jim said.

She looked at Gage's brother. "You did?"

Reed nodded. "It was a good winter project."

"And you paint, too," she said. "Impressive."

I can fly a plane, Gage refrained from blurting out. He tried to conjure up the image of his ex as a reminder that he didn't want to vie for any woman's attention, but his memory couldn't be jarred.

His brother stood from the seat he'd taken and pulled out the chair next to his. "You can sit here," he offered Aurora with a charming grin.

"Thank you," Aurora replied, smiling up at him.

Gage felt a pinch of something that made him want to lift his lip into a snarl. How ridiculous was that? Reed could charm away all he wanted. Even if he'd be wasting his time. Aurora had a life in Seattle. Maybe even a boyfriend, for all Gage knew. Definitely no husband, because he'd overheard her tell Glady that she wasn't married.

The door to the kitchen swung open, and his mother and Julia came out carrying food-laden trays.

"Are you planning to eat standing?" his mother asked Gage as she stepped up to the table next to him.

"Not today," he answered, making his mother smile.

"Then have a seat so we can get everyone served."

"Not there," his sister said as Gage moved to take the closest seat. "I'm sitting there tonight."

He started around the table only to be stopped by his mother. "I was going to sit by your father."

Unless he wanted to sit separate from the others, his only option was to take the seat next to Aurora. Gage dragged the chair back and lowered himself into it, telling himself to focus on dinner and not the woman beside him.

Trays emptied, his mother and Julia scurried back to the kitchen, their stifled giggles followed by fading whispers. They were up to no good. Of that, Gage was pretty certain. He hadn't missed the twinkle of delight that had come into his mother's eyes when Aurora joked about knocking Gage off his game champion podium. He could tell his family liked her, and he was pretty sure his mother and Julia were entertaining matchmaking thoughts as they had done a handful of times since his breakup two years earlier. Well, they could scheme all they wanted. He was not looking for a relationship. His focus needed to be on figuring out a way to keep their family's retreat from being swallowed up by the bigger fish. But that didn't mean he wouldn't enjoy an evening spent in Aurora Daniels's company.

CHAPTER SIX

"This is where Gage knocked my front tooth out."

Aurora's eyes widened in horror at Julia's statement. Lowering her camera, she stood from where she'd knelt to capture an upshot of the towering pine next to her and eyed Gage questioningly.

"It wasn't on purpose," he said in his own defense, splayed hands up in front of him. "And her front tooth was ready to come out anyway, I might add."

"It was," Julia agreed with a grin. "I was almost seven, and that front tooth had been wiggly in my mouth for weeks. Reed, Gage, and I went outside to play a game of hide-and-seek."

"You were hiding outside where bears like Little John are milling about?" Aurora said, eyes rounded.

"We had to stay close to the lodge," Gage told her. "And Dad and Hank were always nearby whenever we went outside to play."

Julia nodded. "Anyway, whenever it was my turn to be the seeker, my brothers, knowing I wasn't very good at it, would help me find them by making noises or poking their heads out."

"Better than hiding for what felt like hours for her to finally find us."

"So that day I was walking past this tree, and Gage popped out from behind it with a ferocious bear growl. It startled me so badly that when I turned to run away my feet got tangled up, and I fell flat on my face."

"I felt terrible about it," Gage said with a nod.

"You were just being a boy," Aurora said with an understanding smile.

"I made out in the deal," Julia said with a grin. "I might have gotten a bloody lip that day, but I also ended up with five dollars to spend the next time we went into Juneau."

Aurora's slender brows lifted. "Gage paid you for causing you to fall?" *Hush money?*

"No." Julia laughed, shaking her head. "The 'tooth fairy' paid me."

"More than double what Reed and I ever got for a tooth," Gage said, sounding playfully salty over it.

"The boys pouted for a week over it."

"I'd love to hear that accident-inducing bear growl," Aurora said with a grin.

"Tell you what," Gage replied. "You do it. I'll do it."

She'd never actually tried to growl like a bear before, but she was game for the challenge. "Okay."

"Okay?" he stuttered, clearly not having expected her to agree.

"This will be entertaining," Julia exclaimed. "I'll be the judge. Loser pays me five dollars."

They both looked her way.

"It was worth a try," Julia said with a shrug.

"Ready?" Gage asked Aurora.

"As I'll ever be," she replied.

"Ladies first."

"Keep in mind that the only bear growls I've heard before have been on TV or my computer."

"She's stalling," Julia whispered to her brother.

"Clearly. How about I go first?" he asked.

Aurora nodded. "Please."

Gage shook his head. "Here goes." Opening his mouth, he let out a ferocious growl that echoed through the trees.

"Wow," Aurora said. "That's impressive."

"I know, right?" Julia replied.

"Your turn," Gage told her.

How had she managed to get herself into a growl-off of all things? Aurora took a deep breath and opened her mouth, but the growl that filtered through the trees around them was not hers. She instinctively jumped toward Gage.

Julia gasped and froze in place.

Gage went on immediate alert, his gaze searching the thicket of trees in the direction the sound had come from. "It's not close, but that could change," he said calmly. "Head back to the lodge," he instructed. "And don't run."

Heart pounding, Aurora turned to follow Julia. Gage brought up the rear.

They were almost to the front porch of the lodge when another ferocious growl erupted behind them. Aurora and Julia shrieked. Gage spun about, fists going up. "Run!" he hollered in a tone that brooked no argument. Then his eyes widened.

Reed burst into a fit of laughter.

"Reed," Gage snarled.

"Were you really going to duke it out with a bear?" he asked in amusement.

"Not funny," Gage grumbled. "And yes, I would have if

it kept the bear from getting to Aurora and our sister while they made their getaway."

"Very realistic growl," Aurora said, but what was playing through her mind was the fact that Gage was prepared to endanger his own life to keep her safe.

"Winner," Julia announced. "Even if that was a dirty trick to play on us."

Reed's guffaws slowed to a few muffled snorts. "Sorry," he replied. "I was on my way out to get some firewood for game night and heard you guys on the path talking. I couldn't resist joining in."

This was exactly the kind of distraction Aurora needed. Her mind wasn't dwelling on the honeymoon she should have been going on in Alaska instead of a job assignment. While she didn't regret the decision she had made, she did mourn the loss of the future she'd been planning for so long. One very like the life Jade was living in Oregon. A husband who loved her. A house of their own. A dog. Well, to be honest, the longing for a dog only came about after she'd called off her wedding. The first time she met Mac, that furry little addition to her sister's family, Aurora was smitten.

"We should probably head back into the lodge now," Julia stated. "The sun is setting fast."

Reed nodded.

After his siblings walked away, Gage turned to Aurora. "Sorry my brother scared you like that. Sometimes he forgets he's thirty."

She laughed. "It's alright. I think the heart needs a good adrenaline-pumping every so often."

"Mission accomplished." He inclined his head toward the porch. "We'd better head in. And be prepared, I intend to defeat my brother soundly tonight."

"Gage," she called after him as he made his way up the porch steps.

Stopping, he glanced back questioningly.

Aurora stepped up to join him on the porch. "I just wanted to say," she began as she looked up into his cobalt-blue eyes, "that you're a very brave and selfless man. Thank you for putting yourself between the bear and Julia and me."

"I did what was right," he told her. "Fortunately for all involved, the bear was my joke-loving little brother."

Aurora wasn't so sure Ben would have reacted the same way if he had been in Gage's position. And Ben and she were still very good friends. Maybe it was Gage having grown up in the wilds of Alaska that had prepared him to take on whatever nature sent his way. Whatever it was, and despite his attempt to play it down, Aurora found it very admirable and incredibly attractive.

"Fish looking out of a fishbowl!" Julia screamed, jumping to her feet.

"That's it," Aurora said with a beaming smile as she stepped forward to toss the scrap of paper she'd been holding onto the discard pile.

"Another point for the girls!" Constance hooted.

Gage's father leaned over on the sofa to give his wife an affectionate kiss on the brow. "That's my girl."

"Hey! Whose team are you on?" Gage asked with an eye roll.

"Yours and Reed's," their father replied. "That doesn't m-mean I can't cheer my sweetheart on when she wins."

"And your daughter," Julia said with a grin.

"And my daughter," he agreed.

Gage looked at Aurora. "Dad occasionally forgets that team competition means not rooting for the bad guys. Or girls, in your case."

His father leaned over to whisper to Aurora, "Looks like I'm about to b-be benched."

Her head tipped back in laughter. Happy, giddy laughter that felt so good.

Reed groaned. "I still can't believe what just happened. How did Julia guess the answer from Aurora making a circle around her head and then puckering her lips?"

"Because I used to have a goldfish," his sister replied. "That's exactly what Bubbles looked like when I'd walk over to his fishbowl to feed him."

Reed dragged his hand down over his face. "Oh, brother."

"Okay, so how did they guess circus bear from Mom prancing around with her arms up in front of her like puppy paws?" Gage said, shaking his head.

"I gave up trying to understand the workings of women's m-minds a very long time ago," Jim admitted with a sigh. "It's much easier to just accept that women know things and c-can share that information without ever speaking a word."

Aurora couldn't keep the smile from her face. Gage's dad was adorable.

"No worry," Julia announced. "Game's over. Girls were the first to score five points."

"Men zero," Reed muttered.

"The ball's in our court now," Gage said determinedly. "The girls chose the last game. We get to choose the next."

"That's right." His father nodded. "So, what do we want to play? C-cards? Maybe trivia?"

"I'm thinking Pictionary," Reed suggested. He looked at Gage. "It's a drawing game, and we know I can draw."

Gage looked at their father. "Dad?"

"Reed does get his artistic ability f-from me. And you can draw a m-mean stick figure."

Aurora snorted, drawing Gage's attention in her direction. "Sorry," she muttered, biting back the giggle that threatened to escape her lips.

"Pictionary it is," Gage declared with a smug grin.

Julia jumped up from the overstuffed chair she'd been sitting in. "I'll get the easel and sketch pad."

"Would anyone like something to drink while Julia sets things up?" their mother asked with a warm smile. "Iced tea, hot tea, a glass of water? Aurora?"

"Iced tea sounds good," Aurora replied. Far less trouble for Gage's mother to make than hot tea.

"I'll have some iced tea, too," Julia called out from the storage closet she was busily digging through across the room next to the check-in counter.

"Same," said Reed.

"Okay. Be right back." She stood up from the sofa and made her way back to the kitchen entrance.

"Just so you know," Julia said as she carried the folded easel and oversized drawing pad back to the sitting area in front of the stone fireplace, "Mom is a way better cook than artist. And I did not inherit Dad's artistic abilities."

Aurora didn't miss the twitch at the corner of Gage's mouth. Ah, so this was the competitive, going-for-the-win side of him his family had talked about. Seeing that fired up her own. "It's not over until it's over," she told Julia.

Gage's mother returned with the drinks, and Reed went up to the drawing pad to start the round. A little less than an hour later, the women were cheering their victory.

Gage looked at his father and brother with a dumbfounded shrug.

"What just happened?" Reed said in clear confusion.

"We just won," Julia announced. "And Aurora is tonight's champion."

"She's good, son," his father said. "Anyone that can guess your sister's misshaped cotton swab on a stick was a matchstick deserves the winner's crown."

"Looked more like a half-eaten cotton candy to me," Reed grumbled.

Julia sent a scowl in their direction. "Aurora figured out what it was. That's all that matters. And she guessed Mom's drawing too. And all she had was a bunch of stars and a curly mustache."

Gage looked at Aurora. "And how is that even possible? You got spaceman from that?"

She shrugged. "Stars are in space. And men have mustaches. Made sense to me."

Reed groaned, rolling his eyes.

"If Reed hadn't taken so long to draw his pictures every time, we might have stood a chance," Gage pointed out.

His brother's gaze swung in Gage's direction. "Art can't be rushed."

"When there's a timer going, it can," their father chimed in.

Aurora loved sitting there listening to their playful post-gameplay chatter, watching Gage's family's antics. This was what she'd grown up with. And proof that she'd made the right decision in giving her engagement ring back. Love was out there. She just hadn't found it yet. But Gage's parents clearly had, as had her parents and her sister. Knowing that gave her hope of someday finding her own heart's connection.

"Morning," Gage greeted, his voice low, when Aurora stepped quietly into the main lodge. "You're up early."

He sat alone at the big table in the main lodge, drinking what Aurora guessed to be coffee. "I guess that makes two of us," she replied softly and then glanced around. "Everyone still asleep?" She kept her voice low as she crossed the room.

"Dad and Reed took a group out fishing this morning, and I've been out back working on the gas fire pit on the patio. It's having some issues with its igniter. Mom and Julia are in the kitchen cleaning up after breakfast."

She sighed, disappointment pulling at her mouth. "I wanted to say my goodbyes to your family before they began their busy day."

He smiled. "Early-riser breakfast for guests scheduled to go out fishing this morning was at six. I ate with Dad and Reed before they left. There's a second breakfast at eight for our remaining guests if you'd like to stick around and have a bite before starting your day."

"I had one of the granola bars from the complimentary snack basket in my cabin and a water from the drink selections your family stocked in the fridge, so I'm not really hungry."

He nodded.

"I'll stop by to see them before we leave for Juneau. When they're not busy feeding their guests. I suppose your father and Reed won't be back in time from fishing for me to see them before I go?"

He shook his head. "Probably not. We'll be flying out before they're scheduled to return."

She frowned. "Please tell them goodbye for me. Hank too."

"I will."

"I had so much fun playing games with your family. Even with Reed, who I'm not sure I've forgiven yet for scaring the daylights out of us."

"He did do that," Gage agreed. "I know Julia really enjoyed having you here. Especially when you girls showed us who ruled the game roost." He smiled. "I appear to have met my match."

Aurora laughed. "I had help. Your mom and sister were so good."

"You weren't so bad yourself."

"Thanks. I had a lot of practice growing up. Julia reminds me so much of my sister, Jade." Who Aurora found herself missing very much. But Jade had a life of her own now. A husband to make new memories with.

"I'm glad you had fun," Gage said.

"I'll let you get back to your coffee. Would you mind very much if I sit by the fire to warm up for a bit?"

"You don't even need to ask," he told her. "The lodge amenities are for our guests as well. In fact, the company is welcome. I'm used to being in the midst of a loud, somewhat nutty family, guests coming in and out of the lodge, and flying people to and from the island. With the exception of when fishing season here comes mostly to an end, and life slows down a bit."

"You're welcome to join me and finish your coffee over by the fire if you like." Pulling off her knit hat, Aurora stuffed it into one of her pockets before removing her jacket.

"I might just take you up on that offer."

She settled in and moved to warm her hands by the fire.

Laying her clothes out near the wood stove in her cabin the night before had helped to dry them out. Only her flannel shirt, which was of a thicker material, was still slightly damp. She'd taken care of that with the hair dryer she'd found in the cabin's bathroom vanity.

"I can add some wood to the fire, if you'd like," Gage said, pulling Aurora from her thoughts.

"No, this is good. I'm warming up already." She rubbed her hands together. "It was chillier out than I expected this morning."

"Only going to get colder now that winter is setting in," Gage said as he settled onto the sofa behind her.

Hands feeling less stiff from the cold, Aurora turned from the fire to find him looking her over with a grin. Immediately self-conscious, she looked down to see what he found so amusing. Had she misaligned her shirt buttons in her hurry to get out and get sunrise shots that morning? Nothing seemed askew.

Aurora lifted her hands, fire-warmed palms up. "What's so amusing?"

Gage shook his head, tempering his grin. "Sorry. Not amusing."

"Then what?" she demanded with a frown.

"I was just thinking that for a city girl, you look like you could have stepped right off the page of one of those outdoor magazines you sell your work to."

She folded her arms across her chest and arched a brow. "So, what you're saying is that I remind you of an elephant trampling down the vegetation in the savanna?"

"What?"

"Or maybe a mountain goat scaling steep cliffs in the Rockies?"

He shook his head. "Not even close. I was referring to the pages in travel magazines and brochures where the pretty girl in casual hiking gear sways readers into traveling to whatever destination she's advertising."

Aurora felt a heated blush creeping up her neck and it wasn't from the fire behind her. "Hardly." She laughed. "I'm just a girl who likes to be prepared for whatever outdoor environment my work takes me to."

She turned back to the fire so he wouldn't see the small smile creeping across her face. *Pretty.* Dressed in faded denim jeans, well-used waterproof hiking boots, and a burgundy and gold plaid flannel shirt. Funny how one simple word could make a person's whole day instantly brighter.

Aurora turned and walked over to join Gage on the sofa.

"Can I get you a cup of coffee or some hot tea?" he asked.

"No, thank you. The fire in the hearth did its job." She bent to grab her camera bag.

"I'm guessing you don't go anywhere without that?"

She sat upright and set the bag on her lap. "You never know when that next great shot is going to happen. Like this morning when I caught a whale breaching the water in the distance from where I stood at the end of the dock."

"That is an incredible moment," Gage replied. "I didn't realize you'd ventured down to the docks this morning."

She nodded. "I woke up early and felt the need for some fresh air, so I went for a walk. And before you say anything, I promise I was vigilant in watching out for Little John."

"That's good to know."

"I'm thinking Big John is more fitting, by the way."

Gage looked at her questioningly.

"I managed to capture a few really amazing shots of the sun's morning glow on Little John's backside as he scrambled away across the grassy area just beyond the larger guest cabins."

Gage's face, definitely a shade lighter than it was when she'd arrived at the lodge, pulled down into a frown. "Lucky for you he wasn't running the other direction."

"I had my bear spray at the ready just in case," she assured him. "That and my treadmill-strengthened lungs."

"Running wouldn't have done you any good if Little John had charged you."

"I know that," she said, rolling her eyes. Did the man think she was completely uneducated when it came to wilderness survival knowledge? "I was referring to my lungs being exercise-strengthened and ready to release ear-splitting screams, should it come to that. Whatever it would have taken to deter Little John from having me for breakfast."

"At least you had a plan," he said, and Aurora could tell he wanted to say more but held back.

"I'm hoping to check out a little more of the island before we leave for Juneau this afternoon. Could you suggest a place to go, time permitting, that would offer the best nature shots?"

"You'd need to stand and turn in circles for that to happen."

She looked at him questioningly.

"Everywhere you look on Conley Island, there's some part of nature that draws you to it. Animals, flowers, waterfalls, gently flowing rivers . . ."

"A northern paradise to be sure," she agreed. "I wish I had more time to experience it all, but I don't," she said with a frown. "That being the case, if you could point me in the direction of the nearest river where guests like to fish, I would really appreciate it. I'm still on assignment for *World Adventures Magazine*, and my remaining time here on Conley Island is quickly running out."

"How about after breakfast I take you to a few spots I think you'll like in one of our utility task vehicles? There will be a little bit of hiking involved once we get to where we're going in the UTV, but you've got the right footwear on for it," he said, his gaze dropping down to her booted feet.

"It's really sweet of you to offer up more of your time, but I'm not about to take you away from the responsibilities you have here at the retreat. I took up enough of your time yesterday."

"You didn't take it," he stated. "I gave it. And until I get you safely back to Juneau, you *are* my responsibility. That being the case, are you sure you wouldn't like a slice or two of toast before we go? I'd hate to have you hungry enough to eat Little John for breakfast should your paths cross again."

Oh, that witty little sense of humor of his, Aurora thought, smiling inwardly as she shook her head. And here she'd believed his grin to be his most charming attribute.

"I think Little John is safe."

"A granola bar and a water," Gage repeated with a husky chuckle. "I'm thinking Little John had better keep right on running in the opposite direction."

CHAPTER SEVEN

"Are you sure I'm not keeping you from anything important?" Aurora asked as Gage assisted her into the side-by-side vehicle.

"The fire pit is repaired, and there are no guests flying in or out today," he replied as he rounded the UTV and stepped into the driver's side. "We're coming to the season's end for guests, so I have a bit more downtime. I was going to fly into Juneau the day after next to pick up some supplies, but I can do that when I take you back. Now buckle up," he told her as he inserted the key in the ignition and started the engine. "Some of the terrain can be a little rough."

Nodding, Aurora did as he instructed. As they drove away from the retreat and into the woods, she said tentatively, "Gage . . ."

He glanced her way.

"Would you mind if I asked about your father?"

Of course she had noticed. Despite his father having come so very far along in his recovery, there were still telltale signs of the stroke he'd had. His gait was still slightly off when he walked. And there was an occasional delay when responding during conversations.

"I don't mind," he told her. "Dad had a stroke last year. Shortly before Thanksgiving. We came close to losing him, but he's a fighter. And after a lot of therapy, both in a rehabilitation facility and then on his own back here at home, he has almost fully recovered. Just an occasional word catching when he speaks and a leg that's taking its time getting back to the way it was before his stroke."

"I'm so glad he's healing," she said with a tender smile. "I know how hard something like that can be on a family. My best friend Emmy's father had a stroke a few years ago. Unfortunately, his recovery wasn't as complete as your father's. But he's still here to be a part of Emmy's and her mother's lives, so they know how blessed they are."

"It definitely makes you look at life a little differently when something like this happens. Things that used to seem so important to me when I was younger have taken a place far lower on my needs and wants list," he replied. "I *want* to appreciate the time I spend with those I love. And I *need* to remember life doesn't always go the way we expect it to, and it's how you choose to deal with the twists and turns that matters most."

There was a shimmer of tears in Aurora's eyes. "So true."

He hadn't meant to bring her down with his response. He was just being honest. Opening up to Aurora felt so easy, so natural. "Prepare your camera. You are about to have a photo opportunity that might just get you the cover of that wildlife magazine."

"Is that so?" she replied, excitement lighting her face.

"Okay, so I might be exaggerating a wee bit, but I do think you'll like the spot I'm taking you to."

She laughed. "I'm on the edge of my seat. Or as close as I can get to it while seat-belted in."

"You should be excited. The sun is shining, and there's no rain on the horizon. A rarity for this time of year."

She looked up at the treetops above them, where rays of sunlight filtered through. "These pines are huge."

"Most of them are Sitka spruce, Alaska's state tree. They can grow over three hundred feet tall."

"They're beautiful," she said as she admired the surrounding pines. "They remind me a lot of some of the trees we have back home in Oregon and up in Olympic National Park."

"I've never been there, but I hear Olympic National Park is something to see."

"It is," she told him. "If you ever have the chance to go there, you won't regret it."

"Maybe someday," he said, his gaze fixed on the path ahead. "Right now, I've taken over the running of our family's retreat until Dad feels like he's ready to take it back on. Until then, my personal life and any adventures I might be tempted to go on are on hold."

"Understandable," she said with a nod. "I'm sure he appreciates what you all have done during his recovery. Hearing him talk about the lodge, about fishing excursions he still gets to join in on, about how he had raised his family here, makes it very clear how much this place means to your father."

Gage frowned. "It really does. He's worked so many years to make this retreat into what it is today. I can only imagine what it would do to Dad's health if we were forced to sell. That's why I have to find a way to build the business back up."

Surprise lit her face. "The retreat's in trouble?"

His frown deepened. "I shouldn't have said anything."

"Oh, Gage, I'm sorry to hear that. I know how much of a financial burden medical issues can be on families."

"It's not that," he said. "The smaller fishing retreats are struggling to compete with money-backed builders who are coming in and building resort-style fishing retreats. I know of two smaller long-running fishing tour businesses that were pretty much squeezed into accepting a buyout."

"That has to be illegal," she said, indignant on his behalf.

"Unfortunately, it's not," he said. "It's a case of the bigger fish swallowing up all the smaller fish. But I have no intention of selling out to the big guys. That's why I was in town when you showed up at Glady's. I had a meeting with the intermediary sent by the private equity firm trying to buy us out. I turned his client's offer down for the second and final time."

She reached out to lay a hand on his arm. "Good for you!"

He shrugged. "I hope I made the right decision. If I can't figure out a way to get back some of the business we've lost to these newer fishing resorts, my family could end up losing it all. That's why I have to stay focused on the end goal. And I'm not about to let some money-hungry investment group turn my father's health issues into their profits."

"I have faith in you," she said, letting her hand fall away. "And I have no doubt your family does as well."

He cast a smile in her direction. "I appreciate that."

The trail they were driving on through the woods widened as it opened to a large, sunlit meadow. In the distance, the winding river he wanted Aurora to see flowed gently around peeking boulders. When it wasn't rainy season and water depths were lower, small islands of time-smoothed stones could be seen with the water trickling over them. Beyond the river was a mountain thick with pines and dotted with trees haloed in shades of yellow and crimson.

"It looks like a postcard," Aurora breathed beside him.

"One of my favorite spots on the island," Gage admitted as he brought the UTV to a stop. Cutting the engine, he climbed out.

"I can understand why." Aurora pulled the camera she'd brought along with her from the padded bag at her side. Then she practically jumped out.

Gage smiled as he followed her.

She paused every few steps to take a few more pictures. "It's so tranquil here. And look how the distant mountain, with the billowy white clouds above it, reflects its mirror image across the water!"

"I thought you would like the view."

"Like it? I love it!" She glanced his way. "Is the fishing good here? Because I could see this river pictured in *World Adventures Magazine*."

No sooner had the question left her lips than an eagle flew past, swooping down over the river to catch a small fish. As fast as it came in, the eagle was gone, flying off with its skillfully caught meal.

"Well," Aurora laughed, "I suppose that answers my question. I'm only sorry I didn't have my camera aimed in the right direction. That would have been a beautiful shot."

"I'm not so sure that poor fish would agree."

"Gage!" she groaned. "Way to turn a majestic moment of power and grace into a fish's worst nightmare."

Gage chuckled. "Sorry. How about we go with the eagle accidentally dropping it further on down the river as he flew off toward his nest."

"Good for that fish," she replied and then sighed. "Bad for the baby eaglets waiting to be fed."

"Thankfully, their mother flew back with a snake that she found, and the eaglets had a fine feast." He glanced her way. "Does the snake part work?"

"Perfectly," she replied, her smile returning.

"Now, getting back to your question, the fishing is plentiful here," he told her. "There are still a few varieties of salmon around for catching this time of year, as well as rainbow trout."

Aurora brought her camera up and took several pictures of the water and the view beyond it. "If I were a fisherman, I'd want to spend hours fishing here just for the view alone."

"I am a fisherman, and I have spent a good part of the day here fishing for that night's dinner at the lodge more times than I can count," he told her as he gazed out over the gently flowing water. "It's peaceful here. A great place to relax and unwind."

"Would you mind if I took a picture of you standing alongside the river?" she asked hopefully. "You just seem to fit so perfectly into this beautifully rugged landscape."

He laughed. "I've never been compared to a landscape before. Thank you. I think."

"Take it as a compliment," she replied with a grin before motioning him closer to the water. "That's it. One more step to the left. We want to get the mountain peak behind you in the background."

Gage took a step to the left.

"Sorry. My left. Your right."

Nodding, he took two steps in the opposite direction. "Better?"

"Perfect," she replied, snapping several shots.

His brows rose. "No one, two, three? Or 'Say cheese'?"

"You can pose if you like," Aurora told him. "But I prefer my shots to be more organic."

He grinned. "You prefer organic over this?" Gage did a playful flexing-muscle pose that made Aurora snort with laughter. Then he switched it up, shifting into his best imitation of a *GQ* model pose.

Giggling, she shook her head. "If you ever give up your piloting career, I think you definitely have a future in modeling."

"Good to know I have options," he said with a chuckle.

She lowered her camera. "I think I have enough river shots."

"How about I take a few of you?" he asked, holding out a hand.

She blinked in surprise. "Of me?"

"If I had to be the subject of some of your pictures, I think it's only fair you are too."

"But I'm the photographer," she countered.

"Whose pretty smile should be captured." He wiggled his fingers. "I promise not to break your camera."

"Well, I suppose since I trusted you with my life when you flew me here, I can trust you with my camera." Aurora handed over her prized possession. "The settings should be good. Just click that button," she said.

"I promise not to let you down. Now, let's have you look out over the water."

"I thought we were going with organic," she said as she followed his instructions.

Gage stepped farther up along the riverbank to get just the right angle. "Tip your head slightly. That's it."

She glanced his way. "Have you done this before?"

"Focus on the water," he reminded her as he adjusted the lens for the shot. The camera was going to love her. He didn't have to be a photographer to know that much. "And yes, I have. About a year or so ago, we had a couple ask if they could get married on one of our fishing boats during their stay. Of course Mom said yes. She's a diehard romantic."

"I could tell," Aurora said, so quiet he almost didn't hear her. "She and your father are so adorable together."

"The couple hired me to fly their preacher in for their version of a perfectly romantic Alaskan wedding." He snapped another shot. "Only they didn't have a photographer to capture their special moment, so I volunteered. They wanted to exchange nuptials while the boat was moving, and Reed had to be at the wheel."

"That was nice of you," she said, turning away to look out over the water.

Was that a quiver he'd heard in her voice when she'd responded?

"Their pictures came out really good, if I should say so myself," he went on as he made his way back to where she stood. "Of course, how could they not when you've got a couple clearly in love and a backdrop of the water and the distant, snowcapped mountain peaks?"

A soft sniffle had Gage lowering the camera and closing the rest of the distance between them. "Hey," he said gently, "everything okay?"

She shrugged. "I thought it was—I was—but now I'm not sure." Another sniffle followed.

That didn't sound like okay to him. With the camera held securely in one hand, he wrapped a comforting arm around her shoulders. "You can have your camera back. I certainly didn't mean to upset you."

Her hand trembled as she took the camera from his

grasp and lowered it to her side. "It's not about the camera. Honestly, it's nothing you did at all."

"Then what's wrong? Are you not feeling well? We can head back to the lodge if you aren't."

She brushed a tear from her cheek. "Today was supposed to be my wedding day."

"What?" he said in surprise. That was not anywhere on his list of possible reasons for this sudden change in her mood. She'd been so happy on the way there.

Aurora looked up, her teary-eyed gaze meeting his. "I was engaged, and Ben had agreed to bring me to Alaska for our honeymoon. I wanted to experience the place that brought my mom and dad together all those years ago. But, as you can see, there was no wedding."

"Aurora," he breathed, "I'm so sorry." He drew her into the circle of his arms.

She nodded, accepting his comforting embrace.

"What happened?" he asked, immediately regretting it. His grimace was lost in her hair as he rested his chin lightly atop her head. What if her fiancé had passed away? He would feel awful for stirring up painful memories for her if that were the case.

Aurora lifted her head from his shoulder and took a step back as Gage released her. Looking up, she met his gaze. "Ben and I have been friends forever," she began.

Have been. Not past tense. Relief for her swept through him.

"Since childhood," she went on. "I think it was second grade. As adults, with no serious relationships for either of us, we decided to give dating a try. It was comfortable."

"Comfortable?" Not exactly how he hoped to describe his connection with the person he'd someday be marrying.

She nodded. "Our parents are friends. We shared the

same friends back home. We both moved to Seattle for work. It was easy enough. Ben and I dated for a little over a year before he proposed. We went through all the motions of planning our wedding, but I couldn't stop thinking about how much I wanted the kind of marriage my parents have. My sister has. *Your* parents have."

"A good thing to strive for. Especially when you are exchanging vows to be together for the rest of your life."

"I realized, thankfully before it was too late, that Ben and I weren't going to have that same special sparkle. We were far better suited to be friends than the married couple we were making plans to become. Six months ago, I asked Ben to come over so we could talk. Before he left, I gave him his ring back, calling off our engagement."

"How did he take your ending things?"

"I didn't want to hurt him, but I think when I sat him down to talk about my feelings, he was. Once it was done and he'd taken some time to think over my reasons, Ben realized I was right. We went back to being just really good friends."

Gage's brows drew together. "Then why did my talking about that couple getting married on one of our fishing boats make you emotional? Are you second-guessing your decision to call off the engagement?" He wasn't so sure he wanted to hear her reply. Did Aurora want to get back together with her ex?

"No," she said, sounding sincere in her response. "I don't have any regrets about not marrying Ben."

"Then why are you upset?"

She thought about the question for a long moment. Just when Gage thought she might not respond to it, she said, "Mine was supposed to be the perfect Alaskan honeymoon with its breathtaking visual backdrop. I began planning it when I was a little girl, listening to my mom's stories of how she met my dad and their time spent here. I've been chasing a dream that isn't ready to be caught, which makes me feel like life is passing me by. My baby sister is happily married, complete with the white picket fence little girls dream about. Only her fence is a bit more on the cream side than white, but it's there all the same, wrapping around their cute little Cape Cod with their adorable little pup racing around their backyard. And where am I?"

"Standing by a river in Alaska," he answered with a grin, trying to lighten the mood.

A hint of a smile tugged at the corners of her mouth. "Besides that," she told him. "Sure, I've got a really good career and friends and family who care about me. But I don't have a family of my own. Or a dog to come home to after a long day of work." She paused. "I suppose I need to focus on the positive in this situation. My toilet seat is always down."

Gage blinked. "Excuse me?"

She giggled. "My sister's one pet peeve is her husband always leaving the toilet seat up. Believe me, I hear about it often."

"And what do you tell her?"

"To glue the seat down."

He threw his head back and gave a hearty chuckle. "Remind me never to get on your bad side."

"I think you're safe."

"I'm sorry about how things turned out with Ben," he told her. But was he really? If she had been on the verge of marrying, he might never have crossed paths with her.

"No, I apologize for taking our beautiful day and making it uncomfortable."

He shook his head. "It wasn't. I just don't like seeing

you upset. I know something, or maybe I should say some-where, that might put that pretty smile back onto your face. Camera at the ready?" he asked, his tone teasing.

"Ready."

"Here we are," Gage announced as they stepped out from the covering of trees they had parked beneath.

Aurora gasped, unable to keep the smile from her face. "Oh my gosh!" she said as they moved toward another body of water. "They're sooo cute!"

"I take it you've never seen beavers frolicking in the wild before," he said, grinning.

She lifted her camera and began snapping away. "This is a first," she replied. "I know these aren't fishing-related pictures and have nothing to do with my assignment, but I can't resist."

"I didn't think you'd be able to," Gage said from behind her.

"I suppose a lot of the pictures I've taken this trip aren't assignment-related. I just think Alaska is amazing." Aurora zoomed in on her subjects. "Look at their flat tails."

"Do you know they use them to warn their families about danger nearby?"

"I didn't."

"They slap the water with their tails, which sends a signal to the other beavers to hide when wolves, bears, or even coyotes, to name their most feared predators, are nearby. That urgent slapping sound sends a warning to the others to swim under the water and hide in their lodges. Their tail serves other purposes, too, like helping them to balance and swim."

She lifted a brow. "You are like a walking Alaskan wilds encyclopedia."

He grinned. "Hey, when you grow up on a fairly remote island in Alaska, you know these things. Not to mention, we need to be knowledgeable to keep our guests safe. For instance, we are watching those beavers from across the water. Some people might try and get an up-close look at them. But beavers can be territorial and have been known to attack by biting and scratching. They also pose a high risk for rabies."

"I'll keep my distance then," Aurora replied, looking up at Gage. "And I won't be hugging any moose either."

"I'd say that's a pretty good plan. More people are injured in Alaska by moose than bears each year."

She lowered her camera. "They're more dangerous than bears? I wouldn't have thought that."

"Actually, bears are more dangerous, but they tend to avoid people. Moose, however, can be found in larger numbers, closer to more populated areas. They can be very aggressive and will charge anything they consider a threat when it's mating season, which runs from September through October."

"Have you ever come close to being charged by a moose?" she asked, her interest now turned fully to Gage. She found his wealth of knowledge about wildlife so mentally attractive. But then, she was a big nature lover. But it wasn't just his mind she found herself drawn to. It was his kind eyes, that make-your-knees-weak smile and, to her shock, because her ex-fiancé had been clean-shaven, Gage's lightly bearded jaw.

"Nope. But I know to keep my distance," he told her. "A lot of tourists don't. You've seen those video uploads of people stepping right up to bison or elk at places like

Yellowstone and suffering the consequences." He glanced in the direction of the beavers. "You all done here?"

"Is it time to head back already?"

"There's so much more here I could show you, but you have a flight to catch. Let's head back and grab a sandwich before we go, because a granola bar isn't enough to sustain you after a morning of hiking about and exploring."

"I am getting a little hungry, but we missed lunch."

He smiled. "You're in luck. I happen to have special access to the fridge and have been known to whip up a mean BLT in times of hunger. Or, if you prefer, I could make you a plain turkey sandwich, additional fixings optional."

"A BLT sounds delicious."

"Good. And you can say your goodbyes to Mom and Julia before we fly out." He inclined his head. "Let's head out."

They walked back to the UTV and took a shortcut back to the lodge. As they pulled up, Julia stepped out onto the porch to greet them with a wave.

"How was your ride?" she asked with a warm smile.

"Incredible," Aurora answered. "We went to a river and saw an eagle swoop in for a fish right in front of us. And then we went to a place where beavers have built a lodge. I took a bunch of pictures and can't wait to load them onto my laptop and go through them all."

"Why don't you go in and warm up by the fire and visit with Julia. I'll head to the kitchen to make us something to eat before flying back to Juneau. I just need to know: mayo or no mayo?"

"Definitely mayo," Aurora replied.

"BLT with mayo coming right up," he called back over

his broad shoulder as he walked toward the entrance to the lodge's kitchen.

"Maybe you can give me a sneak peek of some of the pictures you took on your outing with Gage while you wait."

His sister looked so hopeful. How could Aurora refuse? Besides, it was nice to spend time with someone who shared her love of photography. Aurora smiled as she pulled out her camera. "Maybe you can give me your opinion. Tell me which ones you like best."

"I'd love to."

They crossed the room to the sofa and settled down in front of the warming fire. Aurora turned on the viewing screen and handed her camera over to Julia. "Here you go. It's starting at the end of our ride. When you get to the photos of the docks at sunrise, that will be all of today's photos."

Gage's sister held the camera securely between both hands as she clicked through the pictures. "These are so good," she said in genuine awe. "I can't believe this close-up shot of the beaver swimming with its tail sticking straight up out of the water. The detail and clarity are amazing."

"The lighting was perfect, and I had the camera set in aperture priority mode with a small f-stop. And then—"

"Aurora, wow!" Julia gasped.

Aurora looked down to see what picture had made Julia react that way. To her surprise, it wasn't one of the river with its magnificent backdrop or the whale breaching the water at sunrise; it was Gage playfully flexing his muscles in that pose by the river.

"He didn't want to have his picture taken, but I convinced him to humor my photographic whim. That's what I got."

Julia looked up at her. "It's perfect." She glanced down at the picture on the screen again.

"I thought so too," Aurora agreed. "Even if he was being silly."

"While I will be the first to admit the muscle pose looks a bit awkward, it's what you captured in his eyes that is so wonderful."

His eyes?

"You have had such a positive effect on my brother. I haven't seen any real spark of true happiness in his eyes since Jess . . ." Her words trailed off.

Aurora didn't miss Julia's sudden discomfort. "Jess?"

Julia frowned. "Gage's ex-girlfriend. Hers is a name we avoid speaking around here. Forget I brought it up."

"They were serious?"

Gage's sister glanced in the direction her brother had gone off in and then back to Aurora. "He was," she replied. "Her? Not enough."

"She broke his heart?"

Julia nodded.

"Lunch is served."

Gage's booming voice had both Julia and Aurora jumping guiltily from their perches on the sofa. Julia handed the camera back to Aurora and stood. "Thank you for sharing your pictures with me. Gage can give you my number. Please send me a few, especially the one I loved of Gage. Mom will love it too."

"I will. Thank you for making me feel so at home during my stay here."

"I appreciate you sharing your photography knowledge with me and for giving me so many tips to make my pictures look more professional."

"No problem." Aurora had spent a little time at the end

of game night showing Julia a few different settings she liked to use when taking pictures. Gage's sister soaked the information up like a sponge and had an eye for photography.

Julia leaned in to give Aurora a quick hug. "It was so nice to meet you. I hope you'll come back again to visit someday."

"I would love that," Aurora said, at that moment realizing how much she meant those words. Her time at this completely unplanned stop had been far too short. Conley Island held so many amazing things just waiting to be captured in a photograph.

"Have a safe flight," Julia said with a wave as she walked away, casting a smile at her brother as she passed by him.

"What was that look about?" Gage asked as he set their lunch tray down on the coffee table.

"She might have seen the picture I took of you by the river," Aurora said with a grin.

He rolled his eyes. "I'll never live that one down."

"I'm sure you will someday," she teased. She saw it now. That spark of something in his eyes she hadn't noticed when they'd first met. She knew a little about matters of the heart not working out. You just had to hope there was something better waiting for you out there somewhere. That's what she held onto.

Gage handed her a small lunch plate. "Your BLT with mayo. Can I get you anything else?"

Aurora knew exactly what she wanted. She'd been thinking about it all day. More time. Time to further explore the island for the wealth of perfect shots she knew it harbored. And time to get to know Gage a little better.

She looked up at him with a smile. "How about a cabin at Living the Good Life Fishing Retreat for another week?"

CHAPTER EIGHT

"Are you sure you're okay out here?" Gage asked with a nod toward the cabin behind Aurora. He'd been shocked when Aurora had told him she wanted to extend her time on Conley Island, making it a week's stay instead. He was certain she would be ready to get back to her life in Seattle. To her friends and exciting gallery showings. But Aurora Daniels kept surprising him with her words, her actions, and her ability to make him look at the things in his life with renewed appreciation.

"The answer is the same as it was the first night."

"Thought it might be," he replied with a grin. "Ready for today's adventure?"

"Are you done with your work?"

"Ever the taskmaster," he replied with a grin. "You'll be happy to know I took care of what needed doing first thing this morning. And I don't fly guests back to Juneau until tomorrow morning. So I'm free to take you to see more of the island. Mom's even insisted on packing us a picnic lunch to take so you won't feel rushed to get back here."

"That is so thoughtful of her," Aurora replied.

"We might still find ourselves back here for lunch. There's a forecast of rain for this afternoon. I tried to tell her that, but once Mom had her mind set on making up a picnic, that was it."

"I appreciate that your mother's a positive thinker." Aurora glanced up at the sky through the treetops above them. "Looks like it's already starting to cloud up a little. I'd hate for your mother to go to all that effort and us not be able to enjoy it. We might just have to eat an early lunch fast if the weather requires it while we're out touring the island."

He chuckled. "Sounds like a plan."

"Oh, and speaking of possible rain, I had better run back in and grab my raincoat." Aurora turned and hurried up onto the porch, disappearing into the cabin.

Gage made a mental note to grab his raincoat too when they went back to the lodge to pick up the feast his mother was preparing. Just in case.

The cabin door swung open again, and Aurora came out with light, springy steps, carrying her duck poncho and a happy smile. It was good to see the sadness she'd experienced the day before gone, replaced by that fervor for adventure he'd first seen in her.

A grin slid across his face at the sight of her. Yellow was definitely her color. Bright like the sunshine and her beautiful smile. Gage watched as Aurora made her way down the steps that fronted the cozy little cabin's porch. Steps he and Reed had replaced just that past spring.

Theirs might be a small, family-run fishing retreat, but there was no slacking in the upkeep of it. Even after their father had fallen ill. If anything, it had made him, Reed, and Julia more appreciative of the legacy their father had built. One that all three of them had chosen to remain a part of as adults. A decision that, in the end, had played a big part in his relationship with Jess ending. But it was a choice he'd make again if he had it to do all over. Like Aurora, Gage and his ex had been better off parting ways, because Conley Island was and would always be *home* to him.

"Hello?"

Gage blinked, surprised to find Aurora standing right there in front of him, her expression one of concern. Talk about blanking out for a moment. Since her arrival, Aurora had sent his thoughts and contemplative moments into overdrive.

"You okay?"

He nodded. "Sorry, got a little lost in my thoughts."

"For a moment there, I thought I might have to put this rain poncho on and start waddling around, quacking like a duck to pull you out of that daze you were in."

His gaze dropped to the bundle of bright yellow polyester tucked securely in the crook of her arm. "I should have stayed lost in thought a little longer," he said with a grin. "Your duck waddle imitation would have undoubtedly been a sight to see."

"Too late," she said, starting off down the trail toward the lodge.

For being nearly a foot shorter than his six feet one inches, he'd noticed the woman could cover a lot of ground in a very short amount of time. Gage lengthened his steps to catch up.

"Speedy little thing, aren't you?" he said as they followed the trail through the woods and past the other studio-sized cabins.

"Remember that if we run into Little John or one of his cousins."

"Ah, but it wouldn't matter, because I would stop and

use my big, strong muscles," he said, flexing as he walked, "which you took pictures of yesterday, to save us."

She burst into a fit of giggles. "Stop," she pleaded. "I can't breathe."

"I like it when you laugh," he said.

"I like it when you flex your muscles."

This time it was Gage throwing his head back in laughter. She was quick and witty and made him feel good about who he was. Even if her words were only meant to be playful.

They fell in step with each other, conversation flowing easily.

"I have to be honest," he said as they walked together.

She glanced his way.

"I was more than a little surprised you wanted to stay on."

She glanced his way. "You were? Why?"

He frowned and turned his focus to the trail ahead. "My ex-girlfriend, her name was Jess, found staying here pretty much unbearable. I'm not sure what she expected when she agreed to fly to the island to stay and work here with me and my family, but clearly it wasn't what her dreams were made of. She left three days after she arrived, more than ready to get back to the mainland. I should have known she wouldn't be happy here. That's on me. Life here on the island can be challenging at times."

"Well," Aurora said, "I happen to be enthralled with this little Alaskan island. I'm sorry things didn't work out with Jess the way you hoped they would."

"I'm not so sure I am anymore," he admitted.

Aurora's cell phone rang in the pocket of her jacket. They slowed their pace as she pulled it out to answer it. "It's Emmy," she told him. Then, pressing the answer button, she said, "Hi, Emmy! Hold on. We're walking. I'm going to put you on speaker."

"Aurora . . ."

"Okay, you're on. Say hello to Gage."

"Hello, man who whisked my best friend away and might be holding her hostage for all I know."

"Emmy," Aurora gasped.

Gage laughed. "I would have to be able to catch her first. She's a really fast walker."

"She is fast," her friend agreed.

"Was she ever in the Olympics?" he asked, sending a teasing grin Aurora's way. "I know they have a speed-walking event."

This time it was Emmy who was snorting with laughter. "I never thought about that, but I think she could be a real contender."

"Hello," Aurora said. "I'm still here."

"He's funny," Emmy said. "He scores a point for that."

"He's not trying to score any points," Aurora said, sounding suddenly embarrassed.

"I might be," he countered.

"You're not," Aurora told him. "Emmy, we're almost to the lodge. Can I call you later?"

"Finish your call with your friend," Gage said. "I'll meet you inside when you're through."

He started up the lodge's front steps, hearing Emmy, who was still on speaker, say, "Another point for the pilot."

Grinning, Gage opened the door and stepped inside, giving Aurora some privacy to finish up her conversation with her friend.

"Emmy, stop with the points," Aurora begged after the door closed behind Gage.

"You like him, don't you? Is that why you're staying on the island longer?"

Aurora fell silent. She had never lied to her friend, and she didn't want to start now. But her feelings where Gage was concerned were too new and too unexpected to sort through.

"He's a really nice guy," she said. "And I've enjoyed spending time with him. He knows so much about the wildlife here. We went out on one of the retreat's utility vehicles yesterday so I could get some river pictures for the magazine. A bald eagle swooped right down in front of us to snatch a fish out of the water."

"Eew," her friend replied, and Aurora knew without seeing her what face she was making on the other end of the call. Emmy was not as comfortable with nature.

"You eat fish," Aurora pointed out.

"Already skinned and cooked and laying atop a bed of rice."

Aurora glanced toward the lodge, catching sight of Gage through the wall of windows. He was standing by the table talking to his mother. "Emmy, thank you for checking on me. It means a lot. But I need to go. Gage is taking me out in search of more wildlife to photograph."

"Have fun," her friend replied.

"I will. Talk soon," Aurora said. Ending the call, she slid her phone back into her coat pocket and then made her way inside.

"Hello," Constance greeted with a warm smile.

"Hello," Aurora replied.

"What a surprise to hear you've decided to extend your stay here."

She nodded. "It was a last-minute decision. After going out in the UTV with Gage yesterday afternoon, I realized there's a wealth of photographic opportunities still waiting for me here."

"Will staying on be an issue for you with your job?" Constance asked.

"I'm pretty much self-employed. And as far as my magazine assignment I came to Alaska for, as long as I have internet service, I'm good."

"How nice that you can travel about while you work," his mother said as she reached for the basket on the table beside her. "Here's the picnic lunch I fixed for you."

"That was really thoughtful of you," Aurora said with a grateful smile as Gage took the wicker basket from his mother.

"I have always loved a picnic," Constance said. "Whether it's overly warm out or briskly cold. It's all about being outside and appreciating nature with someone you enjoy being around. And one important thing to remember while you're sitting there on a picnic, surrounded by nature and whatever food you've brought along, is to take a moment to soak in your surroundings." She sighed, as if remembering all the picnics she had gone on.

"I've never been on one," Aurora admitted.

"Never?" Gage said in surprise.

Aurora shook her head. "No, but I do appreciate being away from all the noise and craziness of the city. I like soaking up the peace and tranquility and beauty of nature that most people tend to take for granted."

"Then I'm so glad you will get to experience one before you go home." Gage's mother clapped her hands together. "Okay, you have your picnic lunch. Gage, be sure to grab a blanket, one of the waterproof-bottomed ones, on your way out. You wouldn't want any of the dampness leftover from the recent rain to soak through."

"I thought we would eat in the UTV," he replied. "The seats are comfortable enough. And no worries about our pants having water seep into them."

His mother frowned. "Gage Weston, have I taught you nothing?"

His dark brows lifted. "What did I do?"

She shook her head. "If you're taking a girl on a picnic, you don't eat your food seated in a utility vehicle, comfy seats or not."

"This isn't *that* kind of picnic," he said determinedly, brows drawn in consternation. Gage looked at Aurora, a look of frustration on his handsome face.

"I'm sure she knows that," Aurora said as she stepped over to peek under the flap of the basket Gage was holding clutched in his sturdy grip. She had come to learn that the best tactic in an uncomfortable situation was to redirect focus to something else. "This looks and smells delicious," she said as she released the lid.

Gage's mother smiled. "The cookies are fresh out of the oven."

Aurora looked up at Gage. "I'd really like to see what it's like to experience a real picnic, blanket and all. But you're already taking up your time to show me around, so I'm happy to have lunch wherever makes you the most comfortable."

"I'll go grab a blanket," he said, setting the basket back onto the table and walking off.

"Thatta girl," Constance said, sounding quite pleased. "Sometimes men just need a little push to get them out of their stale old comfort zone."

"Julia told me about Jess," Aurora admitted.

"Oh dear," Constance said with a soft groan. "That wasn't really her place to bring up."

"It wasn't intentional, I promise. But once she'd made mention of her, she offered up a very brief explanation of Gage having had a relationship that hadn't ended well for him. Gage also brought it up in conversation on the way here."

"He did?" his mother said in surprise. "My son rarely talks about that relationship. Thank you for getting him to open up. He keeps his emotions pretty guarded these days. Gage has taken so much on his shoulders since his father's stroke last year."

"We've both gone through relationships that didn't work out," Aurora explained. "I think that made it easier for him to talk to me about her. For her to have walked away from a relationship with a man who is so caring and kind and funny is beyond me. And I, personally, can't imagine what there was for her not to love about this place. It's so remote and enchanting. The only thing that could make being here more perfect would be if I caught a glimpse of the Northern Lights."

"They are truly something to see," Constance said. "And thank you for your kind words about our little piece of Alaska and about my son. If I had the power to paint the colors of the Northern Lights across the night sky for you I most definitely would. But Reed is our painter, and even he can't paint the sky."

"What about the sky?" Gage asked as he returned with the blanket.

"Aurora is hoping to see the Northern Lights before she goes back to Seattle."

He grabbed for the picnic basket, letting hang by his side. "I can take you to see our rivers and creeks, help you find animals to photograph, fly you above the landscape while you take pictures, but I'm afraid bringing the Northern Lights to you is out of my control."

Aurora smiled. "I know it's a matter of chance to see them when I'm only here for a short time. But a girl can hope."

"She most certainly can," his mother agreed with a smile as her gaze shifted to her son. "There's always hope."

"I see what your mother loves about this," Aurora said with a sated sigh as she lay on her back, looking up at the shifting clouds. It was chilly out, but not unbearable, and they were dressed for the weather. "I spend my time photographing things around me, but I rarely take the time to appreciate the sky in all its glory without it being through my camera lens."

"I'm up in that same sky enough to know how beautiful it can be, but this one is promising rain soon," Gage warned as he took in the billowy dark gray clouds drifting in, slowly swallowing up the whisp of gray clouds Aurora had been admiring.

She brought her camera up to her face again, adjusted its focus, and then snapped several more shots.

Gage smiled as he lay stretched out on his side, watching her. His mother was right. This was far better than sharing a meal while sitting in a utility vehicle. Unlike Jess, who didn't eat meat or pasta, avoided potatoes, and hated peanut butter, Aurora ate what his mother had prepared for them without complaint or hesitation. Peanut butter and jelly sandwiches, pasta salad, and homemade chocolate chip cookies. Who hated peanut butter? That alone should have been a sign of their impending doomed relationship.

"So how long have you wanted to be a pilot?" Aurora asked as she made adjustments to her camera.

"Ever since I was a little boy," he replied. "Dad had shown me how to make paper airplanes. Reed drew a cockpit with a pilot inside on each one I'd make. But each time I tried to send them up into the air, expecting a long, smooth glide, those homemade paper planes would do loops and then crash to the ground. I was determined to make it work, so I sat for hours flying plane after plane, making adjustments. Reed gave up drawing pilots inside them after the first dozen or so and went back into the house. When Dad came out to tell me dinner was ready, he was surprised to find me still making paper planes. By then, I was beyond frustrated about not being able to keep any of my planes up in the air for any real length of time."

"I'll bet he felt so bad for you," Aurora said. "But he had to admire your tenacity."

"I'm sure he felt bad, but he didn't comment about my failure. Instead, he sat down on those porch steps beside me and looked up at the sky. He said that if it were me behind the controls instead of those pilots Reed had drawn that he knew I would have soared through the skies for hours." Gage looked up into the sky he'd flown through countless times. "That's when I knew what I wanted to do when I grew up. And do you know what?"

"What?"

"That last plane flew out into the yard in the most impressive glide ever." Gage chuckled. "I think my dad still has that paper plane sitting on the windowsill in his office."

Aurora fell silent.

He looked her way, seeing the sheen of unshed tears in

her eyes. Gage's eyes widened. "Aurora? Did I say something to upset you?"

"No," she replied. "I got emotional hearing your story. What a wonderful father you have. The way he handled your discouragement was so well done. It's no surprise he raised such a wonderful son. Two actually," she hurried to add. "And daughter."

He nodded. "We couldn't have asked for a better father. I realize that more than ever after nearly losing him last year," he added with a hitch of emotion in his voice.

"I can only imagine how scary that time in your life was for you and your family. I know your father has to be so proud of you all for how you kept things going here at the retreat while he was unable to do so. As proud as I'm sure he was of you that day your final paper plane took flight all because you hadn't given up."

Gage took a moment to let her words sink in. *He hadn't given up.* Just as he wouldn't give up on finding a way to make the retreat more profitable so it would remain where it belonged: in his family. He'd recently worked a deal with a friend in Juneau who sold hot tubs, which, apparently, were a popular amenity with travelers according to research he'd done online. It was scheduled to be installed in mid-October. The first of many upgrades Gage hoped to implement as their finances allowed. "How about you? When did you realize you wanted to be a photographer?"

"I was about seven or eight when my parents bought me my first camera for Christmas. I went around taking pictures of all our neighbors' cats and dogs. My mom had the pictures printed out, and we delivered them to their owners. Several were so happy with the pictures that they paid me for them. It was way more money than I had ever gotten from the tooth fairy."

Gage laughed at that.

"I decided that if I could make money doing something that was as fun as taking pictures, that's what I was going to do when I grew up. And there you have it. My road to becoming the me I am today." She brought her camera back up to shoot a few more pictures of the passing clouds.

"I'm glad I got the chance to know the 'me' you grew up to be."

"Same." She snuck a peek his way. "Not about knowing myself but getting to know you."

"I figured as much," he replied with a grin as he watched her slip back into professional photographer mode. This was definitely her life's passion, he decided. And she was good at it. Really good. "I looked you up online."

Lowering the camera, she glanced his way. "What?"

"Not in a creepy stalker kind of way, I promise. I wanted to know more about your photographic work, so I researched you last night."

"So you found out about my past jail sentences?"

His eyes widened in surprise. "Uh, no, that didn't come up."

Aurora giggled softly. "You should see the look on your face."

He was too busy looking at hers.

"In case you haven't figured it out yet, I was only kidding about my having done jail time."

"I would be shocked if you had," he told her. "You don't seem the troubled type. What I did learn was that you have been more than a little humble when talking about your career. I was very impressed by all your achievements. The array of awards you've received for your pictures. Not to mention having several of your photographs picked up by various magazines."

A blush deepened the color in her already weather-pinkened cheeks. "Thank you. I'm pretty impressed by your career choice too. I could never fly a plane."

"Sure, you could."

She shook her head. "Not safely. My attention would be too distracted by all the photographic opportunities around and below me."

"Okay, so we leave the flying to me."

A drop of rain landed on the tip of Aurora's nose. She pushed upright. "I think the rain's here."

"I think you're right," Gage said, jumping to his feet. "Take care of your camera. I'll clean up." He hurried to scoop up their plates and the empty containers his mother had sent their food in as the rain began to fall harder.

Aurora packed her camera away and quickly covered it with her raincoat. Then she stood and grabbed for the basket, opening its lid for Gage.

"Go get in the UTV," he told her as he removed it from her grasp. "You can put your camera bag in the waterproof storage box in the back of the vehicle."

"No need. I have it safely tucked away under my rain-coat," she told him as she bent to gather up the picnic blanket his mother had so wisely insisted they bring with them.

The rain was coming down harder now.

"Aurora, stop folding it. Just bundle it up and let's go," he told her. "You're getting soaked."

"Better me than my camera," she replied with a smile as rain streamed down her face.

Gage didn't miss the slight shiver that followed her words. Guilt filled him. "I should have suggested we pack up as soon as we were done eating," he said with a frown as they returned to the utility vehicle. "I've lived here long enough to know that rain was imminent." But when she'd pulled out her camera and stretched out across the blanket to take pictures of the sky, he couldn't think of anything except how beautiful Aurora looked when she was caught up in her moment of creativity.

They ran together for the cover of the ash tree and the awaiting vehicle. She climbed into her seat while he placed the basket on the floor in front of the rear seats.

Gage grabbed for his raincoat and held it out to her. "Put this on. It'll help keep you warm while we drive back." Her long hair was clinging to her cheeks in wet waves, and her coat and jeans were every bit as rain-soaked as his own, so he knew the chill it brought along with it.

"You need it," she countered with a worried frown. "I'll put mine on and then shove my camera bag underneath it."

"Keep your camera covered and use mine. This coat is weatherproof, so a raincoat for me isn't really necessary," he told her. Reaching down, Gage started the engine.

"Sorry the rain cut our day short," he said as they drove out from under the broad canopy of the ash tree and headed across the meadow they had picnicked in.

"It's a good thing I'm staying for a week," she reminded him with a smile. "There might be time to try this again."

"Rest assured," he told her. His mom had been right. There was nothing like a picnic to brighten up your day. Even when the rain was coming down.

CHAPTER NINE

"Thank you for letting me help out with breakfast this morning," Aurora said as she counted out eleven plates from the hutch in the kitchen. She would be joining Gage and his family, as would their five remaining guests.

"You should be in the great room relaxing and visiting with the other guests," Gage's mother fretted as she pulled the two pans of breakfast casseroles she had made that morning out of the commercial-sized double ovens.

"I'd rather be helping," Aurora assured her. "Eleven people are a lot to prepare breakfast for." And Gage's mother didn't skimp on what she served. That morning's menu was a choice of two different breakfast casseroles. One filled with hash browns, eggs, bacon, ham, sausage, and cheese. The other with eggs, spinach, mushrooms, tomatoes, and feta cheese. And Julia had made fresh biscuits to go with them.

"Eleven is way less than we used to have," Julia said as she filled a tray with coffee cups.

"Your brother is working on that," her mother said in a hushed tone. "Let's not bother Aurora with family business." She picked up a trivet and one of the foil-covered trays and started from the kitchen.

Aurora's heart went out to Gage because she knew he was the brother Constance was referring to. Gage had opened up to Aurora about trying to keep their fishing business from being overtaken by companies that only cared about the dollar earned. She had faith he would find a way to make that happen. What he hadn't told her about was the wonderful breakfasts that guests staying there received. Or about the game nights, where everyone was considered a part of their family. How funny his brother was. How adorable his sister was. The list went on.

"It's hard on her, seeing business slow down," Julia said as she added silverware and napkins to the tray with the coffee cups.

Her words drew Aurora from her thoughts. "I'm sure it is."

"We have to be realistic," Julia added, sounding far older than her years. "Life isn't all fun and games. And all the family love we have for each other might not always be enough to make everything turn out the way you hope it will." She started off in the direction her mother had just gone.

"Julia," Aurora called after her.

Gage's sister stopped in the doorway, glancing back over her shoulder.

"Things will be alright," she said. "Gage will make sure of it."

Julia smiled. "I hope so."

Aurora followed her out into the great room, passing Gage's mother on the way.

"I'll grab the biscuits and butter," the older woman said as she scurried back into the kitchen.

Aurora's gaze skimmed the open room, searching for Gage, who had been busy lubricating the lodge's front door, which had started squeaking.

"He ran down to the docks to help Reed with one of the boats," Gage's father announced from where he sat in one of the recliners going through some paperwork.

"Gage," Julia supplied as if Aurora hadn't realized who the "he" was.

She blushed at their awareness of her visual search for Gage. "We should get the table set," Aurora said, neither confirming nor denying their observation.

Julia nodded in agreement. "The other guests will be here in about five minutes."

Aurora began setting out the plates she'd carried from the kitchen while Julia placed a neatly folded napkin, silverware, and a coffee cup next to each dish. As soon as they were done, Julia headed back to the kitchen.

Aurora went to follow, only to be stopped by Gage's father, who called out, "Aurora . . ."

She stopped and glanced his way.

"I know you prefer ph-photographing animals, but I'd like to hire y-you to take our f-family picture before you go?"

"I'd be honored to take your family's picture," she replied. "And I certainly don't want payment for it. I'd also be happy to take some pictures of your retreat for you to use in your advertising if you'd like."

"That would be wonderful. And you insisted on paying for your stay here. Well, taking pictures is what you do for a living. So you'll be paid for any pictures you take for us. Unless we call it even . . ."

She shook her head. "I can't do that. A week's stay here is worth more than the cost of a family portrait session." She thought about their current financial situation. "What if you give me two nights of my stay at no charge in exchange for my doing your family photo shoot?"

He sat in thought for a long moment before responding, "It's a deal."

She smiled.

The lodge door opened, and several men came inside, laughing and talking among each other.

"I should go see what else I need to do to help," she said quietly to Gage's father, who was rising from his chair to greet their arriving breakfast guests.

Aurora hoped that Gage and Reed would make it back in time for breakfast. She had no idea what they were repairing, so who knew how long it would take? That morning, when he'd walked her to the lodge for breakfast, Gage had asked if she wanted to accompany him to Juneau after they finished eating. He was flying in to pick up the supplies they had on order there. There had been no hesitation in her reply. Not if it meant another chance to take pictures of the beautiful, vast land beneath them as they flew. Not if it meant spending more time with Gage and that adorably charming smile of his.

"I was worried you and Reed might not make it back in time for breakfast this morning," Aurora said as she snapped pictures from where she sat in the front of the floatplane next to Gage.

"Well, you had more than enough company to keep you occupied if I hadn't," he replied. "You were like a sea siren surrounded by a bunch of googly-eyed sailors."

Aurora lowered her camera with a snort. "Googly-eyed?"

He glanced her way. "You know, like this," he said, demonstrating his impression of what he'd found when he and his brother had returned for breakfast.

She burst into a fit of laughter. "Hardly. I asked how their fishing vacation was going and if they had reeled in any big catches. I'm not sure if they were exaggerating or not, but Robert, I believe his name was, said he caught a fish that was over three feet long and weighed more than one hundred and fifty pounds. That's a pretty big fish."

"Pacific halibut," Gage replied. "The world record has one weighing over four hundred and fifty pounds, and that record-setting fish was caught right here in Alaska."

"That's a big fish. How does the fisherman not end up getting yanked into the water while trying to reel one of those fish in?"

"We have our methods," Gage told her. "If you're curious, I'd be happy to take you out on one of our fishing boats before you leave to go back to Seattle. You could see what it's like to fish for those big boys firsthand. And if you get pulled in, I'll jump in and rescue you."

"I would love that!" she said excitedly.

"Seriously?" he said, dark brows lifting. Jess would have turned that opportunity down flat.

"Absolutely."

"Aurora," Gage said, leaning forward to catch a better glimpse out his window, "look down there." He pointed to an area ahead of them. "Right along the edge of the water."

"A momma bear with her cubs!" she gasped, immediately aiming her camera in that direction. "Look how they stick right by her."

"They're learning," he said as the plane passed by the

threesome down below. "Probably yearlings. Won't be long before they are grown enough to set off on their own."

She glanced his way. "Have you ever considered giving tours? You know so much about the wildlife, and the sea life, and even about the land."

He smiled. "What is it they say about great minds? I actually have tossed the idea of giving air tours as an add-on for guests, but not land tours," he replied. "I might have to think about adding that to my list of possible additions to the retreat." It wouldn't cost much to integrate something like that. He already owned a plane for the air tours, and he knew the land around him. Reed also knew the land every bit as well as Gage did. His brother could help with land tours when he wasn't taking guests out on the boat.

"I hope you do," Aurora replied. "I think you would make an awesome tour guide for the retreat. In fact, I should be paying you for taking me all over the place to get shots of the Alaskan wildlife. Not to mention all the interesting facts I've learned from you during our outings."

"I'm not taking your money for doing that," he replied. "Besides, it's been a welcome distraction from the things that have been weighing on my mind."

"I'm glad it's given you a little reprieve," she said. "So if you do start land tours, will you be taking your guests out on UTV picnics?"

"Nope. I only offer UTV picnics to special guests," he replied with his most charming grin.

She smiled. "Well, thank you for including me among your special guests. I can now say that I have gone on a picnic. And not just at some beach or park. I did it on a remote island in Alaska. Between the distant snowcapped mountaintops and the stunningly colorful fall leaves, I know these pictures I've taken here are some of my best ever."

She relaxed against the seat as she pulled up the picture she had just taken of the bears. "This is amazing. I'm so glad you brought me along with you today."

Him too. Aurora had a way of making everything in life seem fresh and new. "You might want to pack up. We're going to be landing in Juneau in a few minutes."

Nodding, she grabbed for her camera bag and began to prepare for their arrival. The landing was smooth, and the skies were clear. A far cry from the flight they had from Juneau to the island days before.

"If you keep an eye on the treetops, you might find spy eagles nested in some. Hopefully, we can get you a shot of one. Even though it's not as exciting as having it swoop down past you."

"That would have been such an incredible picture, but it wasn't meant to be. I'd be more than happy to settle for one in a treetop."

"I have to pick up a supply order at the hardware store," he said. "You're welcome to come along or visit the shops while I take care of that. I can just find you when I'm finished."

"Do what you need to do," she said. "I'll spend time exploring and doing a little store browsing while you're gone."

"If we have time, we can stop by Glady's place to say hello before we fly back."

"That would be nice." She glanced his way. "Do we have time to fit all that in? I know Reed's expecting you back."

He smiled. "We should. Unless you get caught up in an all-day shopping spree. And if that happens, we'll simply have to catch up with Glady on another trip."

"Okay. That sounds like a good plan."

"Come on," Gage said, inclining his head, "I'll walk with you to the start of the port shops and then head off to take care of retreat business."

The port area in Juneau was filled with people scurrying about, mostly cruise passengers, according to Gage. Their haste was understandable, seeing as how time allotted in port was never enough for one to really take in all the beauty Juneau had to offer.

Women clutching various shopping bags hurried from one store to the next, while several men stood talking outside each of those stores. No doubt waiting for their significant others to finish up with their day's purchases.

"So this is what the cruise port looks like when the ships are docked here," Aurora noted with interest.

He nodded. "Pretty busy. The ships stop docking here by the end of September and won't come back again until sometime in April. There's a new agreement the town made with the cruise lines, limiting visitors brought in daily, with less allowed on Saturdays."

"That's so many people."

Gage nodded. "Residents here were getting fed up with the post-pandemic crowds that were swarming the town and sought to change things. The agreement allows them to have both the income the ship passengers bring to Juneau, while also giving Juneau more of a community feel, rather than overwhelmingly touristy."

"I can't say that I blame the people who live here full-time for wanting to take back a little bit of their town," Aurora said.

Looking around the busy street, Gage said, "This is why I choose to live on an island."

"The most incredible little island," Aurora agreed.

"I'm glad you like it," he said and meant it.

"Well, hello there!"

Aurora looked down the sidewalk to see Mr. Wilson heading their way, his adorable companion, Bailey, at his side. She smiled and waved her greeting. "Hello!'

"Mr. Wilson," Gage said with a nod of greeting.

"Hope you're enjoying your stay here," he said to Aurora as they stepped aside to converse for a moment on the busy sidewalk.

"I am," Aurora replied. "Thank you." She looked down at the golden retriever who had seated herself next to her owner. "Hello, Bailey. It's so good to see you again."

The dog's tail thumped happily on the sidewalk.

"We're just out for our daily walk." Mr. Wilson looked down at his faithful companion.

"Aurora's hoping to do a little browsing through some of our shops today," Gage told him.

"Don't let us hold you up," Mr. Wilson replied. "Bailey and I need to finish our walk and get back to the diner. Glady is making us meatloaf."

"Hers is the best," Gage noted.

"Come on, girl," Mr. Wilson said. "Rest time is over. Let's go get our meatloaf."

As if prompted by the promise of food, Bailey bound to her feet, tail wagging even harder.

Mr. Wilson looked their way. "Have a good rest of your day, you two."

"We will," Gage replied. "Same to you."

Aurora and Gage had only continued on a short distance when she stopped in her tracks. "Do you smell that?" she asked Gage, her gaze sweeping the area. "Mmm ... whatever it is, it smells wonderful."

Gage knew exactly what she smelled. Apples and spices. He pointed to a black storefront about ten or so feet away. On a small, white distressed-wood table next to the entrance step, a two-wick candle burned, luring shoppers in to try the various candle scents offered there.

Aurora read the gold lettering that stretched out over the door aloud, "1820 House Candle Company. Ooh, I love a good candle!"

"Well, these are the best," Gage said. "At least, according to my mom. This is the only place she'll buy candles. They're all soy and burn for a really long time. She likes them so much she buys the scents in multiples of two. Like she's preparing for some sort of candle ark."

Aurora laughed. "If they're that good, I think I'll start my perusing of the stores here," she said with barely concealed excitement.

He stepped over and swung the door open, then made a sweeping gesture with his hand. "After you."

"You're coming in?"

"I might as well pick Mom up a couple of her favorite candles while I'm here."

"You're sweet."

"Sweet like the candle," he replied and then bit back a groan at how corny that response sounded. He never tossed out silly one-liners with his ex. But then Jess wouldn't have smiled or laughed the way Aurora did when he tossed those things out. She would have pursed her lips in irritation. His gaze sought out his family's pretty guest, only to confirm his musings as she stood shaking her head at him with a grin.

Aurora groaned aloud. "Oh my gosh, the smell is even better inside."

"Morning, Gage."

"Morning, Sidney," he replied to the dark-haired, twenty-seven-year-old entrepreneur-in-the-making as she came over to greet them. Just as he and his siblings would someday take over the retreat completely, Sidney would someday step into her mother's role of owning and running the candle shop. He looked at Aurora. "Sidney and Julia studied marketing in college together."

"How nice," Aurora replied. "That's how my best friend Emmy and I met. We were both pursuing our Bachelor of Fine Arts degree with a minor in business at Seattle University."

"Julia and I knew each other growing up but didn't become close friends until college. But I'm so grateful we did." Sidney smiled. "Anyway, welcome to 1820 House."

"Thank you."

"Aurora wanted to see what other scents you have while we're in town. I told her how much Mom loves 1820 House candles."

Sidney's slender brows arched slightly. "You're here together?" she asked as if trying to decipher what kind of *together* they were.

He could see why Sidney and his sister had become such good friends. They were both inquisitive and not afraid to ask questions. "Aurora's just a guest at the retreat," he quickly explained, not wanting Sidney to misread the situation and add fuel to the fire with his sister and mother wanting him to find someone special.

"Uh, yes, I'm just a guest," Aurora agreed, glancing his way.

She wasn't smiling. Why did it feel as though he'd just hurt her feelings? That's the last thing he ever wanted to do.

Aurora pulled her gaze away from his and turned to Sidney. "That candle I smelled burning outside of your shop stopped me in my tracks."

"It's part of our Northern Candlelights Collection," she

replied. "We call it Solar Flare. It's a blend of apple and cinnamon with a hint of clove."

"I love the play on the Northern Lights," Aurora told her. "But then I was named after them, so I tend to like everything that has to do with the Northern Lights. Even if I have yet to see them for myself."

"I hope you get to someday," Sidney replied. "They're spectacular. The collection was my idea. Mom came up with the five scents for the line. Solar Flare, mixing apple, cinnamon, and clove. Spectacular Sky, which is pumpkin and vanilla. Dancing Lights, vanilla and cardamom. All Aglow, which is vanilla, clove, and dried orange peel. And Beautiful Aurora, which smells just like a sugar cookie, because seeing the Northern Lights is the sweetest, most breathtaking moment ever."

Beautiful Aurora. Sweet. Breathtaking. She was definitely all of that, Gage thought. Her parents couldn't have given her a more fitting name. "Beautiful Aurora sounds like one Mom would love," he said. "Can you please wrap one up for her?"

"Only one?" Sidney asked, clearly knowing better.

"You're right," he said with a chuckle. "Make it two. Actually, make it three. I'd like to get one for Aurora."

Aurora looked surprised by the gesture. "Gage, that's—"

"Sweet of me," he finished for her. "We've already covered that part. I'm just a sweet guy."

Sidney snorted, drawing both their gazes her way. "Sorry," she said, waving their attention away. "I'm just going to go about my business."

"Gage, I'd love to take some candles home with me, but I'm pretty sure they're not permitted in a carry-on," Aurora said.

"Then I'll mail them to you in Seattle."

"If she finds any other candles she wants, I can mail them all to her together," Sidney offered. "It would save on postage."

"I'll accept your gift," Aurora said with an appreciative smile, "but I insist on paying for my own shipping for anything I buy, plus the candle you're buying for me."

He nodded. At least, she was accepting his gift.

Looking to Sidney, she said, "Can I smell the candles in the Northern Candlelights Collection?"

"Absolutely," the younger woman replied. "They're over here on this wall," she said, motioning for Aurora to follow as she crossed the room.

Gage walked over and took a seat in one of two leather armchairs in front of a large candle display window. The perfect spot for husbands to wait while their wives shopped. Or, in his case, while his guest, who felt oddly like something more, shopped.

"So, what was the candle I smelled coming in called again?" Aurora asked.

"That was Solar Flare."

"It smelled so unbelievably good," Aurora told her. "I absolutely love the candle scents that come out in the fall and at Christmas."

Sidney beamed with pride. "Then you've come to the right place." She motioned around the shop where dark metal shelves held rows and rows of single and two-wick candles for purchase. "These are all made from one hundred percent soy wax and are handmade daily in the back of the shop by my mother."

"I'm guessing Melissa is busy at work right now, creating her next incredible scent," Gage said from the other side of the room.

"She is." Sidney turned to Aurora. "Mom is the candle

chemist around here. She pours and packages the candles while I handle the sales, shipping, and marketing. We've started working on our line for the upcoming holidays, so she's been really busy with perfecting festive scents. Our candles sell well, but go like hotcakes over the holiday season."

"Maybe we should offer some in our gift shop at the retreat," Gage thought aloud.

"You should." Aurora moved along the towering shelf, smelling each of the special collection's candle scents. "I can't speak for men, but most women enjoy candles. Especially when there is a variety of scents to choose from."

After about five minutes of sampling the scents of every candle in the Northern Candlelights Collection, along with a few others, Aurora turned toward the checkout counter where Sidney stood talking to Gage.

"Do you sell your candles online?" Aurora asked. "There are so many I would love to try."

"We do," Sidney replied.

Picking up one of the jars she hadn't gotten to yet, Aurora lowered her head and took a slow, studying sniff. "Mmm . . . I get vanilla, I think, and possibly nutmeg."

"She has a great nose," Sidney told Gage.

And a great smile. Gage somehow managed to keep that thought to himself.

"These would make the most perfect Christmas gift." She looked at Gage. "And before you say anything, I know Christmas is still three months away. I happen to be one of those who likes to start shopping early."

He put up his hands. "Hey, I wasn't going to say anything, but since you brought it up . . ."

Ignoring his teasing, she set that candle down and picked up another from the neatly organized black shelf, one of several that lined the wall from ceiling to floor. Lifting its lid, she sniffed the scented soy wax. "All of these candles smell so good. This is definitely pumpkin and something else that I can't quite put a mental finger on."

"Autumn fig," Sidney said. "The scents are printed on the sides of the jar labels."

Aurora turned the jar and laughed. "I guess they are. I was so distracted by the incredibly yummy smell that I didn't even notice."

Gage was soaking up everything about Aurora. The simplest things made her so happy. And seeing her joy made *him* happy.

"The sampler packs with their assorted two-point-five-ounce candles make wonderful little stocking stuffers."

"I guess the only way to really know which scents are my favorite is to burn them. So I'll have you ship me one of the sampler sets also. Once I get them and have a chance to try them out, I'll no doubt be ordering more."

"Be sure to burn the Northern Candlelights Collection ones first," Sidney warned. "In case you want more. We're only offering them for a limited time."

"I think it should be a year-round selection," Gage suggested. "The marketing is spot on for this area."

Sidney beamed with pride. "I suppose that's something Mom and I should take into consideration."

If Aurora got this excited over the candles, he had to imagine some of the women who come to the retreat might as well. Men, too, for that matter, because they even carried a line of candles geared more toward men's tastes. It would be another way to offer more to their retreat guests while helping another local business in the process.

Gage looked at Sidney. "I'll be in touch about ordering some of your candles for the retreat."

"Really?" she said excitedly.

He nodded.

"Gage, that would be great. Just let us know what you need and when you need it."

"I'll be in touch."

Turning back to Aurora, Sidney said, "I'll need to get your information for shipping. After that, we'll get you checked out."

Aurora set the candle she'd been sniffing back on the shelf and crossed the room to where Sidney waited. After giving Sidney her mailing information in Seattle, Aurora placed her order, including some candles for her mother and sister.

After saying their goodbyes, Gage opened the door for Aurora as they stepped outside. "If I had known how happy it would make you to go into a candle store, I would have brought you here that day you came sloshing into Glady's place in your adorable bright yellow duck poncho."

Aurora rolled her eyes. "Must you continue to remind me about that mostly embarrassing moment?"

"I must," he replied with a grin. "It was one of the most memorable moments of my life."

"Of your life?" she repeated as they started down the sidewalk toward Glady's.

"Without a doubt. It's the day I met you."

That simple statement touched her more than he could ever know. Embarrassed by the unexpected rush of tears that threatened to pool in her eyes, she looked away. "I'm glad I was able to create a memorable moment for you."

"The first of many since your arrival," he admitted with a chuckle.

"Sorry for taking so long in the candle shop," she said, wanting to talk about something other than the memories they'd shared. Memories she'd soon be taking with her when she returned to Seattle.

"Don't be sorry," he told her. "It made you happy being in there."

"But it took a lot of time. You still need to pick up your order at the hardware store, and Reed's waiting for you to get back to help him with the landscape lighting."

"It just gives me an excuse to bring you back to town again. Check out a few more stores, and we'll come back another day to visit with Glady."

Aurora nodded. "If you're sure."

He nodded. "I'm sure."

"It did make me happy," she confided. "I didn't think about my canceled wedding even once while I was in there."

"Glad to hear it." Even more glad that her ex hadn't been in Aurora's thoughts that afternoon. Gage suddenly found himself wondering if he had been hers, because Aurora had definitely taken over his thoughts.

CHAPTER TEN

"Did you get the work done you needed to see to this morning?" Gage asked from beneath the lowered hood of his raincoat when Aurora opened the door of her cabin.

She laughed. "You're starting to sound like me. Come on in out of that rain." She opened the door wider and then moved aside.

Gage shoved back his hood and then stepped into the cabin, stopping just inside the threshold. Water from his wet raincoat and boots sluiced off onto the rubberized entrance mat. He looked down with a frown. "Probably not the best idea to have come inside. I should have stayed out on the porch."

She followed his gaze downward, stopping at the misshapen bulge beneath the front of his raincoat. "What in the world . . .?" Looking up into Gage's mirth-filled eyes, she said, "Did you come across Little John on your way here and swallow him whole for lunch?"

"And miss having lunch with you? Not a chance."

One arm still wrapped around the bottom side of the protruding lump, he unzipped his raincoat, revealing a tall pair of boots. "For you to wear up to the lodge," he told her as he pulled them free.

"I have waterproof hiking boots."

"No sense in you getting them all muddy. These take five seconds to hose off." He handed them to her. "I guessed on the size. Hope they at least come close to fitting. If not, I'll be carrying you to the lodge."

She laughed. "I don't think that will be necessary. Like I said, I have my own boots."

"The trail to the main lodge gets pretty muddy when it pours like this. So humor me. Please."

"Fine." As she set the boots on the floor beside her to step into them, Aurora saw the forgotten pools of water surrounding his booted feet. "The floor," she gasped.

"I'm sure it's not the first time someone dragged water and a bit of mud into the cabin with them," he said, his tone calm. "There should be some utility towels stored in the cupboard underneath the kitchen sink. Would you mind grabbing one so I can clean this mess up? Then I'll stand on it until you're ready to go."

Nodding, she set the boots down and hurried to grab one of the neatly folded utility towels from the stack in the very back of the sink cupboard.

"It's expected to be an all-nighter, and my family is looking forward to having you there for the rainy-day activity Mom has planned for this afternoon. She always has a backup activity on days like this for our guests. Certain conditions keep the boats from being able to safely take them out fishing. Such as today's inclement weather. Guests are welcome to join in if they want to, or if they prefer to just relax in their cabins, or take a walk in the rain, they have those options as well."

"That's really thoughtful of her," Aurora said as she

hurried across the room to where Gage remained standing. "Let me guess what activity your mother has planned for us this afternoon," Aurora said as she moved to dry up the water with the towel. "I'm thinking trivia."

Gage shook his head as he knelt beside her.

Aurora looked up as he placed his large hand over hers, stilling her attempt to clean up the puddles of water.

"My mess," he told her. "I'll take care of it."

"Okay," was all she could muster as he gazed into her eyes for several long moments.

Gage cleared his throat, then redirected his attention to sopping up the puddles. "Would you like for me to tell you what we're going to be doing today?"

"And take the fun out of trying to guess it?"

"Have at it," he told her, keeping his gaze fixed firmly on the floor in front of him.

"I have to warn you, I'm pretty good at guessing games," she said as she rose to her feet. "Jade and I used to play them all the time as kids."

"Let's see how good you are then," he replied with a grin, finally glancing up at her. "If you guess right, I'll take you to Juneau for lunch, weather permitting. Maybe we'll even see about finding you some moose to photograph while we're out."

"Moose! Seriously?"

He chuckled. "Seriously."

"And if I guess wrong?"

"*You'll* take me to lunch in Juneau instead."

Her heart pounded with far more enthusiasm than usual. "I accept the challenge." Spending time with Gage anywhere excited her to the point of being almost embarrassing. She was going to miss him when she returned to Seattle.

Gage took one last swipe across the mat and the floor around it with the towel and then spread it out, stepping onto it. "Okay, I'm ready. Let's have that guess."

"Keep in mind that this is my warm-up. It doesn't count if I get it wrong."

"Noted," he said with a refrained grin. "Was this how you and Jade used to play this game?"

"Maybe."

He shook his head. "Okay, your rules."

"Is it bingo?" Aurora asked hesitantly. Not that her answer really mattered. They would be going to lunch either way. Was this his way of asking her out on a real date? Or was that just wishful thinking? That last thought took her by surprise. Was she even ready for something like that? Her heart had certainly grown fond of Gage and seemed to be growing fonder by the minute.

"Cold."

Gage's response pulled Aurora from the tangled web of her post-engagement breakup thoughts. "Excuse me?"

"Cold," he repeated. "Meaning your answer was nowhere near to being correct."

Of course. Okay, she had to think. What did her mom like to play when entertaining? It came to her. "How about euchre?" A bit more confidently this time.

"Iceberg," came Gage's exaggerated response.

Aurora laughed. "Oh no. Can I try one more time?"

He shrugged. "It's your rules, remember?"

In truth, there was no telling what Gage's mother had planned for that afternoon. They played games every evening, and Aurora had enjoyed every one of them. "Hangman?"

"Antarctica," he said, one side of his mouth pulling

upward in humor. "You can't get any colder than that. Looks like you're taking me to lunch."

She feigned a frustrated sigh. "If I have to."

"A deal's a deal," he told her.

"So, what are we doing today?"

He smiled. "We're going to be painting."

She wouldn't have guessed that as a possibility. "You know I'm a photographer, not an artist, right?"

He nodded. "You don't have to worry about Reed making any of us look bad. I think he's going to be instructing and giving help where help is needed."

"Well, that's a relief. I'd better grab my raincoat so we can get up to the lodge. I don't want anyone having to wait because of me."

"Before we go, you never did answer. Did you finish the work you needed to have done today?"

She couldn't help but smile. Usually, it was her asking Gage that same question. "I did. I got up early and sent a few teaser shots to my editor."

"I've seen your work," Gage replied, "so there's no need to ask if you've heard back and what his or her thoughts are on them."

"His," she clarified. "Eugene Watkins is the editorial manager at *World Adventures Magazine*, and my contact. He's the one who hired me for this assignment." She slipped her rain poncho on. "I've been trying to get in with this magazine for years. Thankfully, the stars finally aligned for me, and my dream has become a reality."

"You deserve it," Gage said sincerely. "I've seen you in action, and you live and breathe for the moment you get that perfect shot. Which pretty much describes all the photos you take, from what I observed online."

"They weren't always that good," she told him. "And to

answer your question, no, I haven't heard back from Eugene yet. But I'm sure he has his hands full making sure everything is falling into place for next month's issue." Rain splattering harder against the cabin window drew her attention that way. "It's a deluge out there," she groaned.

"That's September in Alaska for you," Gage replied. "Pull on those boots I brought you. You're going to be needing them for our walk up to the lodge."

Aurora reached for the boots, which she hadn't paid much attention to when Gage had pulled them from his coat. She'd been too distracted by his playful smile to notice. Lifting one of the very tall rubber boots, she held it up, dangling it in the air in front of her. "Are you serious? You expect me to wear these?"

His smile sagged ever so slightly. "That's up to you," he told her. "I'm just trying to keep your jeans and your nice hiking boots from becoming a wet, muddied mess. But I know Jess hated them, so you might too."

"Jess was out of her element here," Aurora told him, trying to be understanding of Jess's reasons for acting the way she had when she'd been there, yet be supportive for Gage, who had been hurt by those actions. "I'm not." Smiling, she grabbed the oversized boots and walked over to sit on the small sofa. "They just look so big."

"Way off on the size?" he asked with a frown.

"No." She stood with the boots on. "They actually don't fit too bad where my foot is. They're just really tall on me. They go up over my knees."

"And half of your thighs," he agreed with a nod. "I suppose that's because they're sized for men."

She glanced up. "All those pairs of boots up at the lodge, and none of them are made specifically for women?"

"Uh . . . no," he answered.

"But you have women come here to fish too?"

He shrugged. "We do. Not as often, but there have been women who have gone out on the fishing boats. Most of them bring their own boots."

"Gage, your family might think about having better boot options for the women who come here. Even if it's not as often as men come to your retreat for a fishing getaway."

He nodded in agreement. "You're probably right. Do you want to change into your own boots or—"

"Have you carry me?" she cut in with a grin. "I do believe that was my other option if these didn't work out."

He threw his head back with a husky chuckle. "Aurora Daniels, you are truly a breath of fresh air."

"I wasn't being serious about your carrying me to the lodge," Aurora said with a giggle from beneath the drooping hood of her raincoat as the water poured down around them.

"Looks like you're not as good at the guessing game as you think you are," Gage said as he moved hurriedly along the trail, Aurora held securely in his arms.

"Gage, it's raining harder. You're going to slip. Put me down. I can walk the rest of the way."

"Me fall? Ha!" he scoffed. "I'm as sure-footed as a mountain goat. Besides, the lodge's front porch is in view."

The words were no sooner out of his mouth than the toe of Gage's boot caught a root protruding from the rain-washed earth.

Aurora shrieked, wrapping her arms tightly around his neck as he struggled for balance.

There was no stopping it. His hurried pace when his boot slipped on the slick ground left him struggling to remain upright. The effort was futile. Though Gage managed to turn them so he landed on the ground backside first, skidding across the wet trail. Mud and water sprayed everywhere.

"Hold on," he told Aurora, who had ended up seated safely on his lap.

When they came to a stop, Aurora lifted her head from where she'd buried it against his neck. "Gage," she said worriedly. "Are you okay?"

"Other than being completely and utterly embarrassed," he replied, his own hood having fallen off his head when he went down. Rain ran down his hair and face, even finding its way inside his jacket. "Are you okay?" he asked.

"I'm fine," she assured him.

He looked her over and groaned. "But you're a muddy mess."

"Seems to be my thing in Alaska," she said with a grin as rain ran down her face too. "I hate to break it to you, but you fared no better."

Of that, he had no doubt. Gage felt awful. He'd acted on a momentary lapse of judgment because it had felt like a good idea at the time. He'd wanted to make Aurora laugh, and he had. And now they sat, wallowing together in the mud.

The lodge's main entrance door flew open, and his entire family spilled out onto the porch, looking around.

"I know I heard a scream," Julia said worriedly.

"Aurora?" his mother called out.

"We're over here," Aurora replied as she and Gage scrambled to their feet.

Gage's mother squinted to see them through the coursing rain. "Is Gage with you?"

"I am," he answered with a frown. Reed was going to have a field day with this.

They started toward the porch. Gage wrapped an arm around Aurora's waist as she struggled to move in the too-high boots he'd brought her to wear, which was why he'd been carrying her in the first place.

"Son?" his father said hoarsely when they reached the porch and started up the front steps.

"It's a little slick out there," Gage replied.

"Oh my goodness," his mother said, moving to meet them at the edge of the porch. "Are you two alright?"

"We're fine," Aurora hurried to assure her. "Just a little wet."

"And muddy," Julia noted.

"How on earth d-did that happen?" his father inquired as he looked them both over.

"Caught a root with the toe of my boot on the way here," Gage explained.

"And you pulled Aurora down with you?" Reed said, clicking his tongue. "Not very gallant of you."

Gage shook his head. "I didn't pull her down. I was carrying her when I fell."

"He didn't want me to trip in these big boots on our way to the lodge, so he very thoughtfully offered to carry me," Aurora said, meeting Reed's skeptical gaze. "And he sacrificed himself in the fall to keep me from hitting the ground."

"That was pretty thoughtful," Julia agreed with a nod.

"Can we discuss this inside where it's warm and dry?" Gage said in frustration. Mostly at himself for being overly confident of his mountain goat nimbleness during an outright downpour.

"Of course. Jim, honey, get the door," his mother directed. "Reed, go on inside and add some wood to the fire. These two are going to need to warm up. Julia, sweetie, go to the kitchen and heat up some water for hot chocolate."

They all moved to do his mother's bidding, his father's off gait a little more noticeable that evening as it was at times.

She looked at him and Aurora. "Hang your coats out here and leave your boots on the porch below. Gage can rinse them off in the morning." She frowned as she eyed their wet hair and jeans. "Honey, no sense trying to get back to your cabin in this rain. We'll find you something dry to change into. You can wash up in one of the empty guest bathrooms. There will be a basket of toiletries on the vanity counter. The hair dryer is under the sink."

"Thank you," Aurora said as she peeled her wet raincoat off.

Gage grimaced as he took in the long, wet, slightly muddied hair hanging down over Aurora's shoulders.

"I'll see you two inside," his mother said.

After his mother and the rest of his family had gone, Gage turned to Aurora. "I'm so sorry."

"Accidents happen," she said with a sweet smile.

"I'm beginning to see why Jess couldn't imagine spending her life here with me on the island."

Aurora hung her raincoat and then turned. Reaching out, she placed a gentle hand on his cheek. "I'm beginning to wonder how she couldn't imagine spending her life here with you. You're fun and adventurous. You're sweet and caring. You're—" Her words fell off as Gage drew her to him.

"Finding it very hard not to kiss you right now."

Her eyes widened in surprise. "Really?"

"Really."

"I think I'd like that," she replied, looking up into his searching gaze.

Gage lowered his head and covered her mouth with his, closing his eyes as he lost himself in the moment. The kiss was sweet and tender. It felt like he'd been waiting his whole life for this. Suddenly, it was like fireworks were going off all around him.

"Umm, Gage," Aurora mumbled against his mouth before pushing away.

Opening his eyes, Gage looked to find Reed flicking the porch light on and off as he stood in the open doorway. He asked with a frown, "What do you think you're doing?"

"Trying to get your attention," his brother replied. "Mom said whenever Aurora is ready, she and Julia will take her upstairs to the Bear's Den."

Gage grumbled, "We'll be in as soon as we get our boots off."

The door closed, leaving Gage to focus on the woman standing next to him and the unplanned kiss that left his heart thudding hard inside his chest.

Aurora looked up at him, cheeks flushed. "Well, that was poor timing."

He nodded with a slow grin. "The worst."

"Actually," she said, "it was probably for the best."

His dark brow lifted as he looked down at Aurora's pretty face.

"I like you, Gage," she admitted. "But we can't allow ourselves to get swept away by a vacation romance. I need to focus on the assignment I was sent to Alaska to do, because the work I do here could land me my dream job. And you need to focus on the retreat."

He gave a reluctant nod. "I like you too. But you're

right. We both have obligations we can't afford to get distracted from." Gage caught the regret in her eyes before it gave way to acceptance.

Aurora offered up a soft smile. "The Bear's Den, huh?"

"Julia named all the guest rooms here as well," Gage explained. "There's the Bear's Den, the Bee's Hive, and the Eagle's Nest.

"How cute!"

"That's my sister for you."

"She's very creative."

He nodded. "She should be. That's what she got her degree in." He hesitated for a long moment before saying, "I'm not sure whether I need to apologize for that kiss or not."

"It wasn't that bad," she said, pulling a boot off.

"Not that bad?" he repeated, pretty sure that wasn't a compliment.

Aurora burst into giggles. "You should have seen your face, mud and all. And to address your concerns, in all seriousness, there's no need to apologize. Truth is, that kiss is one I will remember long after I go home. And not because it was bad."

"Same." Grinning, Gage inclined his head toward the door. "Ready?"

"Ready."

As soon as they stepped inside, his mother and Julia were waiting to whisk Aurora away. Gage stood, watching them go.

"There are easier ways to get a guest to leave than dragging them through the mud or kissing them."

Gage looked away from the door that had closed behind the departing women to see his brother grinning at him from over the back of one of the dark brown leather recliners by the hearth.

"First of all, I didn't drag her," Gage said as he walked over to where Reed and his father sat. "I slipped while I was carrying her, which you already know."

"You kissed her?" his father said, eyes widening.

"It just sort of happened," Gage replied with a frown, because he wouldn't mind it happening again. "Don't read anything into it. We both have other commitments we have to focus on right now." He looked at his brother. "And I wasn't trying to get Aurora to leave. I was trying to make her laugh, because she's going through something right now that's been emotionally hard for her."

Reed's expression sobered. "I'm sorry to hear that. I'll try and remember to back off the teasing comments whenever she's around."

"As if you can help it," their father chimed in.

"True," Gage agreed. "I don't think you need to be anything other than yourself. Aurora actually finds your snarky comments quite amusing."

His brother perked up, a gratified smile etching its way across his cheeks.

Gage shook his head. "I probably should have kept that tidbit of information to myself. You're bad enough as it is, without feeding your comedic ego."

That made Reed chuckle. Then he glanced across the room in the direction Aurora had gone. Shifting his gaze back to Gage, he said with a concerned expression, "Having been around Aurora this past week, I would never have known there was anything weighing on her. She always seems so happy."

"She's happiest in her element, which is anywhere she

can find wildlife to photograph," Gage explained. "As you already know, she came to Alaska to take pictures for *World Adventures Magazine.* What you don't know is that this was supposed to be Aurora's honeymoon. Unfortunate timing for her to be sent here on a photo assignment."

"What happened?" their father asked, his graying brows creased with worry. "Please tell me he didn't b-break her heart like . . ." He paused as if searching his memory and then said, ". . . Jess did yours."

Gage shook his head. "Aurora called off the engagement."

Surprise lit his father's and brother's faces.

"She's a runner too?" Reed asked, disapproval in his tone.

"It wasn't like mine and Jess's situation," Gage said, coming to her defense. "Aurora was engaged to a man she'd known since childhood. They were good friends who thought that would be enough to start a life together. Six months ago, Aurora told him she couldn't marry him because she wanted both of them to be able to find the kind of love her parents have."

"What if the kind of love she's looking for doesn't really exist?" Reed challenged.

"It exists," their father said with a confirming nod.

"I'm just telling Gage to be careful," his brother said with a frown. "I like Aurora a lot, but I see him getting his emotions tangled up in her." He turned to Gage. "I never want you to have to go through what you did with Jess again."

"Aurora isn't Jess," Gage said. Despite that, he understood his brother's concern. Was he ready to invest his feelings, and possibly his heart, in another relationship? He wasn't so certain. Reed was only trying to keep him grounded.

It didn't matter how much he was drawn to Aurora. Her career would have her off traveling the world while his was on Conley Island, where his family had long ago put down roots. Even if she agreed to give a long-distance relationship a try and it moved toward them having a future together, Gage had no idea if he would have a steady source of income to support a wife. The business was floundering, and there was no guarantee he would be able to turn things around. But he was going to try his best to make it happen.

"Son," his father said, clearly seeing Gage's battling thoughts, "sometimes you just have to p-put your all into things, even knowing that might not be enough. If it doesn't happen the way you'd hoped it w-would, then you will at least know you gave it your all. No regrets. And if things do go in your f-favor, then you know they were meant to be."

"Thanks, Dad," he said. While his father had made so much progress from those first few days following his stroke, he still dealt with some occasional trouble getting a word out here and there. And there were also moments when he had to search hard to pull up a memory. The doctors remained hopeful for even further recovery but had prepared the family for the possibility that he might not progress from where he was now. Gage prayed for the best but was grateful his father was as good as he was.

The lodge's main entrance door swung open, and three men in stockinged feet came in.

"I hope lunch is still on," one of the men said with a smile.

Their guests knew to leave wet or muddied footwear out on the porch. Judging by the men's mostly dry clothes, they had hung their jackets out on the porch as well.

"Like clockwork," Gage's father replied.

"And the post-lunch activity?" another man inquired.

"Will also be going on as planned," Reed assured them. "Mom is like the U.S. Postal Service. Rain, snow, sleet, or shine."

"Good to know." The man still stood near the door, looking at that week's information flyer that hung next to it.

"Quite a day," one of the other two men stated as he moved farther into the room.

"Coming down like cats and dogs out there," another man said as he followed his friend over to the warming fire.

"More like moose and bears," Reed amended with a grin.

Gage looked at his father. "He just can't help himself."

Their father chuckled. "Nope. Not at all."

"I need to get showered and change into some clean clothes. Wouldn't want to hold up lunch."

"Much appreciated," said the man who had been reading the lodge flyer as he joined his friends in front of the hearth.

Gage turned and headed for the doorway to the section of the lodge where the rooms were, his father's advice front and foremost in his mind. *No regrets.*

***

"Ah, you look much more comfortable," Constance said as Aurora started down the stairs, carrying the canvas tote she'd been given to place her muddied clothes in.

Julia and her mother sat smiling up at her from the small sitting area adjacent to the base of the stairs. The two barrel-shaped chairs were covered in a rustic cabin pattern that included fish, bears, and pine cones. A few feet away, on the same side of the hallway, was the door that led to the lodge's great room.

"You look great!" Julia said with delight as she got to her feet. "I knew that color would be perfect with your dark hair."

Gage's mother rose to her feet with a warm smile. "You do look pretty in pink."

"It's not a color I've really worn before," Aurora admitted. She usually went for warmer, more earthy tones with an occasional pop of color in plums or darker greens. Definitely never hot pink. "My sister Jade, however, wears lots of bright colors. In fact, her closet is filled with a rainbow assortment of colorful clothing options."

"You should borrow some from her every now and then," Julia suggested. "That is what sisters do, isn't it? Of course, I wouldn't know as I have two big brothers who dress like lumberjacks."

Aurora couldn't help but laugh at Julia's description of her brothers. She'd never considered that comparison when she was with Gage. He liked flannel shirts, and they seemed to like him because he always looked roguishly handsome in them. She felt for Julia for never having had the chance to experience the joy of growing up with a sister. It was definitely a special bond that Aurora wouldn't trade for the world.

"I suppose it depends on the sisters and their relationship," Aurora told her. "My sister and I used to borrow each other's shoes and purses. But then I moved to Seattle for my career, and Jade still lives in Oregon, in the town we grew up in. That tends to make borrowing from each other a little bit harder to do."

"I suppose it would. Do you miss living in Oregon?" Julia asked, her curiosity that Gage had spoken about clearly piqued. "I can't imagine living that far away from my brothers. Even if they can be intentionally annoying at times," she added with a grin.

"I don't miss Oregon as much as I miss my family," Aurora replied. "You know what they say about home being where the heart is."

Gage's mother nodded. "So true. Here, let me go throw those muddy clothes in our washer."

"You don't have to do that," Aurora said with a shake of her head. "Gage said you have a guest laundry here. I can run them through myself."

"I don't mind," Constance countered as she removed the bag of dirty clothes from Aurora's grasp. "I'll go throw them in our family washer right now, so we'll have them all clean and dry before you go back to your cabin tonight."

"Thank you, Constance."

Julia held out the ceramic mug she'd been holding. Wisps of steam curled slowly upward from it. "Here's some hot chocolate to warm you up." A worried expression came over her face. "You do like hot chocolate, don't you? I could make you some coffee if you don't."

"I love it," Aurora replied with a grateful smile as she accepted the cup. Bringing it to her nose, she inhaled slowly. "Mmm . . . this smells so yummy. Thank you so much. For this and for letting me borrow your clothes. I'll bring them back to wash them tomorrow morning."

"You're more than welcome for the loan," Julia replied. "There's no rush getting them back to me. You're here for a few more days."

Only a few? How had the time passed by so quickly?

"How are you feeling?" Constance asked in concern.

Aurora smiled. "Much better. Thank you."

"Are you sure you didn't get hurt when you and Gage fell?"

"Your son made sure I didn't," Aurora assured her. "Gage did go down hard, though. Is he okay?"

"You can see for yourself," Constance replied. "He just came downstairs from washing up about five or so minutes before you. He's in the great room, talking to some of our guests who were determined enough to venture out into that miserable rain to have lunch and join in the activity afterward."

"I know I'm looking forward to it."

"I'll go throw these in the washer and meet you girls in the great room." That said, Constance headed off in the opposite direction than they were going.

Aurora followed Julia down the carpeted hallway to the door that led to the lodge's main entertainment area. "I hope everyone will keep in mind that I'm not a painter of any sort. That would be my friend Emmy."

"Neither are any of us, with the exception of Reed, of course," Julia replied and then frowned in thought. "We certainly wouldn't want any of our guests feeling intimidated by my brother's artistic ability when it comes to painting. I'm going to suggest to Mom that Reed paint opposite-handed."

Gage's sister pushed open the door and stepped through. Aurora followed. Julia pointed across the room. "You can head on over to the hearth to warm up a bit more. I still don't know what my brother was thinking, convincing you to come out in this weather. He could have delivered lunch to you after we had finished eating."

"I'm glad he came to get me," Aurora told her, drawing the younger woman's gaze her way. *So glad.* But she wasn't going to admit aloud that it was one of the most fun and carefree moments she had ever had.

His family was already up to a little well-intended mischief where she and Gage were concerned, even if that tree wasn't going to bear any fruit for their efforts. She lived in Washington and Gage in Alaska, for starters. Then there was the travel she did for her job. But it went beyond geographical issues. Gage was still working to put his past relationship behind him, and she had just come out of a broken engagement that never should have happened in the first place. Reminding herself of these things helped to keep Aurora's heart from getting too caught up in all the reasons she and Gage could be good together.

They moved farther into the great room. For a room so large, it was wonderfully cozy with its large, glowing hearth and dimmable lighting. Aurora's gaze drifted across the room to where Gage stood conversing with one of their guests next to the hearth.

As if sensing her arrival, he stopped talking and glanced her way. Then a slow smile spread across his face.

"Told you pink looks good on you," Julia whispered near Aurora's ear before stepping away.

Aurora turned her focus back to Gage, only to find him coming toward her.

"While I've never seen you awash in the vibrant hue of the setting sun, I can now say, without a doubt, it looks really good on you."

Aurora blushed. Something he seemed to have her doing often. "Are you this flattering to all your guests?"

"Definitely not the ones with beards," he replied with a grin. "Or the ones here with their significant others. I have found that I tend to throw out ridiculously flowery comments only to guests who get all giddy photographing something as simple as a dragonfly."

She shook a finger. "Not just any dragonfly. A blue dasher. And I was able to actually get a decent shot of him before he flew off."

He chuckled. "Now you're beginning to sound like me. How did you know the name of that particular species of dragonfly?"

"You have inspired me to be more knowledgeable of the places I travel to for my job. So thank you for that."

He laughed. "And you've taught me to be more appreciative of all the creatures, big and small, that inhabit this island. Even if I'm not chasing after them with a camera."

"I don't chase after my photographic subjects," she said, her brows pinching together.

"Tell that to that blue dasher you stalked for that perfectly shot picture."

Aurora laughed. "Okay, so maybe I went about it a little aggressively. But you of all people should know all about going about things aggressively, *Mr. Mountain Goat*."

"Just be glad I didn't try to impress you by taking on the persona of *Mr. Orangutan*. The landing would have been a lot more uncomfortable if we had fallen while I was swinging through the trees with you."

Aurora let out a snort of laughter, drawing gazes her direction. She smiled and then looked at Gage. "Please stop," she pleaded in a hushed whisper.

"Sorry." He chuckled. "I'll be good."

"Lunch is almost ready," Constance announced as she entered the room. "Please have a seat."

Gage held out a hand, motioning for Aurora to go and he would follow.

"You're more like your brother than you think," she told

him as she passed by. He was the best combination of responsible and focused, and, like Reed, humorous and playful. Jess was a fool to let this man go. Her loss was definitely going to be some other woman's gain. Was there any possibility that other woman could ever be her? Despite Aurora's head telling her that was a question she shouldn't be asking at this time in her life, her heart wasn't as easily convinced.

CHAPTER ELEVEN

"Are we done yet?" Gage asked with more than a little impatience as he stood in front of the window, where it was a bit cooler than the rest of the room. His mother had the great idea to have her guests paint a "fisherman" celebrating his catch. She'd even told their guests, Aurora included, that she planned to display their artwork on the wall behind the check-in desk.

Gage had the misfortune of being the chosen one for that day's art project. At his mother's request, he had changed into a pair of his fishing bibs, his raincoat, boots, and had topped off his wardrobe with a pair of polarized sunglasses. If standing inside his house dressed like a fisherman wasn't enough to make him feel ridiculous, his mother had brought out a fish that she'd mostly thawed and instructed him to hold it up in the air in front of him as if admiring his catch. If he didn't love his mother so much . . .

"Is everyone close to being finished with their painting?" his mother asked the group seated around the long dining table that she and his father had covered in a plastic sheet and set up with easels and painting palettes.

"Not quite," Reed said from the far end of the table as he dipped his paintbrush into the glass of water next to his tabletop easel.

"Oh, come on," Gage groaned.

"Hey, I'm right-handed, painting with my left," his brother countered. "It's going to take me a little longer than usual."

Their mother looked at Aurora and her other three guests who had traversed through the rainstorm to have lunch and then join in that afternoon's planned activity. "Would any of you like more time?"

"I'm about done," one of the fishermen replied.

The man beside him leaned back to take a good look at his creation. "I might have to give up fishing and start painting for a hobby."

The third fisherman gave a hearty chuckle. "Might be a good idea. I've seen how small the fish were that you reeled in this week."

They all laughed at that.

"Mine's done," Julia announced, holding hers up for everyone to see.

"You're supposed to wait for the group's collective reveal," their mother said.

"Oopsy. I forgot."

The only thing in his sister's painting that resembled Gage, or his pose, was the black blobs meant to represent his fishing boots. The rest consisted of a stick figure with dark, slanted sunglasses that looked more like big, black alien eyes.

"I stood here for nearly a half hour for that?" Gage complained with a frown. Thankfully, he hadn't had to hold the fish up the entire time.

"It's not my fault Mom drew your name instead of Reed's."

Standing in that silly pose for what felt like hours made Gage incredibly thankful that he flew a floatplane for a living and was not a model.

"Aurora?" his mother said, reminding Gage that his brother wasn't the only one who might not be finished painting him.

Gage sought out Aurora's gaze, silently pleading with her to help set him free.

She smiled back at him and set her brush down on the paper towel his mother had placed next to every easel. "I'm good. More time isn't going to make this painting any better."

"Oh, honey, I'm sure it's way better than you think it is," his mother said supportively.

His father leaned over to peek at Aurora's painting.

Gage watched his father's thick, graying brows lift slowly upward. Then a twitch appeared at the corners of his mouth. He was battling the urge to grin for Aurora's sake. "I can s-see the resemblance."

"You can?" she said, sounding adorably delighted by his father's comment.

"More than my painting of Gage," he replied with a nod. "Reed clearly does not get his artistic ability from me."

His mother tilted her head ever so slightly to study hers. "Judging by my painting," she began, "I'm starting to think Reed was switched at birth."

Julia snorted.

"Impossible," Reed said defensively as he placed his paintbrush in the glass of water beside him. "At least, according to the DNA tests we all got last Christmas. And you'll be happy to know that I'm done."

Gage lowered his arm, letting the fish he was holding by its open mouth dangle at his side. He was thankful it was one of the smaller catches his mother had stored in their commercial freezer for the amount of time he'd had to hold it up in the air above him.

"Okay," his mother said, rising from her seat, "since everyone is finished, go ahead and turn your easels around so Gage can see your artistic renderings of him."

Raucous laughter arose as the paintings of Gage were revealed.

"You all did such a wonderful job!" his mother said, clapping her hands together.

It sounded like she really meant it, but Gage couldn't imagine how his mother thought they were anything close to wonderful. Creative? Yes. Realistic? No. His gaze traveled the length of the table where everyone was seated facing him, taking in all the paintings on display.

When he got to Aurora's painting, his mouth pulled up into a wide grin. Although the details of his face were pretty abstract, what really caught his attention were the broad shoulders she'd painted on him.

Gage nodded. "Not bad."

"I'm not so sure Emmy would share your opinion, but thanks," she replied with an appreciative smile.

He continued down the table with his visual inspection, commenting on each of the paintings. It was kind of amusing, seeing everyone's rendering of him. Gage's perusal came to a dead stop when he got to the end and saw his brother's work of art. Gage blinked, brows slowly lifting. "That isn't a fish I'm holding. It's a box of fish sticks."

"I was supposed to draw what I saw when I looked at you standing there. You made me think about that guy on the fish stick commercial," Reed admitted with an unabashed grin.

Aurora giggled.

"It's so good," Julia groaned. "And he painted him opposite-handed too. Ugh."

"It's not good," Gage argued. "I'm not even wearing a hat. And I certainly don't look like I should be selling fish sticks."

"Oh, I don't know if I'd say Reed's painting doesn't resemble you," Aurora joined in.

Gage glanced her way with a questioning look.

"You and your brother's artistic rendering of you are both wearing raincoats and boots," she explained.

He rolled his eyes and groaned in defeat.

The three men who had joined in threw their heads back in laughter.

"I'm going to return this fish to the kitchen," Gage announced. "And wash my hands," he added, not wanting Aurora to think he was leaving because he was upset by her support of Reed's efforts.

"There are so many stars out this evening," Aurora said as she sat bathed in the warm glow of the fire pit on the lodge's back patio. "It's so beautiful. I'm glad it finally stopped raining so I could experience this." They'd sat around and visited with his family after the other guests departed following the painting challenge, which had been way more fun than she'd expected it to be.

"You think that's something," Gage told her, drawing her back from her thoughts, "you should see the night sky when the Northern Lights are painted across it."

"I would love more than anything to see them in person, but it doesn't seem to be in the cards for me this trip," she said with a sigh. "Mom and Dad always talked about how magical they were when Jade and I were growing up." She looked his way. "They fell in love under the Northern Lights when they were here."

He smiled. "I never really thought about them as magical. Maybe because I grew up with them being fairly common in my life. But you're right, they really are something special to behold. Especially for your parents, it seems. Maybe you'll have the chance to see them for yourself before you leave for Seattle. There's still time."

"I really hope so," she said softly. "But I'm not going to hold my breath."

"If they're as magical as your parents say they are, you just have to believe you will see them before you go home," he said.

She nodded and lifted her gaze upward once more. The second she did, a shooting star raced across the dark velvet sky. "Did you see that?" she exclaimed.

"I did. Be sure to make a wish," he replied.

She laughed softly. "I don't believe in wishing on shooting stars," she admitted. Not anymore. She'd wished on them so many times before. Always the same silent plea. Aurora wanted to find that one special love. She thought she had found it with Ben, only that wish hadn't ended up coming true.

"You believe that the Northern Lights are magical but won't wish on shooting stars?" he said, his curiosity clearly aroused.

"Wishing on them was something I did as a child," she told him.

"There's no age limit for wishing. I think you should go ahead and make one. Just in case it decides to come true."

She sighed. "Okay." Closing her eyes, she made her wish. Then she looked up at Gage. "Happy?"

His smile lifted a little more. "Happy."

Aurora shivered and pulled the wool blanket Gage's mother had given her before they'd gone outside around her tighter.

"Are you cold?"

She shook her head. "No. This blanket and the fire are keeping the evening's chill at bay. I'm not sure where that shudder came from."

"Well, if you get cold, just tell me and I'll turn up the fire. Or we can go back inside," Gage told her as he joined her in admiring the starlit sky.

"Gage . . ."

He looked her way. "Yes?"

"Can I ask how you met Jess?" Aurora quickly added, "If you don't mind my asking. I know it's none of my business."

He hesitated for a long moment and then shook his head. "For some reason, when it comes to you, I don't mind opening up about things I don't normally share with others."

"I feel the same."

"She and I met when I flew to Anchorage to pick up some supplies and a couple of parts Dad had ordered for our fishing boats," he explained. "We try and keep the boats, the UTVs, and my plane updated and properly running. That's where we first crossed paths."

"She worked there?"

"No," he said with a tight chuckle that showed little emotion. "Her father owned the boating supply business. I was checking out when she came in from getting her nails done. Or maybe it was her hair. Whatever it was, she came to drop off lunch for her father, and we got to talking. That discussion led to us exchanging numbers. We would mostly talk on the phone, but I also traveled to Anchorage once a month to see her. My family wanted to meet her because they knew I was getting pretty serious. She suggested moving to Conley Island and helping at the lodge for a while so we would have more time to get to know each other. So I flew her here. I have no idea what she was expecting, but this place evidently was not it." Gage shook his head. "I don't know how I could have been so wrong about her."

"You loved her," Aurora stated. Gage didn't seem like the type to bring a woman home to meet his family unless he was all in.

"I thought I did," he admitted. "But I realize now that I read more into our relationship than was actually there. On the phone, and when we met in person, she said all the right things. Things she thought I wanted to hear. But that all changed shortly after she arrived here. She was disappointed in the man she chose and made no effort to hide it."

"Disappointed? In you?" How could that ever be possible? Aurora wondered, feeling angry that this woman had made Gage feel unworthy of having her love.

"Me," he answered. "And my life," he went on with a troubled frown. "I think Jess was expecting something far more glamorous. Like the fishing resorts that are taking over the smaller businesses. The same ones I am fighting against taking over our small family-run business. The woman I had gotten to know over the phone and through brief visits to her place in Anchorage wasn't the same one I brought here. After coming to Conley Island, Jess chose to spend hours on her phone in the great room instead of joining conversations or family gameplay. Meals were a challenge for my mom because Jess had an aversion to fish, which, as you know, we serve our guests often. Not that Mom had to worry over many meals. Jess's stay lasted only a few days."

"Oh my," Aurora said. How awful that visit must have been for him. "She sounds . . . not nice." That was the kindest thing she could think to say about the woman who'd treated Gage so unfairly.

He laughed, some of the tension the conversation had stirred up leaving his handsome, moonlit face. "Not nice at all," he agreed. "But the truth is she wanted a life in the city or one on a fancy resort. That was not the life I had to offer her. In the end, I was not her person."

"I'm so sorry she hurt you," she said.

"It kept me from making the biggest mistake of my life."

"You deserve someone who appreciates you for who you are. There are so many things in life that can make a person rich, and not all of them are connected to financial wealth. Like having a loving, caring family. Like having the ability to step outside and soak in the tranquility around you every day. Like the feeling you get when you do for others without having been asked to do so."

"Going by that, I'm a very wealthy man," he said with a smile.

"Filthy rich," she agreed with a grin.

They turned their gazes back to the fire, sitting in companionable silence.

"Hot cocoa and s'mores, anyone?"

Aurora looked back over her shoulder to see Julia coming toward them carrying a large metal tray. "Yes, please."

"Sounds good," Gage agreed.

When Julia reached them, Aurora glanced over the tray

and its contents. Next to the necessities for s'mores were two steaming mugs. "You're not having a hot chocolate with us?"

"I already had some with Mom and Dad in by the fireplace," his sister answered as they took the offered cups of hot cocoa. "These are for you two. And I brought out everything you need to make s'mores if you have room left for some dessert. I'll set the tray over here."

"I always have room," Gage told her as he stood and walked over to join his sister, where she placed the tray on a long, narrow table that sat against the rear outer wall of the lodge. A few feet above it, a strip of wood with several hooks lined up across it held a fire poker and several stainless steel marshmallow roasting sticks.

"I suppose I could force a s'more down as well," Aurora called over to Julia with a grateful smile. It was so sweet of Gage's sister to think about them. "Maybe two."

Julia returned the smile. "Enjoy," she said before starting for the lodge's rear door.

"You're not going to have a s'more with us?" Aurora asked.

Gage's sister paused and then turned to look at Aurora, surprise lighting her features. "You want me to join you?" She looked at Gage, who had returned with several roasting sticks, her expression now anxious.

"She's not Jess," he said, sounding confident in his words.

Aurora couldn't help but smile. She'd been trying to get Gage to accept that for the truth it was. It seemed that he finally had. That meant a lot to her. Gage had somehow begun to mean a lot to her too, much to Aurora's chagrin. For so long, she had been trying to get in with *World Adventures Magazine* and had finally been given that opportunity. A full-time job with the magazine was within her reach if the photos she took this trip wowed them enough. This was not the time to let her heart lead her down some other path.

"You are more than welcome to join us," Aurora said. "Come on over and fix yourself a s'more."

Julia smiled. "I do love a toasted marshmallow."

"You and me both," Aurora agreed as Gage handed her a roasting stick.

He handed Julia one, keeping one for himself. Then he held up the bag of marshmallows he'd carried over with the roasting sticks. "Ladies first," he said, handing the bag over to Aurora.

She opened it and pulled out a fluffy, white marshmallow, then handed the open bag to Julia, who sat on the opposite side of her. "This brings me back to my childhood, making s'mores by a campfire with Jade."

"Was that the last time you had one?" Julia asked as she placed her marshmallow onto the pointed tip of her roasting stick.

Aurora nodded as she pushed her marshmallow farther up the tine she'd placed it on. "Yes. There isn't much opportunity for me to sit around a campfire in downtown Seattle."

"I can't imagine living somewhere surrounded by concrete," Julia replied as she stuck her loaded stick in the flames.

"Plenty of people do it," Gage said. "We're just used to a different kind of life."

"I have to admit that I'm a little envious of your life here," Aurora told them. "It's so much slower-paced and relaxing. And being surrounded by nature with all its breathtaking views is the biggest plus of all."

"Most people think that when they come here for a

stay," Gage said as he turned his marshmallow, which had cooked to a golden brown on one side. "But they're ready to get back to their kind of civilization by the time their stay is up."

"I think you'd be surprised," Aurora told him as she pulled her stick from the fire and stood to go fix her s'more. She was not one of those people Gage was referring to. She was nowhere near ready to leave Conley Island, but she had a life to get back to in Seattle.

"I loved your painting of Gage," Julia said when she joined her at the table to fix her campfire treat.

"I loved Reed's," Aurora said in a hushed whisper.

"Hey, I heard that," Gage said from behind her as he reached past them for two graham cracker squares.

The two women giggled.

"You know," Aurora said to Julia, "I'd be happy to show you how to get the most out of your pictures for the retreat's website."

"Are you serious?"

Aurora smiled. "Very. I could even have a look at the website and give you my two cents on its layout if you'd like. I designed my site that I use to sell photos and prints online. And I did my friend Emmy's website for her new art gallery."

"I would never turn down a chance to better my skills," Julia replied. "Thank you so much."

"You are so very welcome," Aurora said as she placed the perfectly golden-brown puff atop a graham cracker, topping it off with a square of chocolate, and then another graham cracker. She took a bite and groaned, thoroughly enjoying their campfire masterpieces. "This is sooo good."

Gage grinned. "I had no idea that s'mores were the way to—"

Gage's words were cut off by the ringing of a phone. Aurora pulled hers out from her jacket pocket and glanced at the screen. "It's my sister," she told them with a worried frown. "She doesn't usually call me this late in the evening." Jade and her husband were the early-to-bed type.

"Take it," Gage said without hesitation.

"I hope everything's okay," Julia said as Aurora stood and stepped away from the fire pit to take her sister's call.

Her stomach knotting in worry, she hit the answer button and brought the phone to her ear. "Jade? Is everything alright?"

Her sister laughed, the sound immediately sending relief coursing through Aurora. "Everything is wonderful," she said.

"You sound pretty perky for this time of night," Aurora told her in confusion.

"The correct term would be giddy," her younger sister corrected. "And I'm up because David had to work overtime this evening, and I didn't want to make this call without him."

"Hi, Aurora!" her brother-in-law called out in the background.

"Hold on," Jade told her. "I'm going to put my phone on speaker. Okay, go ahead."

"Hi, David," Aurora replied, trying to remember when she'd ever heard him sound so bubbly.

"Hope you're ready to be an aunt."

"Ready to . . . wait a minute! Did you just say aunt?"

"He did," her sister confirmed with a happy giggle. "We're going to be adding a little one to our family."

"As in another puppy?" Aurora said. Jade and David always called their dog, Mac, their child. Maybe they were adopting again and giving Mac a playmate.

"No, silly," Jade said, her voice filled with unrestrained joy, "we're having a baby!"

A wave of emotion washed over Aurora. She had never felt so many things at one time. Surprise and joy for her sister and David. Sadness for herself, because she was the oldest daughter. She should have been the one telling her little sister that she was going to be an aunt. But Aurora hadn't even made it to the altar. At that moment, it felt as if life was passing her by. She wanted all those things her sister had been so blessed to find.

"Aurora?" she heard Jade say, her excitement replaced by concern.

Aurora fought back an unexpected rush of hot tears. "I'm here." She forced a smile because she really was happy for her sister. But her heart ached at the realization that while she had put an end to the life she'd thought she wanted, her sister was adding to hers. "I'm just speechless. I had no idea you and David were trying."

"We didn't want to say anything to anyone, not even Mom and Dad, until it happened and we were safely through the first trimester. Today was day one in my second trimester!"

"I have to say your sister dealt with the first three months of pregnancy like a champ," Aurora's brother-in-law said with pride. "Even with morning sickness that lasted beyond the mornings."

"Jade, David," Aurora said, her throat tight, "I am so very happy for you both. And for Mac," she added. "He's going to be the best big brother."

"He will," Jade agreed. "I can't wait to hear all about your trip to Alaska. It must be pretty special for you to extend your stay a week longer than planned. Hope you're getting all the photos you need for the magazine."

"I am," Aurora replied with confidence. "And it is," she said, her thoughts going to Gage.

"I'm glad," her sister replied. "Enjoy the rest of your stay. I need to get going. David and I still have to call Mom and Dad and then David's family with our news."

She was touched that her sister had shared their big news with her before anyone else. "We'll talk more when I drive home for early Thanksgiving dinner," Aurora said. "Love you guys."

"Love you, too," Jade said, and then the call disconnected.

Aurora stood in contemplative silence, staring off into the darkness that surrounded the lodge's back patio.

Gage stood watching Aurora as she paced about on the phone. "She looks upset," he said to his sister, keeping his voice low.

Julia nodded. "I hope everything's okay."

"I should go check on her," he said, rising to his feet.

Across the starlit patio, Aurora stood gazing out, phone still clutched in one hand by her side.

Gage stepped up behind her and stopped, not wanting to intrude on her thoughts, but needing to know she was alright. "Aurora," he said softly, "everything okay?"

She nodded, but didn't turn around. "I'm going to be an aunt," she told him, her reply ending in a muffled sob.

"So those are happy tears," he surmised, relief sweeping through him.

"Yes," she said and then added, "and no."

No? "Is your sister having problems with her pregnancy?"

Aurora shook her head. "She's wonderful. It's me. And I feel awful for feeling the way I do. And it's not just my sister's pregnancy announcement. Being here makes me feel homesick, because it feels so much like home did before I moved to Seattle, and Jade got married and moved into a home of her own. I miss the quality time you still get to have with your family."

A brow lifted as understanding settled in. Stepping forward, Gage wrapped his arms around her in a comforting embrace. "It's okay to be happy for someone yet feel sad at the same time. You are dealing with a lot on this trip. Give yourself some grace."

"I'm going to take this tray back to the kitchen," his sister said as she darted past Gage and Aurora. She paused halfway to the back door of the lodge and glanced back. "If you ever need to talk, Aurora, I'm a great listener."

"Thank you, Julia," Aurora replied. "I appreciate the offer."

Gage's sister nodded. "Night, all."

"Night, Julia," Aurora managed, with a hiccupping sob.

"Night," Gage said, his focus centered on the woman he held in his arms. He hated seeing Aurora hurting. Outwardly, she'd been happy, easygoing, and fun-loving, but she was here during what should have been her honeymoon. That had to stir up a lot of emotions. Emotions made even more raw when she learned her sister was starting the family Aurora had no doubt been hoping for.

Resting his chin on the top of her head, Gage said, "You are going to be the best aunt."

She laughed. That was followed by a soft sniffle. "I intend to be." Wiping her eyes, she turned to look up at him. "I'm so embarrassed for getting all emotional and chasing your sister away."

"Don't be," he said as he looked down into her dark, moisture-filled eyes. "And thank you for including her in our marshmallow roasting. I know it meant a lot to her."

"I enjoy spending time with your sister," Aurora replied.

"Speaking of marshmallows, you have some on your face."

"I do?" she said, hand coming to her face. "Where?"

He smiled. "It's only a speck of marshmallow. Right here," he said, brushing the side of his thumb along the corner of her mouth.

"Is that all?" she asked, her teary gaze lowering to his mouth.

"Maybe a little bit more," he said, running his thumb in a tender path across her lower lip.

"Gage," she said softly.

"Gage . . ." his father called out.

Aurora and Gage separated. "Over here," he replied.

"Can I get you to lend me and Reed a hand for a moment?"

Frowning, Gage looked at Aurora.

"It's okay," she said. "I should be getting back to my cabin anyway. You have guests to fly out tomorrow."

"You do realize I'm not about to let you walk back to your cabin alone? Especially when you're feeling out of sorts."

"Gage," she argued with a frown.

"Aurora, humor me," he said. "I'm trying to be a good host."

She smiled. "You're an above-and-beyond host.

"Glad to hear you've been satisfied with your stay here so far," he told her with a grin. "But seriously, a lot of our bookings come by word of mouth. As Dad likes to say, 'A happy guest brings the rest.'"

"That's really good. And so true," she replied. "It's the same in my business. If people are satisfied with what you have to offer them, they tell other prospective clients. I intend to spread the word about Living the Good Life Fishing Retreat when I get home."

"Any bit of good word put out there is appreciated," he told her. Although he wasn't certain the friends she'd spoken to him about were the remote retreat in Alaska type. But her offering to promote his family's business in any way when she had so many other things on her plate was really thoughtful.

"Come on in and wait by the fireplace," Gage said. "I'll go see what Dad needs me for, and then I'll walk you back to your cabin."

"I'm beginning to think I should have taken a room at the lodge," she said as they started for the door. "Then you wouldn't have felt the need to escort me back and forth my entire stay here."

"And miss out on all the stimulating conversation we've shared during those walks?" he teased with a grin. "Not to mention the free mud bath."

Aurora's laughter returned full force, letting Gage know he had accomplished what he set out to do—put that happy light back in her beautiful brown eyes.

CHAPTER TWELVE

"I'm so glad the two of you stopped by for lunch during your outing today," Glady said as she gathered up Aurora and Gage's empty plates and bowls.

"Aurora was paying up on a bet she lost to me," Gage told the older woman with a grin.

Glady looked at Aurora questioningly.

"I lost a bet and owed him lunch out," she explained. "But I got to choose where we went."

"And you chose to come here," Glady said, sounding quite pleased by Aurora's choice. "You've crossed my mind a time or two since I sent you flying off into the wild blue, or as is the case here now, gray yonder with Gage. I thought you'd be long gone by now."

Aurora shook her head. "After visiting Conley Island, I knew there was so much more there to be photographed. I couldn't leave. An evening spent with Gage and his wonderful family only reinforced my decision to stay on."

"I take it you were able to get the pictures you were hoping for during your visit here?"

Aurora looked across the table and smiled. "I did. More

than I ever hoped for. Gage, as it turns out, is not only a terrific pilot, he's also a very knowledgeable tour guide. He knows all the right spots for the best wildlife shots."

He shrugged. "Comes with having grown up on the island and being able to answer our guests' questions."

He kept saying that, but Aurora knew Gage put a little something extra into helping her.

Gage's cell rang, playing a lively country tune. Pulling it from his pocket, he glanced at the screen and then stood. "I need to take this," he said with a frown.

"Of course," Aurora replied. "I hope everything's okay," she muttered as he stepped outside of the diner to talk.

"That boy is far too serious," Glady decided with a shake of her head as she stared at the closed door. "But then Gage has been shouldering the responsibility of running the family retreat since his father took ill last year."

"I know. And Gage is actually very funny," Aurora said in Gage's defense. "In fact, he's always trying to make me laugh."

Glady looked her way with a speculative eye. "Does he now?"

"I can't ever remember laughing so hard so often before. And my best friend Emmy can be really funny."

"I'm so glad to hear that," Glady told her. "I know Constance worries that they're asking too much of Gage, but he insisted on shouldering most of the weight of running their business after Jim got sick. I suppose his having a business degree along with his pilot license makes him the most qualified to step in. Of course, Reed and Julia are also pitching in more."

"I'm so glad his father is recovering so well," Aurora said. "It's clear to see where Gage and Reed got their silly sense of humor from."

The door to the diner opened, and Gage came back inside, the frown he'd worn going out the door cut even deeper into his face now.

"I'll just take these dirty dishes to the kitchen," Glady said before hurrying off.

Gage slid his phone back into his coat pocket and then settled into his chair once again. "That was Clive."

"That look on your face when you came in tells me the call didn't go well," Aurora said with a worried frown.

"The private equity firm just upped their offer." He met her tense gaze across the table. "It's a good one. But it's not about the money. It's our home. Our business."

"I hope you told him that," she replied.

"I did," he said with a sigh. "But was it the right thing to do? If the business continues to lose guests to these newfangled fishing resorts, my family could end up with nothing. I also know that the stress of financial issues could put my father's health at risk."

"Gage, I have some money saved . . ." she heard herself offering, yet no regret followed.

"No," he said adamantly, and Aurora found herself wishing she could take her well-meant offer back.

"I'm so sorry. I shouldn't have tried to involve myself in your family's business." She hadn't considered the embarrassment he or his family might feel by her offering to lend them some money until Gage turned things around. She had just wanted to help.

"We're not at that place yet," he told her. "Please don't think that I don't appreciate your offer to help if we need it. I just can't accept it. That would be like me quitting on the promise I made my family to make things right."

"I understand," Aurora said with a nod.

"Enough of all this serious talk," Gage decided. "We

need to get out of here because I have a surprise I've been setting up for you."

She smiled. "Ooh, I love surprises."

After saying their goodbyes to Glady, they returned to Gage's floatplane and took off out of Juneau for whatever surprise he had planned. Aurora had tried unsuccessfully to get it out of him when they were walking back to the marina where his floatplane was docked.

Aurora watched out the plane's front windshield as they flew away from downtown Juneau, past the cruise ship terminal with its impressive ships that were there on their last runs of the season.

Aurora looked at Gage. "No hints, huh?"

"Nope."

"Can I buy a vowel?"

He chuckled. "Why do I feel like your parents had to hide all your Christmas presents somewhere really good so you couldn't find them when you were growing up? Because I'm sure you tried to."

"Still do," she answered with a grin as she turned to look out the window beside her.

"I knew it," Gage replied. "But I'm about to verbally unwrap your surprise."

Her head snapped around. "You are?"

He nodded. "We are currently traveling over part of Alaska's picturesque landscape on our way to fifteen hundred square miles of the Juneau Icefield. Be on the lookout for wildlife roaming about the mountain peaks. Bear. Moose. Goats. To name a few." He glanced her way. "Sound tour guide-ish enough for you?"

Aurora smiled. "Very professional and informative," she replied as she retrieved her camera. "Now I know why you told me not to forget my camera."

"As if that would ever happen." He chuckled again. "Now pay attention. You might catch a glimpse of some waterfalls along the way. I'll try and give you a heads up in case you want to snap a few pictures of them."

"I would love that. Thank you." She couldn't imagine seeing the beauty of a waterfall among the lush forest from a view high above it all. A whole new perspective for her wildlife shots.

The view was even better than Aurora had hoped it would be. Gage not only pointed out two waterfalls, but he also flew her over several glaciers. The best one of all—the Taku Glacier.

"I never expected glaciers to be so amazing, but they are," Aurora admitted in awe as she snapped pictures of the land below.

"Only thirty-six of the glaciers in this icefield are named. And only a scant few of those are accessible."

"The Taku Glacier was definitely my favorite."

"Understandable," he said with a nod. "It's the deepest and thickest alpine temperature glacier in the world. I believe it's just under five thousand feet thick and thirty-five or so miles long."

"How do you know so much?"

"I read a lot growing up and have always been able to store away even the most useless facts."

"It's a gift," Aurora said with a smile as she glanced back out her window. "Gage! There's a moose!" she exclaimed as she fumbled with her camera to get a shot.

"Good eye," he told her. "Did you get it?"

She sighed, her shoulders sagging. "Not clearly. But it was magnificent all the same."

"Hold on," he told her. "We're going back around to see

if we can get you that picture. Then we need to head back to Conley Island."

I love you! That's what she came far too close to exclaiming in her excitement. Thankfully, she did not. "It's going to be the most amazing shot," Aurora said with forced calm. "I've never ever seen a moose before. Not in real life anyway."

"Well, you have now."

She had experienced so many new things since missing her flight that day. Who would have thought a road-blocking mudslide could lead to the wonderful adventure of a lifetime that she had been on since coming to Juneau? To a newfound friendship with a very special Alaskan pilot. To the kind of happiness she'd been seeking. Yet, the stars weren't aligning for her and Gage as they had for her mother and father. They were both on different paths in their lives. She was trying to move up in her photography career. And Gage needed to be there for his family and their guests. Other than after the unexpected kiss they'd shared, one Gage had not sought to repeat, he'd made no mention of having any romantic feelings for her. Like those final grains of sand in an hourglass, her time there was running out. She had to get back to her life and responsibilities in Seattle, and Gage had to save his family's business.

"Penny for your thoughts," he said, glancing her way. "Better make that a dollar. Inflation and all, you know."

Aurora managed a weak laugh, despite the slight heaviness in her heart. In a few days, she wouldn't be seeing that warm, knee-weakening smile every day.

"Aurora?"

She gave her troubled thoughts a mental shove aside. "I was just thinking about how much I'm going to miss all of this," she replied. *And you.* "Thank you for being such a thoughtful and helpful host. Without you and your knowledgeable tour guidance, I wouldn't have taken some of the best nature shots I've ever taken."

"It was a nice change of pace," he said with a nod, his gaze returning to the cloud-dotted sky view in front of them. "Seeing the things I've come to take for granted through your eyes, and your lens," he added with a grin, "has given me a whole new appreciation for the place I have, and always will, call home."

It seemed their chance encounter had left a lasting impression on both of them. "Gage . . ." she began, wanting to tell him she was grateful for more than his escorting her around the island during her stay there.

"Yes?"

Don't complicate his life any more than it is, a voice in the back of her head warned. "I hope to come back again someday." She would make certain of it. She had come to love everything about this visually breathtaking part of the world. From its quiet remoteness, to its abundance of wildlife just waiting to be photographed. From the views to be found while flying above it all in Gage's plane, to time spent with his warm and welcoming family.

"I . . . uh, I mean *we* look forward to having you come back to visit us again someday," Gage replied.

Aurora tried not to smile. It was nice to know she would be welcomed back by both Gage and his family.

"I can't believe you leave tomorrow," Julia said with an effective pout.

"I know," Aurora agreed as she packed her camera equipment away. She'd come to the lodge early that morning to take the family pictures she'd promised Gage's father she would take before she left Conley Island. She knew how important they were to him after coming so close to not being there for family pictures.

"I'm so excited to see those pictures," Constance said as she set a platter of crispy bacon on the table with the rest of their breakfast selections.

"I will email them to Gage as soon as I get back and can edit them," Aurora promised. "The earthy shades you all chose to wear for your family portrait blend together so perfectly. Like the colors of nature that surround your home."

They were dressed in black dress pants. Each wore a sweater, in different styles and colors. Gage in a dark blue like the water that surrounded the island. Reed in a dark brown like the earth under them. Their parents in dark green like the woods around them. And Julia in a warm gold sweater she said represented fall on the island, but as far as Aurora was concerned, it was more of a reflection of her warm and caring heart of gold.

"I can't remember the last time our family got all dressed up for a family photo," Jim said as he took his seat at the table.

Aurora was thankful he was there to share in the moment with his family, considering how things could have turned out.

"Don't get too used to it," Reed muttered. "Unless I'm allowed to wear jeans for the next one."

"We can do that," their mother replied. Then she looked at Aurora. "Maybe we could hire you to come out and take our family pictures again next year?"

Aurora smiled. "I'm sure we can work something out. I

already told Gage I hope to come back to visit again. I still can't believe my visit here is over. It went by so fast."

Reed took a seat at the dining table and reached out to scoop a spoonful of potatoes onto his plate. "You know what they say. Time flies when you're having fun."

Aurora nodded in agreement as she took her seat. Hank had taken the other guests out fishing, allowing Aurora to share time alone with Gage and his family. "I've had the best time here." She glanced around the table. "You've all been so welcoming. I feel like I've known you all forever."

Julia sniffled.

"Are you crying?" Reed asked his sister with a quirked brow.

"No," she said, dabbing at her eyes with her napkin. "I think we put too much onion in the fried potatoes."

"If you're ever looking for a n-new job," Gage's father said, "I'd be happy to hire you to be in charge of game n-night here at the retreat."

Aurora laughed. "I will keep that in mind should I need a career switch."

As they had at every breakfast she'd spent with Gage's family, everyone talked and laughed. Gage's father told funny stories about Gage and his siblings when they were growing up. Aurora told them about some of her and Jade's silly antics when they were young girls. She was going to miss these moments, just as she missed the time she used to spend with her family after she'd moved away. She would be going back to a coffee and bagel from her local coffee shop, which she would take back to her condo to eat while working.

Gage set his napkin on the table next to his plate. Then he looked at Aurora. "We'd better get moving if we're going to get you out on the water to experience a fishing trip the way we do it here."

Reed swiped a napkin across his mouth. "True. We want to get you out there while the fish are biting." Pushing away from the table, he stood. "Good breakfast, Mom." He looked at Gage. "I'll go get the boat ready while you and Aurora suit up."

"Are you sure you want to go out fishing on a drizzly day like this?" Gage's mother asked Aurora.

"The weather is supposed to clear up," she replied with an affirmative nod. "This is my last chance to do it. I'm not about to miss out because of a little rain."

"She's a trooper," Jim said, meeting Gage's gaze.

"I try to be," Aurora said with a laugh.

"I'm sorry we couldn't get you out sooner," Gage said.

"You had guests that were already booked to go out," Aurora replied. "I'm just glad to have the opportunity to give it a try before I go back to Seattle." Conversation stopped as her cell phone went off across the room. "I should get that," she said. "I sent a batch of photos out to Eugene late last night. He might have had issues receiving them, since internet service here isn't quite the same as on the mainland."

Reed, who had already stood to leave, hurried over to grab Aurora's jacket from the back of the sofa, since she was on the opposite side of the table. By the time he returned and handed it to her across the table, the ringing had ceased. "Sorry," he apologized.

"You tried," she told him. Retrieving her phone from her pocket, she pulled up her missed call screen. Her brows knitted together as she read the caller's name.

"Mr. Watkins?" Gage asked.

"No," she answered.

"Emmy, making sure you're actually coming home tomorrow?" he teased with a grin.

Aurora shook her head. "No. It's—" The cell phone rang again, this time in her hand. She hadn't spoken to her ex for months, but then they were both busy with their careers. Answering the call, she brought the phone to her ear. "Hello, Ben."

"Hey, Aurora," her ex-fiancé said. "I was hoping we might be able to get together for dinner soon. I have something pretty important I want to talk to you about."

"I'm not in Seattle right now," she told him, wondering what it was he needed to meet up with her to discuss. "I'm in Alaska on an assignment. I have a few things going on when I get back. Can I call you then, and we'll set something up that fits both our schedules?"

"Alaska?" he replied.

"It's where *World Adventures Magazine* needed me to go."

"I see. Hope you're doing okay."

She looked at Gage. "I'm doing better than expected."

"I'm glad. Same here."

She glanced over to find Gage watching her, his expression unreadable. Why did she feel so guilty sitting there talking to her ex about a proposed dinner date?

"Talk to you when I get back." Disconnecting the call, she smiled sheepishly at Gage's family. "Ben and I have been friends since we were children."

"Friends?" Julia repeated with a studying glance.

Aurora looked back up at Gage to find his gaze no longer fixed on her but on the eggs he was shoveling around on his plate.

"I guess you'll be able to catch your *friend* up on everything you've been doing here during your stay," Reed said with an intentional glance in Gage's direction.

She knew Reed was thinking about the kiss he'd interrupted on the porch the afternoon they had arrived in the rainstorm. "I'm not sure he'll bring it up when I see him again. Ben and I were engaged," she admitted, feeling the need to be honest with Gage's family, "until I called off our wedding."

"Oh," Constance said, surprise in her eyes.

Oh, great. Now Gage's mother thought she was like Gage's ex. "We both agreed that we were not each other's person and deserved something more than friendship in a marriage. Even if friendship is an important basis to build something more on, I knew in my heart that was all there would ever be between us. I'm just thankful Ben and I were able to remain friends."

"You don't owe us any explanations," Gage told her. "Your personal life isn't our business."

Why did he suddenly sound so businesslike?

"Gage is right," his father said.

"Unless your friend is having second thoughts about the breakup," Julia said with a pout.

Aurora felt guilty, but allowing herself to feel that way because a good friend wanted to meet up with her was silly. Especially when she and Gage had no sort of commitment between them.

"Well, I'd better go get our rain gear ready so we can get down to the dock. Time is running out," Gage said as he rose to his feet.

As if Aurora needed any reminding of that fact.

"I'll walk out with you," Reed said.

Gage looked at Aurora. "I'll meet you out on the porch when you're ready."

She nodded, watching them go.

"I hope things work out for you," Constance said as she stood and began clearing the dishes from the table.

"There really isn't anything to work out," Aurora told her. "Ben and I didn't have the kind of relationship that I truly want with the person I intend to spend the rest of my life with."

"Honey, I was referring to your magazine assignment," she said. "I hope it works out and you get that in-house job you're hoping for."

"Same," Julia said. "Although I really wish things had turned out differently for you and my brother."

"I really like Gage."

"I hear a 'but' coming," Julia said.

Aurora smiled. Gage's sister was perceptive. "If I get an offer for a full-time position with *World Adventures Magazine*, I'll be traveling more than I do already. Not just to places in the states. I'll be flying to other countries too."

"Oh," Constance said, her expression one of disappointment.

Aurora nodded. "I know Gage's life is here. He loves Conley Island, and I can certainly see why. I've learned that the stars don't always align the way you hoped they would," she admitted. "I'm just grateful to have met Gage and all of you."

"Same," Julia said with a soft smile.

Aurora glanced toward the retreat's main entrance door. "I shouldn't keep Gage waiting." Standing, she said, "Thank you for breakfast. It was delicious, as usual." That said, she stepped away from the table and made her way out to the porch where Gage waited patiently for her to join him.

"Are you standing out here sniffing one of Mom's candles?"

Gage lowered his arm, along with the scented wax-filled jar. It wasn't something he could deny. Reed had caught him red-handed. "It was sitting on the table by the door when I went out," he replied, and then felt the need to add, "I bought it for her."

"Well, that makes all the difference," his brother replied as he moved to stand next to Gage. "Sniff away."

"This is from the 1820 House's special candle collection," Gage told him. "It's called Beautiful Aurora. She loves this scent."

"Sniffing a candle, no matter how good its scent is, is not going to keep Aurora here on Conley Island," Reed said, as if Gage didn't already know that. "Are you really going to let her get away?"

Gage looked to his brother, who was pulling on his rain boots. "You have to have someone for them to get away from you," he told Reed with a frown.

"You were so close to reeling her in," his brother insisted.

"Aurora isn't a fish."

"True."

His brother was hitting far too close to home. "I'm not fishing," Gage snarled in frustration, the phone call Aurora had received that morning still fresh in his mind.

"Okay, she's not a fish," Reed agreed, his tone calm. "When you spend most of your days out on a boat, that's the kind of analogies you make. But in all seriousness, I've seen the way you and Aurora are when you're together. There's something special there."

"I think you all are so eager to see me in a relationship again that you're reading more into what you see between me and Aurora."

His brother's frown mirrored his own. "It has nothing to do with our wanting to push you into a relationship. We want you to move past what Jess did to you," Reed told him. "I know how she made you feel. Like you weren't enough." He looked around. "Like this wasn't enough."

"Maybe right after she left," Gage admitted. "But once she was gone, I took a look at my life again and had no second thoughts about keeping it just the way it is. I'm over Jess. Have been for a very long time."

"Maybe so. But will you be able to get over Aurora?"

Gage fell silent.

"Thought that might be your response."

Mouth pulling down into a frown, Gage said, "I can't do this with her. Not right now. You and I both know we have to focus on saving the retreat."

"We're making upgrades," Reed said. "You've been coming up with ideas to draw more guests in. We will save the retreat. Of that, I have complete faith. But none of us want you to do so at the cost of your happiness."

"I'm happy," Gage said, not very convincingly.

"But you're truly happy when you're with Aurora," his brother countered. "We've all seen it. However, you're determined to keep that wall up around your heart because you're afraid you won't be enough. That our life won't be enough."

"It's not the easiest place to live," Gage conceded.

"Jess might not have been cut out for our life here on the island, but Aurora could be," Reed pointed out with a frustrated frown. "Remove that emotional safety chain you've put on the door to your heart, and let her in. You will be so much happier for it."

Gage grabbed for his raincoat. "What are you, my therapist?"

"Your brother, who happens to love you. As does the rest of your family," Reed told him as he crossed the porch. "I'll meet you two down at the boat." Turning, he made his way down the front porch steps and out into the light drizzle that was falling from the gray September sky.

Was he holding back? Gage wondered. He'd kissed Aurora. Yet, he thought with more than a hint of regret, he hadn't expressed how he'd felt at that moment. Maybe if Reed hadn't interrupted that kiss . . .

The lodge's main door creaked open as Aurora stepped out to join him on the porch. Gage hurried to set the candle on a nearby table while making a mental note to add some petroleum jelly to the door's hinges. Focusing on that helped steer his thoughts away from Aurora's upcoming dinner date with her ex.

"Where's Reed?" she asked, glancing around.

"He went on ahead to the boat to get it ready." He handed Aurora a pair of rain pants, making another mental note to order ones with shorter inseam lengths for their female guests. "They're going to be long, but we'll roll them up, and you'll be good to go."

Smiling, she took the pants from him and walked over to sit down on the edge of one of the porch chairs. "Is everything okay?"

He met her worried gaze. "Sure. Why?"

"You left the lodge kind of abruptly," she told him. "Was it because of Ben's phone call?"

He hesitated before nodding. "I know you want what your sister has. But I don't want to see you settle for less than you deserve out of life."

She laughed. "You think I would reconsider getting back together with Ben?"

Gage shrugged.

"We are not getting back together in that way. He just has something important he wants to talk to me about."

"What's more important than talking to you about how he hopes to win your heart back?"

She fell quiet for a long moment, studying him closely. "Would that bother you?"

He met her scrutinizing stare. "Yes." Well, it was out there now. He'd just taken the chain off his heart's door. That didn't mean he wasn't keeping the toe of his mental shoe against it to keep the door from swinging all the way open.

"Gage," she said with a soft smile. "You're the most thoughtful, caring man I have ever met. Thank you for protecting me where Ben is concerned. I promise not to settle for less than my heart deserves."

Gage felt a mixture of relief and frustration with her reply. Aurora thought he was being protective of her because of what he knew about her broken engagement. Not because he couldn't stomach the thought of her with Ben or any man, sharing time, and laughter, and silly inside jokes. The way Aurora and he had during her stay there.

"Okay," Aurora said, "I'm ready for my boots."

He grabbed a pair that was closest to the door. "These are Mom's. She said for you to wear them out on the boat today. Even if they're a little big, they'll be better than the ones we have for guests," he said, inclining his head toward the row of boots lining the wall beneath the rain jackets and pants.

"That was nice of your mother," Aurora said as she slipped them on. "Perfect fit," she announced as she bent over to work her cuffed rain pants carefully down over them.

Gage watched as she straightened and moved to the

edge of the porch. No awkward wobble. "Looks like I won't need to carry you to the boat."

"It is raining," she replied with a mischievous grin. "There's bound to be lots of mud."

Gage's brows lifted. "You didn't learn your lesson the last time I carried you in the rain?"

She laughed, a beautiful, lilting sound that Gage would never forget. "Apparently not."

CHAPTER THIRTEEN

"I was only kidding," Aurora said, her laughter filling the air.

"I can't have you going home thinking I'm not the sure-footed mountain goat I claimed to be," Gage told her with a grin. Thankfully, the rain was light and the ground far less slick. His mother would never let him hear the end of it if he and Aurora ended up covered in mud again or worse.

"You've definitely proven yourself today."

Gage slowed his gait as they neared the dock where the boat Reed would be taking them out on was waiting.

His brother looked up from the rope he was coiling, his eyes widening beneath the hood of his raincoat. A slow smile spread across his face. "What are you?" he asked. "The island taxi service?"

"Only for special guests," Gage called back as he carefully lowered Aurora to her feet on the wet dock.

"It was a do-over," Aurora explained as they made their way along the dock. "Gage needed to have his pride restored."

"Truth," Gage said with a chuckle as his brother reached out a hand to help Aurora onto the boat.

"The boat's ready to go," Reed announced. Then his gaze took in Aurora's altered rain gear. "Only you could make an oversized raincoat and pants look fashionable."

"It's all in having the proper cuff-folding technique for both pants and jacket sleeves," she explained with a grin. "Today I am attempting the fold-under to keep the rain from pooling in my pants."

After a short safety briefing from Reed, they pulled away from the dock.

"Any word from Hank?" Gage asked.

"Fish are biting. Vick, Mario, and his boys hope to get a full day of fishing in before they leave tomorrow," his brother replied. Then he looked at Aurora. "You haven't met them because they prefer to cook at their cabin. Mario brought his teenage sons for this fishing trip."

"I'll bet the boys have enjoyed being included in this trip. I came across them on my walk one morning." She looked at Gage. "So it appears you're going to have a full flight out in the morning."

Gage nodded. "Last of our guests for the week leave tomorrow." He wished it were going to be just him and Aurora on the flight to Juneau, but it was his job to shuttle guests back and forth, which meant that wasn't going to happen. So he'd set up this private fishing outing with his brother's help.

Aurora moved to stand at the side of the boat, arms crossed in front of her.

"Cold?" Gage asked as he stepped up beside her. There was a bit of a breeze, mixed with the misting rain, making it feel chillier than it actually was.

"No," she replied, shaking her head. "Just trying to take

it all in. I've only really seen these waters from the plane flying in from Seattle and then from your plane. It's a whole different view when you're on a boat right in the middle of it all. The rain-dappled water. The snowy mountain peaks."

A loud whistle sounded from behind them.

They looked to see Reed pointing off to the other side of the boat, just ahead of where they were. "You might want to aim your camera that way," he called out as he slowed the boat.

"Oh, Gage, look!" she exclaimed, frantically scrambling for her camera as she hurried over to the opposite side of the fishing boat.

He followed right behind her, prepared to catch Aurora should she slip on the wet deck in her haste to get another perfect shot. When they reached the rail at the front of the boat, Aurora quickly aimed her camera in the direction of the pod of whales Reed had caught sight of. They were breaching, spouts of water bursting upward as air released from their blowholes mixed with the surface water just above it. Always a sight to behold.

"Those are humpback whales," Gage told Aurora as she snapped pictures of the natural spectacle the boat would soon be passing.

"This is so incredible! I don't even care if it's drizzling out today, or that the water isn't as calm as it could be," she assured him, the awe clear in her voice. "I got to see whales! A whole school of them."

"That's what's known as a pod of whales," Gage explained. "You're catching the tail end of them. By the end of September, they'll be migrating to warmer waters. Some traveling as far as Hawaii before returning to Alaska some-time in April."

She smiled up at him. "There you go again. You know

so much about everything. It's like having my own personal tour guide along with me on this trip." She brought up her camera to snap another shot of the beautiful creatures as they continued their journey.

Gage stood watching, thinking about how intricate and amazing nature was. And how beautiful Aurora was when she was lost in her photographic passion for it all.

Aurora sighed. "It's moments like this that make you forget all about the weather and just appreciate everything around you. From the emerging tails of passing whales to the pine-covered mountains with their snow-capped peaks visible through the light mist of the falling rain."

"You know," Gage said, "I grew up with all of this a part of my everyday life. But when I'm with you, I better understand the saying about living vicariously through someone else. You make me feel like I'm experiencing all of this for the first time."

"I'm so happy I've been able to do that for you," she said, looking up into his eyes.

She had no idea how much her coming into his life had done for him.

"We're going to drop anchor up ahead and see if we can't turn you into a fisherman," Reed called out from where he sat at the wheel.

Delight written all over her face, Aurora hurried to wipe her camera off before returning it to the waterproof bag. "That would be fisher*woman*," she corrected with a grin.

Reed laughed. "My bad."

"Your brother reminds me a lot of Emmy," she told Gage. Reaching out, she braced herself on the aluminum railing as the boat picked up speed again.

"I'm sure he'll appreciate knowing that he reminds you of a woman," Gage said with a chuckle.

Aurora rolled her eyes. "He reminds me of Emmy because they are both artistic. He has the same snarky sense of humor. And he says whatever's on his mind, even if he has to backtrack after the fact."

Gage nodded. "That would be Reed. Truth is, I thought the same thing that evening I spoke to Emmy during our walk to the main lodge."

"Thankfully, she didn't try and track me down when she was questioning your trustworthiness. Can you imagine if those two ever joined forces to torment us?"

The boat slowed to a stop.

"Looks like we're at our spot," Gage told her.

Reed came over to join them, carrying a rod. "Weather's clearing up. Should be a good time to fish."

"I'm so excited for this," she told him. "I used to have a bright pink fishing pole I fished with whenever my family went camping when I was a little girl. But the minuscule fish I would catch back then wouldn't even qualify as bait for some of the ones I've seen caught by your family, and your guests, in that album on the great room's coffee table."

"Maybe we can add one of your catches from today to our 'Big Catch' photo album."

"Count on it." Gage joined in as he took the rod Reed had brought over for Aurora to use.

"I'll leave you to help Aurora get her line cast in," Reed told him. "I'm going to go grab a pole and drop a line of my own."

"We'll cast from the rear of the boat," Gage told her, leading Aurora in the direction Reed had gone, only he moved to the opposite side of the boat.

Aurora listened intently as Gage instructed her on the

weight he'd added to the line to get it to drop down and stay at a good depth. He told her about the lure they were using and how to cast it.

"Now, let's get your line in that water," Gage said once he'd finished going over the basics. "Come on." He motioned for Aurora to come stand close to him. "I'll help you with this first cast."

Together, they cast her line out into the water, and then he instructed her on how to place the base of her rod into one of the mounted holders along the rear side of the charter boat.

"Thatta girl," Gage said as he stepped away. "Now, we wait."

The tip of the rod bowed down seconds later and then bounced back up. Aurora looked at Gage in a panic. "Surely I don't have a bite already."

He chuckled. "I'd say you do."

The rod's shaft curved more sharply.

Aurora let out a startled shriek.

"Wait's over," Gage said with a grin. "Time to reel your catch in."

"Way to go, Aurora!" Reed cheered from where he had cast his line in.

"What do I do?" she asked, eyeing the holder.

Gage moved to stand behind her, instructing Aurora on how to reel her catch in, assisting her when needed. As the caught fish neared the boat, Gage took a large net and scooped it out of the water. Pulling it free, he removed the hook from its mouth and then held up the coho, or silver salmon, as it was also known, for Aurora to see.

Reed let out a low whistle. "That's a beauty!"

"Hold on," she said excitedly, pulling her camera from its bag. "I have to get a picture."

"Oh no, you don't," he told her. "Your catch. Your picture." He held the fish out.

Her eyes widened. "You want me to hold it?"

His brows lifted. "You have no fear of crossing paths with a bear in the woods, but you're nervous about holding a fish up for a picture?"

"A very big fish," she corrected him with a sheepish smile.

Reed snorted.

"Come on, Aurora," Gage said, "you live your life on the edge with all your photographic adventures. You can do this. I'll take a picture so you'll have it to remember your first big catch in Alaska."

After a long hesitation, she sighed. "Okay, I'll hold it. But you had better take the picture quick." She handed her camera over to Reed to hold until Gage made the transfer.

Gage made sure Aurora gripped the fish correctly before wiping his hands off and then taking the camera from his brother. Turning back to face her, he raised the camera and said, "Smile." With a single click, he captured the image of Aurora beaming proudly with her prize catch. One he wouldn't need a picture to remember. It was a memory that would be forever embedded in his mind.

Seeing how comfortable Aurora was while hiking through the woods, flying in his floatplane, even reeling in a fish for dinner, at least with the fish she'd caught after that first one, Gage found himself thinking about how well she would fit into his life if things were different.

Time was running out to sort through his feelings where Aurora was concerned. A part of him wanted to let her go to save himself the heartbreak of another relationship ending due to their two different worlds. But the other part of him already felt the gaping hole she was going to leave behind.

"Dinner was so delicious tonight," Aurora said as Gage walked her back to her cabin.

"It tastes even better when it's your catch," he said as they stepped up onto the tiny rental cabin's front porch.

They stood in silence for a long moment, before Gage said, "Aurora . . ."

Her cell phone rang. She looked fretful. "I'm sorry," she apologized.

"Answer it," he told her.

She pulled her phone from her jacket pocket. Her face lit up. "It's my editor," she said excitedly.

Nodding, he stepped away to give her a bit of privacy.

"Hello . . .? Yes, this is Aurora."

Silence as her editor spoke on the other end of the line.

Gage suddenly felt as anxious as Aurora did, but for different reasons.

"You do?" she gasped. "Yes, I would be very interested." Her gaze snapped up to meet Gage's. "I see. Yes, we can talk more when I get back to Seattle."

Gage couldn't help but catch bits and pieces of her conversation. It sounded promising for Aurora's career.

"That would be wonderful," she replied. "Thank you for calling as soon as you'd made a decision. I know it's fairly late there in New York. I'll be in touch soon."

Gage looked up to see Aurora return her phone to her pocket. "Good news?" he asked as he joined her back on the porch.

"Very," she answered, her eyes alight with happiness. "That was my editor. He called to tell me that they love what I've sent them so far and want to offer me a full-time position with *World Adventures Magazine*."

"That's great news," he told her.

"Except I'll be traveling on their schedule instead of my own," she added with a nervous frown. "To places far away from Emmy and my family in Oregon *and* here."

Gage saw the panic come into her eyes. "This is your dream," he gently reminded her.

"But what if it turns into a 'be careful what you wish for' situation? What if they don't like my photos? What if I don't like traveling so much?"

He smiled. "And what if it turns out to be even better than you dreamed it would be? I've seen your work, Aurora. They are going to love anything you give them."

She looked up, meeting his gaze.

"As far as travel goes," he went on, "I think you were born to do it. You happily soak up any environment you're in with ease, and you will be doing what you love to do. Definitely what I'd call a dream job."

Her mouth lifted into a grateful smile. "Thank you for talking me down. This truly is what I've wanted for so long. I can do this."

"Thatta girl. I'd better head back to the lodge and let you get inside where it's warm," Gage told her. "I'm sure you'll want to make some calls to share your good news with your family and friends."

"And I've taken up your entire day," she agreed. "I guess I'll see you at breakfast in the morning."

"I'll be there."

"Thank you so much for making my last day here so wonderful."

"It was my pleasure," he replied, looking down at her

beautiful face. Trying to burn it into his memory. "See you in the morning."

Aurora rose up on her toes and pressed her lips to his, taking Gage by surprise.

He returned the kiss, his heart filled with all the things he wanted to say to her, wished he'd said to her before that call came in and pulled her life in a new direction.

When the kiss ended, Aurora said, "I'll never forget my time here. Or you, Gage. Good night."

He nodded, unable to speak, and stood there until she had disappeared into the cabin. Then Gage started back to the lodge, his heart heavy. Aurora was sweet, kind, and beautiful, inside and out. Where things had been off between him and Jess, Aurora felt *right*. Emotions he hadn't expected gnawed at his gut.

The retreat wouldn't be the same when Aurora was gone. Her effervescent energy and never-ending desire for adventure had breathed new life into his family. Something that had been missing since his father's stroke. Hiking around the island wouldn't have the same sense of adventure. Gage had truly enjoyed seeing his world anew through Aurora's eyes. And family game nights would lack the challenge Aurora gave him with such glee. Night walks around the retreat would be just that—walks. No more shared laughter beneath star-filled skies.

Gage sighed. He'd known from the beginning that Aurora's being there was only temporary. She had a life and a career she had to return to in Seattle.

"I'm so excited for you!" Emmy shrieked through the phone.

"It's what I've wanted," Aurora replied as she paced the

cabin that had been her home away from home during her stay on Conley Island.

"For forever," Emmy told her. "So why don't you sound more excited about this job offer?"

"I am," Aurora said, trying to have a bit more gusto in her voice.

"Well, that was convincing," her friend said sarcastically. "Now, do you want to tell me what's really going on here?"

Hot tears rushed to Aurora's eyes. "I'm going to miss seeing you as often as I usually do."

"We can video chat when you're out of the country," Emmy assured her.

"I know that," Aurora replied. "So I'm not really sure why I feel so sad. I should be dancing around my cabin."

"Maybe this has more to do with that handsome pilot you've been getting to know during your stay there . . ."

"It has everything to do with Gage," Aurora admitted with a troubled frown. She could always count on Emmy to be her emotional sounding board. She did the same for Emmy.

"So this really isn't some sort of fleeting Alaskan vacation crush," Emmy surmised.

"I wish," Aurora groaned. "How silly am I? Falling for a guy who's not at a place in his life where he's free to put time into a relationship?"

"Why not?" Emmy asked. "People commit to long-distance relationships all the time."

"Right now, Gage's father and the family business have to come first. His father had a stroke last year, and when he came home to continue his rehabilitation, they made a family decision to close off new bookings for a brief period.

That allowed Gage, Reed, and Julia to help their mother with his care."

"I definitely get that," Emmy replied. "Recovery can be a long process. Look at Dad."

Aurora nodded with a frown. "Gage's father was fortunate they were able to fly him to the hospital in Juneau as soon as it happened." Sadly, for Emmy's father, his stroke happened while he was home alone, and getting to the hospital within hours of a stroke made such a difference. "He's made almost a full recovery. The retreat, however, is struggling to get back to what it was. Mostly because guests are being lured away to the Reel and Relax Resort, another fishing retreat that recently opened not far from Conley Island. One that has all the bells and whistles of a luxury resort, including guest spa services."

"Luxury isn't everyone's cup of tea."

"Agreed," Aurora replied. "Places like Living the Good Life Fishing Resort make you feel completely at home while away on a vacation surrounded by nature."

"Sounds like the perfect advertising pitch," Emmy said.

Her friend was right. That pretty much said it all. Aurora filed that away in her mind to run past Gage later.

"Getting back to Gage," her friend said, "we know a lot of people who like to travel. Maybe we can send some their way. If we can help get things turned around for his family's retreat, then he would be free to pursue something with you."

"You're assuming that's what he would want to happen. But other than the kiss we shared, he—"

"Kiss!" her friend exclaimed, cutting Aurora off. "Gage kissed you, and you kept that little tidbit of very important info to yourself?"

Aurora groaned. "I'm sorry, Emmy. I didn't intentionally keep it from you. I've just been dealing with a lot of mixed emotions since coming here. This was supposed to be my honeymoon."

"I know," Emmy said empathetically. "I was hoping that being there would be enough of a distraction to keep you from dwelling on that. I know you have developed some feelings for Gage, but are you also having second thoughts about ending things with Ben?"

"I have no regrets about calling off my engagement. This trip has helped me know for certain that I made the right choice. It's also helped me to discover a lot of things about myself, some of which were things I had forgotten that I enjoyed so much."

"Like what?" her friend asked.

"Like being part of a family game night. And being able to reel in a fish that I caught all by myself," she said proudly. "A really big fish."

"You went fishing?"

"Don't sound so surprised," Aurora told her.

"Sorry. I'm just used to you taking pictures of animals and sea creatures like dolphins or stingrays. I've never known you to actually go fishing."

"I used to when Jade and I were little. Dad would put the worms on the hook for us, and then we'd try our best to cast our lines in. The fish we'd reel in back then could have been canned as sardines. Today's catch, however—a silver salmon—happened to be big enough to keep and cook for dinner at the lodge. It was so good."

"Sounds like you had a pretty good day," Emmy surmised. "So if your mood a little bit ago didn't have anything to do with Ben, does it have anything to do with Gage?"

"Being here, spending time with Gage and his family,

and also finding out that Jade and David are expecting, has me thinking about the family of my own I had hoped to have someday. But with no relationship to speak of and having just committed to a new job, I can't help but fear my dream of having a family of my own is slipping further and further away."

"Why can't you have it all?" her friend asked, direct as always. "I know plenty of women who juggle careers, marriages, and children."

Why couldn't she? Maybe because she didn't want just any man to be a part of her dream future. She wanted—

A knock at the door cut Aurora's thought short.

"Emmy, I have to go. Someone's at the door."

"At this time of night?" her friend replied. "It's after eleven."

Aurora glanced at the time on her phone. "I guess it is."

"Do not open that door," Emmy told her. "Have you never seen those scary movies where the killer stalks the cabin in the woods?"

Aurora rolled her eyes, yet even as she did so, she found herself stepping over to the window to ease the curtain back and take a peek outside. "It's Gage," she told her friend, noting that he looked anxious.

"All the same," her friend replied, "I'll stay on the phone until you find out why he's there."

Aurora walked over to open the door. "Hi."

"I know it's late," he admitted. "But I thought you'd want to see this."

"This?" she repeated.

He smiled and motioned for her to join him out on the porch. As she did so, he pointed up toward the night sky. "Looks like Alaska has a special going-away gift for you."

"The Northern Lights!" Aurora gasped, her heart skipping a beat as she took in the vibrant green and purple glow visible through the openings in the treetops. "Oh, Gage! Thank you so much for coming to get me." She brought her phone back up to her ear. "Emmy, I have to go! The Northern Lights are out!"

"Aurora," her friend replied.

"Yes?" she said distractedly.

"He scores double-digit points for this. Go enjoy."

Aurora hung up and said, "I have to grab my jacket and my camera."

"No need to rush," he told her. "I think the Northern Lights are going to be out for a while."

She hurried to grab her things anyway, not wanting to miss a single moment of the colorful display painted across Alaska's night sky.

"I think our best option for viewing tonight's light display will be down at the dock," Gage told her when she came back out.

"You don't need to walk me down there," she told him. "I know you have to work tomorrow morning. I grabbed the flashlight from the cabin. I'll find my way there."

"I've seen how excited you get over something as simple as a dam-building beaver," he said with a husky chuckle. "There's no way I'm going to miss your reaction to seeing the Northern Lights for the very first time. Beyond this small glimpse of them through the treetops." He took her hand, and they moved down the steps, out onto the path leading down to the docks.

"My heart is pounding," she admitted.

"I tend to have that effect on women," he said with a grin, visible under the glow of the lit sky above.

Aurora laughed giddily. "Not denying it." She felt close to bursting with the happiness she felt inside.

Moments later, they were walking carefully out onto the dock, boats on both sides of them. Thankfully, Gage still held her hand because Aurora surely would have fallen off the side in her distraction. Her gaze was fixed solely on the sky above with its brilliant streaks and swirls of green, blue, and purple.

She couldn't look away from the mesmerizing glow of the Northern Lights as they whirled about in a glorious dance. To add to the beauty, the gently rippling water below mirrored the brilliant colors stretched out across the night sky.

Lifting her camera, Aurora hurried to adjust her settings and snapped a shot, paused, and then several seconds later snapped another. "It's so beautiful," she breathed as she stood capturing the wondrous moment in pictures.

"Like you," Gage said.

Lowering her camera, she looked his way. The ever-changing rainbow of colors above reflected in those brilliant blue eyes. Overcome with emotion, she said, "I don't know how I'm ever going to be able to leave this place."

He drew her into his arms. "I don't know how I'm ever going to let you leave." His gaze slid down to her lips, and then his head lowered.

Closing her eyes, Aurora melted into his sweet kiss. Gage was right. He did have a way of making a woman's heart pound. When the kiss ended, they stood for a long moment, gazing into each other's eyes.

Gage was the first to collect his senses and take a step back. "I shouldn't be keeping you from capturing this incredible sky."

I don't mind, she wanted to say. But as her gaze lifted past him, Aurora saw the ribbons of bright pink that had woven their way through the myriad of colors already lighting up the night sky. A soft gasp left her lips. "It's even more breathtaking than it was moments ago."

"I agree," he said with a smile that carried unspoken words. Gage moved to stand behind her, watching as she captured the mesmerizing light display.

When she was through, she placed her camera back into its bag.

Gage stepped forward, wrapping his arms around her.

Aurora leaned her head back against his broad chest, staring up into the sky above as they stood together in wondrous silence, just taking it all in.

CHAPTER FOURTEEN

As soon as Emmy spotted Aurora standing just inside the doorway of her art gallery, she hurried over to greet her. "I wasn't certain you'd be able to swing by before driving back to Oregon this morning, but I'm so glad you did." Leaning in, she gave Aurora a quick hug and then a kiss on the cheek.

"How could I not support my best friend when she's unveiling her newest pottery creations?" One Emmy had kept secreted away, even from her, until its grand reveal.

Her friend beamed with pride as her attention shifted to the acrylic display table, which held a half dozen handmade glazed pottery plates, each one depicting her friend's artistic envisioning of a stick moose in various settings. Along the water. In a flower-dotted meadow. On a mountainside. And so on.

Aurora was taken back to those special moments she'd had on Conley Island. To the memories she'd created there with Gage. How could it have already been almost two months since she'd returned to her life in Seattle?

Her gaze lowered to the art label in front of the display,

a white card with black lettering. She laughed out loud. "Never Hug a Moose Clay Imaginings?"

Emmy shrugged with a grin. "My trip to Alaska for the conference, along with the pictures you took of the moose there, helped inspire me."

Shaking her head, Aurora said, "I think your moose needs to eat more. Those are far scrawnier than the ones I saw."

Emmy laughed. "Art is subjective. For this collection, the backgrounds are the focal point. Thus, the minimalized abstract moose."

"It's bound to be the hit of your art show," Aurora told her, and then frowned. "I hate to pop in and run, but I have to get on my way to Mom and Dad's." It was a good thing they were having early Thanksgiving, since *World Adventures Magazine* was sending Aurora to Madagascar a few days before Thanksgiving for an article they planned to run in an upcoming publication.

"Tell everyone I said Happy Thanksgiving."

"I will do that."

"And be sure to give your sister a huge hug for me."

"If I can get my arms around her," Aurora said with a grin. "Dad said Jade is really showing already. I told her I'm hoping for twins, after which Jade threatened to sew my lips shut."

Emmy snorted. "Let's hope that doesn't happen. You won't be able to have your bi-weekly phone conversation with Gage."

"True," Aurora said happily. "I definitely need to remember to stay on my sister's good side."

"And don't forget," Emmy said, "you're going to be showing your fabulous photo display *Into the Alaskan Wilds* here next Saturday."

Aurora laughed. "How could I forget? You remind me every time we talk."

"Only because I'm so excited to have my best friend display her incredible photos at my art gallery before she heads off to exotic wildlife shoots all over the world. Getting back to those prints you're going to be showing at my art show," Emmy said, "you have to know they're your best work yet."

"I love my *Sunsets of the World* photograph collection," Aurora said, and then nodded. "But I have to agree, the ones I took in Alaska are truly special."

"And we both know why those pictures turned out as incredible as they did. Do we not?" Emmy asked with a challenging grin.

"I'm just that good?" Aurora replied, trying to avoid a conversation that included her feelings for Gage. Emmy had certainly changed her tune where he was concerned. To her, he was no longer a crazed kidnapper of stranded travelers. He was the man who had rescued her friend's struggling heart. A heart she'd left behind in Alaska with Gage. Even if he didn't know it.

"You are, but I think it's more due to the fact that you were the happiest I've ever known you to be when you were on that island. I heard it in your voice every time we talked. When you filled me in on where Gage had taken you that day to get pictures. When you talked about flying over those glaciers. About picnicking in the rain. Seeing a pod of whales in person for the first time ever. Even playing games at the lodge. And what do all those activities have in common?"

"I had fun?"

"Yes, with Gage," Emmy pointed out. "So I credit him with the extra bit of sparkle I see in the pictures you took while you were there. Clearly, *World Adventures Magazine* saw it, too, because they hired you after only seeing a handful of them. Now get going before I get in trouble for delaying your arrival for Early-Thanksgiving dinner."

Aurora smiled and then leaned in to give her friend a quick hug. "Good luck today. I'll see you when I get back."

"Safe trip," Emmy said with a wave as she turned and melted into the crowd of art-goers, living her best life.

Aurora took one last glance around the art gallery her friend had opened earlier that year. It was something Emmy had been dreaming about most of her adult life. She had renovated an old shoe store she was leasing, added feature walls and had painted everything calm, soothing colors that allowed whatever artwork was on display to take center stage. She'd also put in new flooring, which helped eliminate the creaking you heard when walking on the old wood plank floor. Aurora had helped pick out the modern light fixtures, and Emmy added dimmable spotlights to allow the best lighting possible for each artist's display during art shows. She and Emmy were so fortunate to have seen their career dreams come true. Now, if only they could do the same with their personal lives.

Aurora made her way out of the gathering crowd inside the gallery and walked to her car, which was loaded with baby gifts she hadn't been able to resist buying. Jade might just threaten to sew Aurora's wallet shut, instead of her lips, once she saw everything. Her sister tended to be more of a minimalist. Aurora was not. If anything, Gage was to blame for her out-of-control gift buying. She had discovered that shopping, especially for her soon-to-be niece or nephew, helped take her mind off her unsettled feelings for a certain Alaskan pilot.

It was hard to believe that it had been nearly two

months since she'd stood under that breathtaking Northern Lights sky with him. Or had it been Gage making her breathless that night? She'd been both surprised and elated to receive a call from him the very evening she'd flown back from Juneau. He'd said he was making sure she'd gotten home alright. The calls continued, coming once or twice a week, allowing them to catch up on each other's lives. Their continuing friendship wasn't something she had expected, but she was so grateful Gage made the effort to keep it going. Even if it was a challenge for Aurora to keep her heart from wanting more.

Gage had mentioned, during one of their more recent phone calls, that things were looking up for his family's retreat. Oddly enough, guest reservations had started picking up over the past couple of weeks, despite it being the off-season. People were coming to see the island and its varied wildlife, to stargaze, and to simply spend evenings playing games by the warming fire in the hearth at the lodge.

Aurora hadn't been able to suppress her glee at the news. She had done her best to put the word out about his family's warm and welcoming fishing retreat. Gage and his family had done so much for her during her stay there. If Gage hadn't invested so much of his personal time into helping her get those perfect shots, Aurora wasn't sure her editor would have offered her the position with their magazine over other equally qualified photographers.

When she was about half an hour away from the exit she would get off at to go to her parents' place, Aurora called her sister.

"Sis!" Jade answered.

"Almost home," Aurora said happily.

"I can't wait to see you!"

Aurora smiled. "Same. How are you feeling?"

"I couldn't be better," her sister replied. "Morning sickness is gone. Thank goodness for that. And I'm able to eat all the pistachio ice cream with peanut butter on top that I want and not have anyone question why."

"Ew," Aurora said, cringing at the thought of eating that mixture. Pistachio ice cream was bad enough.

"You say that now," Jade retorted. "Someday you will find yourself also craving things like steak with strawberry jelly, garlic pickles with chocolate milk."

"Again, ew," Aurora told her. "Please stop before I completely lose my appetite." And she wasn't so sure that day her sister spoke about was ever going to come for her. She was twenty-eight years old and doubting she would ever find herself saying *I do*. Mostly because the man she saw herself marrying in her dreams had chosen to keep their relationship on a friendship level.

Her sister's giddy laughter filtered through the phone. "Okay. Just don't look my way at the dinner table when we're eating this evening."

"Noted," Aurora said with a smile. "See you soon."

The call disconnected, and Aurora felt that rush of excitement she got whenever she went home to visit. It was where she needed to be right now. By now, there would be some other town gossip or excitement going on, and her broken engagement would be old news. Truth was, if Ben's mother had anything to do with it, everyone would be fully aware that her son was dating again and head over heels with his new sweetheart.

Ben's new love interest was the reason he'd contacted her in Alaska. He'd wanted to get together so he could introduce her to Charlene. Aurora had to admit she really liked her. And Ben had a special light in his eyes when he looked at Charlene that he hadn't had whenever he'd looked at Aurora. Even when he'd proposed. That dinner with her ex-fiancé had eased any of the remaining guilt Aurora harbored over calling off their wedding. Her decision to set them both free to find the people they were meant to be with had been the right one. Aurora could say, without a doubt, that she was genuinely happy for her still-very-dear friend.

Flipping on her turn signal, Aurora eased over into the exit lane and onto the off-ramp that led to her hometown. Soon, she was passing all the old, familiar landmarks she'd grown up around. Her excitement to be home again grew. She really hoped they would play games like they used to before she graduated from college and moved away to Seattle to start her photography career. Those game nights she'd shared with Gage and his family at the lodge had reminded her of how much she missed out on living so far away from her family.

She also missed spending time with Gage. And, if she were being totally honest with herself, she had to admit that night they'd stood watching the Northern Lights on the dock, she'd felt a spark of hope that things might be able to work out between them somehow. Then, the next morning, while they waited for the other guests to arrive at the float-plane, Gage fed into that hope as he admitted to having feelings for her. Inner exuberance and joy had filled Aurora. And then he'd followed that unexpected statement by saying he wished his situation was different, but they both knew that he wasn't at a place in his life where he was free to pursue a relationship with anyone.

Aurora understood his whys, truly she did, but that didn't stop his words from feeling like the tip of a very sharp needle, bursting her balloon of hopes and dreams. The only response she'd been able to give Gage at that moment had been an offer to show him around Seattle if he was ever in the area. He'd told her he might just take her up on that someday. And that was it, because the other guests arrived and their chance for any further personal conversation came to an end.

She had tried to accept that she and Gage could be nothing more than friends, but his unexpected call that same evening and every week since threatened to reignite that spark of hope she'd felt that night on the dock. Aurora had to constantly remind herself that theirs was only friendship, and if she pushed for more than that, she would find herself in Ben's shoes—on the receiving end of a breakup.

Gage stood on the boat dock, watching Reed and Hank lead their newly arriving guests away to the main lodge. Despite it being late in the season for their usual bookings, guests were still coming in. If not to fish, then to just get away from it all and unwind, which was a new reason they were being given when some of their guests booked a stay. He wasn't about to question intentions. A reservation was a reservation. Besides, Julia had said she'd been working on getting their retreat information out on more online social platforms. Apparently, whatever his sister was doing was working.

Turning, Gage walked out to the end of the dock, the wintry wind gusting between the two docked fishing boats tossing his wavy hair about. After raising the collar of his winter jacket, he tucked his hands into its pockets to warm them. How was it even possible that it had been almost two months since he'd stood on that same dock with Aurora, watching the brilliance of the Northern Lights dance across the fall night sky?

Forty-three days to be exact. Sharing nature's light show with Aurora that night had been an unexpectedly profound moment in his life. So much so that the memory surfaced every time he stepped back out onto that dock. And in his dreams. And when he took walks. Thankfully, his plane had been put in storage for the winter. He couldn't afford to be distracted when flying guests back and forth from Juneau. This time of year, they used one of their boats for runs into Juneau and back.

Gage's phone vibrated in the back pocket of his jeans, its ringtone cutting into the surrounding silence and his distracted thoughts. Slipping it free, he glanced down at the lit screen. Then he quickly brought the phone to his ear.

"Hello," he answered with a widening smile.

"Hi," Aurora replied on the other end. "Am I catching you at a bad time?"

Gage frowned as the call dropped in and out. "I'm out on the boat dock, and the connection here isn't the best."

"I can let you go."

"No," he practically shouted in protest. "I mean, there's no need to hang up. Give me a moment to walk up closer to the cabins. The signal should get a little clearer there."

"Okay. I can . . ." The rest of her words were too muffled to make out.

"If you can hear me," he told her, "I'm heading up to the main lodge."

The call disconnected.

Gage growled in frustration. The weather wasn't helping the phone service that afternoon. He quickly punched in Aurora's number, which he had memorized, despite having it already saved in his phone's contact list.

"Hello again," she answered.

"Any better yet?"

"A little," she replied. "It sounds windy there."

"We're expecting a little bit of a squall here shortly," he told her. "The winds are starting to kick up, but I'm almost to the path. The trees should help block some of the wind." He wasn't as confident in the cell service.

"Well, we can give this one more try," she said. "I'm on my way up to Oregon and am almost to my parents' place. We're having what Mom is calling Early-Thanksgiving dinner because my sister's husband is going to be working at the hospital over the actual holiday, and I'm going to be leaving for Madagascar on assignment that same week."

"Madagascar?" he repeated, not sure he had heard her correctly.

"Yes!" she replied. "Isn't it exciting? The magazine is doing an article on lemurs. I'll be—" Static washed out the rest of her words.

She sounded so happy.

"Gage? You still there?"

"I'm here."

"I was saying that I'm really looking forward to seeing my family again," she repeated. "Especially Jade."

"How is your sister doing?" he asked, his stride length-ening as he moved along the path that led up to the lodge.

"Wonderful, except she's craving the most unappealing food combinations."

Gage laughed. "And how are things going with you? Besides getting to travel all over the world."

"You cut out," she said. "Can you repeat that?"

He frowned, wishing he were already back at the lodge. He'd have a much better connection there. "Anything new in your life?" he asked.

"I was finally able to meet up with Ben," she told him.

Gage's gut twisted. "And how did that go?"

She began to speak, but her words were garbled. Then the reception cleared up long enough for him to hear, "It just felt right, and I couldn't be happier."

Before Gage could respond, not that he even knew how he was supposed to reply to that, the call disconnected. He stood staring at the phone. Aurora and Ben had worked things out? The knot in his gut grew.

Gage looked down at his phone, wanting to call Aurora back and ask her if she was sure about her decision to reconcile, but he wasn't in the right head space at that moment to hear about her and Ben's reunion. He would touch base with her after she returned from her visit with her family, after he'd had time to process the news and could react less emotionally.

He continued up to the main lodge, where he stepped up onto the porch. But instead of going inside, he moved to stand at the railing, looking out over the land that he had spent most of his life traversing. His gaze came to the spot in the path where he and Aurora had taken their spill in the mud. She hadn't panicked when she'd gotten mud all over herself. She never complained about the cold when she was here. Or the rain. Unlike his ex, Aurora thrived on the remoteness of Conley Island. Endured the elements with nothing but appreciation. Like the phenomenon she was named after, Aurora was a rare beauty.

He'd let her get away without telling her how he felt. Well, he'd opened up a little bit, but then he'd put that proverbial chain back on his heart's door and given her all the reasons why things wouldn't work between them. He'd been trying to woo her back through phone calls. Too slowly, it seemed. Because now it was too late. She and Ben had reconciled. The pain in his heart at losing her again, this time for good, nearly threatened to suck all the air from his lungs. How had he ever thought himself in love with Jess? He hadn't felt anything close to what he felt after Aurora left Juneau. What he felt now. Aurora was the only one his heart had ever truly wanted.

The lodge's main door opened, and Gage heard footsteps on the porch behind him. He stood silent, hoping whoever it was would just continue on their way to their cabin without trying to strike up friendly conversation. He wasn't feeling sociable at that moment. Just empty.

"Last time I saw you standing in that very spot, you were caught in a lip lock with a pretty and somewhat muddied photographer."

His brother. "Not now, Reed," he said through gritted teeth as he fought to keep his emotions at bay.

"Gage?" his brother said as he moved to stand beside him. "What's wrong?"

Gage shook his head.

"Are you ill?" Reed pressed.

Sick to his stomach? Yes. "Aurora and Ben are back together," he said, knowing Reed was stubborn and would press until he found out what was wrong. "Aurora called me on her way to her parents'."

"You must have misunderstood her," Reed replied. "She was very clear that their relationship was over."

"Apparently, Aurora had a change of heart." The words came out tight and chock-full of the emotion he felt at that moment.

"Or is she taking what she can get because she doesn't think she can have what she wants?"

Gage turned to look at his brother. "I've been calling her, and that didn't make a difference."

"Calling her and laying your heart out on the line are two different things. Have you told her that you're in love with her during any of your phone calls?"

"I open up to her about what's going on in my life," he said in his own defense. "I always ask about hers. I've told her how grateful I am to have her in my life."

"I'm no expert," Reed admitted, "but I'm not sure that screams 'you have my heart.' Think about it, Gage. Flannel shirts are in your life. Your floatplane is in your life. That doesn't mean you would marry either of them."

Gage frowned. His brother was right. "I should have been more open with my feelings." He met Reed's worried gaze. "I can't let Aurora walk away from what we could have had to settle for a life with Ben that's not what she's always dreamed of having."

"Then don't."

"I can't call her right now," Gage said. "She's at her parents' place having their family's early Thanksgiving dinner. But I intend to call her when she gets back to Seattle. Before she leaves for her next assignment." Before things progressed too far with her ex.

"Speaking of Aurora's job," Reed said, "I almost forgot the reason I came out to find you."

Gage looked up questioningly.

Reed pulled out his phone, tapped the screen, and then turned it so Gage could see.

He looked down, seeing a photograph of the main lodge from probably fifty or so feet away. "Why are you showing me a picture you took of the lodge?"

"I didn't take it," his brother replied. He zoomed out, showing more of the page. "Read the caption."

"*Fishing and Frolicking in This Alaskan Island Paradise,*" Gage read, then looked to Reed in confusion.

"Mom was checking in our new guests, and one of them mentioned reading about our place in *World Adventures Magazine.*"

Gage's eyes widened. "What?"

"Apparently, they also have a digital magazine as well as their print subscription, and our guests found us through that write-up about our place. Scroll down. Read the article."

Gage scrolled slowly down through the brief write-up. It referred to the island fishing retreat being so much more than reeling in that perfect catch. How this hidden gem in the Alaskan wilderness offered both the comforts of home and the excitement of experiencing all the wondrous things that nature has to offer. Then the writer talked about how she'd not only fallen in love with Conley Island and the cozy little retreat but had also left her heart there with a fun, dependable, mountain goat of a man when she'd returned to her life in Seattle.

Gage's heart drummed hard in his chest in response to the words she'd written. Lowering the phone, he looked at his brother.

"I suppose I don't have to scroll up to the top to show you who wrote this article," Reed said as he retrieved his phone from Gage's grasp.

"Aurora," Gage breathed, his mind still reeling over her ending words. She'd left her heart here—with him.

CHAPTER FIFTEEN

"I can't believe I have to head back to Seattle tomorrow," Aurora said, tears in her eyes. "Even worse, my relocation deadline is getting closer. I'm not sure I'm ready to leave Seattle. Or this little one I haven't even had the chance to meet and love up yet." Reaching out, she ran a hand over her sister's adorable little baby bump.

"You have to be here when I have her," Jade said with a pout.

"The moment I hear you've gone into labor, I'll catch the first flight out from wherever I am at that time." Because she would be traveling. That was a given. Hopefully, her sister would deliver on time. Aurora would plan her travel schedule around Jade's due date, give or take a week on either side, just to be safe.

But what if she couldn't get there right away because the flights were all booked? Or a mandatory meeting in the editorial offices that she had to take part in? What if something happened that Aurora didn't even want to think about, and she wasn't here with her sister when she needed her most?

"I know you'll do your best to get here," her sister replied with a loving smile. "But you've been given this wonderful opportunity that you've been dreaming of for so long. If getting home puts your dream job in jeopardy, I don't want you to risk it."

"I love being a professional wildlife photographer," Aurora admitted, "but I've been doing a lot of thinking since flying home from Alaska."

"Thinking about what?"

"About whether or not the timing was right for this career opportunity to come into my life."

"Aurora," Jade gasped, "you're not seriously thinking about quitting the magazine."

Aurora frowned. For the first time since she'd received the call telling her *World Adventures Magazine* wanted to offer her a position with their company, she was considering not only the positives of doing so, but the negatives as well. She didn't want to constantly be in some far-away country when everyone she cared about was on the West Coast. Especially now that her sister was expecting. "I want this job, but I also want to be around for long enough periods of time to allow me to be a part of my new little nephew's or niece's life as they're growing up. Not easily done when you're thousands of miles away."

"Niece," her sister interjected.

Aurora's gaze lifted from the loose piece of thread on the quilt she'd been fidgeting with. "What?"

Jade giggled, something Aurora noticed she did far more often than she used to. Pregnancy and the nearing arrival of her first child had softened her sister, made her so much happier with everything in the world around her.

Jade leaned in and, in a conspiratorial whisper, said, "David and I are having a girl."

Scrambling to her knees on the queen-size bed, Aurora leaned over to give her little sister a hug. "Oh, Jade, I'm so happy for you! And how exciting to know what your baby is going to be!"

"Shhh . . . not so loud," she said, hushing Aurora. "Mom and Dad don't know yet."

"Oops," she replied in a hushed tone.

"We're telling them at family dinner tonight, but I couldn't wait to share my little secret with my lifelong best friend and sister," Jade told Aurora as she smoothed a hand down over her rounded abdomen.

"Mom is going to be so excited when she finds out you're having a girl," Aurora said with glee.

Her sister's smile widened. "I know."

"I certainly am," Aurora told her. "Oh my goodness, knowing that I'm going to have a niece soon makes this all seem so much more real."

"Tell me about it."

"I promise to be the best aunt ever for that precious little one you're carrying."

"I have no doubt about that whatsoever," Jade said with a tender smile. "I also know, without a doubt, that you are going to be her favorite aunt."

Aurora laughed. "I would certainly hope so, seeing as I'm her only aunt."

"Knock, knock."

They looked up as the bedroom door creaked open, and their mother poked her head inside. "I thought I would find you girls in here reminiscing."

Aurora's bedroom was where she and her sister had spent hours upon hours of sisterly bonding time while growing up, sharing troubles, joys, secrets, and talking about boys.

"Come in and join us," Aurora said, patting the empty spot on the bed beside her.

Their mother crossed the room and settled comfortably onto the edge of the bed. "I'm so happy to have both of my girls here with me." Her smile quivered as she looked at Aurora. "I'm so proud of you for going after your dream. I just wish that dream didn't take you to places so far away. Motherly whining aside, I know this new job opportunity is going to be so very exciting for you."

"I'll be home as often as I can to visit," Aurora assured her. Her mother and father always made time to drive up to Seattle to visit her once or twice a year.

"Of course you will," Jade agreed. "This little one is going to need to have his or her aunt in their life." She looked at Aurora with a conspiratorial wink.

Guilt filled Aurora, knowing she might not be able to be there for her niece as much as she would like to be. But there were phone calls and video chats. She would make it a priority to use every source of communication she had to build that special relationship.

"Mom . . ." she said.

"Yes?" her mother replied.

"How did you know Dad was the one?"

Her mother looked surprised by the question and then smiled. "I would have to say that my heart knew first," she told her. "My head, however, took a little bit longer to catch up. I knew I was almost done with the job I was sent there to do in Alaska and would be heading to Glacier National Park next. I couldn't allow myself to start something I wouldn't be around to continue. Your father's job in Alaska was permanent. It hurt my heart, knowing that our time there was coming to an end."

Aurora understood that feeling. She had experienced it during her last few days there on Conley Island.

"A few nights before I was supposed to leave Alaska," their mother went on, "your father asked me out for a goodbye dinner. On our way back after eating, the night sky came alive with the most wondrous colors. We pulled off the main road and then sat on the hood of his car, watching the Northern Lights swirl all around us."

"How romantic," Jade said, tearing up. Something she also did more often since becoming pregnant.

Their mother nodded. "The Northern Lights took my breath away. At least, I thought it was the colorful phenomenon above us causing it. But the longer I sat there with your father, the more I realized it was being there with him that made it hard for me to breathe. I was in love with this man I had worked alongside professionally. That night, your father told me he loved me, and I knew I couldn't walk away from what we had between us. I ended up staying and going to work for his company. We married and stayed in Alaska until we started our family. Then, we moved here to Oregon, where your father's family was from, and have been here ever since."

"I just love that story," Aurora said with a sigh.

Their mother looked her way. "Trust your heart, sweetie. When it's right, your heart will let you know."

Aurora was pretty certain hers already did. She nodded her response.

"Is it almost time to eat?" Jade asked. "I'm starving."

"You've been eating all day," Aurora teased.

"*We've* been eating all day," her sister replied with a playful jab at her expanding abdomen.

Aurora's cell phone vibrated in the back pocket of her jeans, signaling the arrival of a text. Slipping it free, she glanced down to see that Gage had sent her a text. As it always did whenever he called or texted, her heart did a little flip.

Clicking on the screen to open the message, Aurora read what he'd sent her:

> I just wanted to wish you and your family a Happy 'Early' Thanksgiving!

"What, or maybe we should ask who, just put that big ol' smile on your face?" her mother inquired with a querying glance.

"I bet I know," Jade said in a singsong reply.

Aurora smiled. "Gage texted me to wish all of us a happy Early Thanksgiving."

"Oh, that was really sweet of him," her mother said.

"That's Gage," Aurora told them. "Always thinking of others."

If he only knew how often she thought of him. When Aurora had least expected it, she had found love under the Northern Lights, just as her parents had all those years ago. Things hadn't worked out as easily for her and Gage as they had for her mother and father. But anything worth having was worth investing the time into getting. She loved Gage. That was the first time she admitted that to herself.

"I love him," Aurora said aloud.

Both her mother's and Jade's eyes widened with that blurted-out admission, joy lighting their faces.

"I knew it!" Jade exclaimed.

"The Northern Lights did it again!" her mother declared in delight.

"I think the connection happened long before that," Aurora told them. "I think something special sparked between us the moment I shoved the rain-soaked hood of my poncho back, and our eyes met. Not that I'm saying he felt the same way. That's just how I felt. It's just taken me a while to acknowledge it for what it is."

"That meet-cute is right up there with Mom and Dad's," Jade decided. "So, what are you going to do about it?"

"It's not a conversation I want to have with Gage over the phone," Aurora replied. "I have that art show this coming Saturday at Emmy's studio. If I can get a flight out on Sunday, I'm going to make my way back to Conley Island to tell Gage in person how I really feel."

"Oh, honey," her mom said, "I'm so happy you found someone who makes your heart smile."

"He does, Mom," Aurora replied wistfully. "More than I ever thought possible."

"As your mother, I should probably be asking about your career," her mother said with a tender smile. "But I know firsthand that you can have love and still follow your career dreams."

Aurora returned her smile. "You've always been my role model. Both as a mother and as a career professional." Her mother had taken some time off to raise her daughters, and when the time was right, she had gone back to work.

Her mother leaned in to hug her. "Love you, sweetie." Then she straightened and looked at Jade. "Both of you."

"Love you back," Aurora said.

"Ditto," Jade chimed in.

It was possible to have it all, Aurora thought excitedly. But you have to be willing to take a risk to make your dreams come true. A future with Gage was so worth the risk.

"Welcome back," Emmy greeted with a hug when Aurora arrived at her art studio.

"Sorry I'm late," Aurora said. "I had an unexpected conference call with my editor that ran over."

"The magazine isn't having second thoughts on the new arrangement they agreed to, are they?" her best friend asked with a worried frown.

Aurora smiled. "Not at all. Eugene wanted to tell me their online numbers for my article on Gage's family retreat were beyond their expectations and that they'd like me to do a follow-up article about river fishing on Conley Island in the spring."

"Oh, Aurora," her friend exclaimed. "How perfect!"

Aurora nodded. "It was definitely an assignment I couldn't refuse." She glanced around. "Great turnout."

"Beyond expectations," Emmy replied. "Just like your article."

Aurora smiled, catching sight of her *Into the Alaskan Wilds* prints displayed prominently on one of two focal walls across the room. She crossed over to it, her gaze fixed on the largest framed picture in the center, and her heart tugged. She would never think about the Northern Lights again without Gage being included. Oh, how she missed that charming grin of his. Aurora sighed.

"You didn't have to be here today," Emmy said as she joined her at the wall. "I would have understood if your heart urged you to leave a day sooner to see him."

Aurora glanced over at her dear, sweet, always-supportive friend. "I want to be here."

"But not as much as you want to be somewhere else," Emmy replied with a knowing smile.

Aurora's mouth curled upward as she shook her head, answering honestly, "No, not as much." Emmy wouldn't take offense. She knew how Aurora felt about Gage and about her plans to fly out the next morning to Juneau. There, she intended to take a boat she'd hired to Conley Island to pay Gage and his family a surprise visit.

"I'm glad you came in anyway," Emmy said. "I know you have packing to do."

"Of course I'm going to be here," Aurora said, laughing softly. "I might be in love with Gage, but you will always be my best friend. I'm honored to be a part of your art show."

"Well, that's convenient," a deep voice said from behind, "because Gage is in love with you."

Aurora spun to face him with a gasp. "Gage?"

Emmy's smile widened. "If you two will excuse me, I have guests to see to." Her gaze went to Gage. "Took you long enough."

Gage chuckled, his focus solely on Aurora. "Too long."

Stepping forward, Emmy gave Aurora a hug, whispering in her ear, "Dreams do come true." Then she released her and walked away humming a happy tune.

"Gage?" Aurora said again, still shocked to see him standing there. Was she dreaming this? She looked around. Everything looked real. Felt real.

"Has it been that long?" he replied with a grin. "Long enough that you aren't even sure it's me?"

Her hand flew to her pounding heart. "I can't believe you're really here."

He nodded. "I'm here."

"But I'm supposed to be there."

"There?" he repeated.

"At your family's retreat," she told him. "I have a ticket booked for Juneau tomorrow morning."

"Your magazine is sending you back for more pictures?"

She laughed. "Not this trip. My going back to Conley

Island has nothing to do with my job and everything to do with you."

He stepped forward, drawing her into his strong arms. "Apparently, great minds really do think alike, because my being here has everything to do with you." He searched her eyes. "I've missed you like crazy, Aurora."

"I've missed you, too," she said, heart pounding.

"I look at those pictures you sent me, the ones you took when you were staying at the retreat, every morning when I wake up and every night when I go to bed. I remember with so much clarity each and every one of those moments we shared together."

"I do too."

His gaze lifted to the picture displayed on the wall behind her. "Your parents were right about the magic of the Northern Lights. That night out on the dock, I knew I wasn't just falling. I knew I was totally and completely in love with you."

"Same," she breathed.

"I never should have let you go without telling you how deeply I feel for you. Even if I couldn't make any real commitment at that time." His attention returned to her, love and adoration so clear in his eyes. "Thank you for what you did for me and my family."

"You know about the article?"

He nodded. "I do. Guests staying at the retreat this past week mentioned they had read about Living the Good Life Fishing Retreat in an online article through your magazine. They were intrigued enough by your write-up and the accompanying photos to book a stay. Despite it being the off-season for most things, we still have guests coming in. Reed showed me the article he found online."

"I wanted to repay your family's kindness," she told him.

"I'd say you went above and beyond," he told her with an appreciative smile. "And my whole family is indebted to you for it."

"When you care about someone, you want the best for them. If there was any chance I could help, I had to try."

"You helped us more than you'll ever know, and for that, I'll be forever grateful. But I'm not here because of my gratitude; I'm here for you," he said, smiling tenderly down at her.

Tears filled Aurora's eyes, blurring Gage's handsome, hopeful face.

"When you left Alaska, I thought I might lose you to Ben, but he never came up in our conversations, so I didn't know where the two of you stood. I was too afraid to ask."

"Ben?" she repeated in surprise and then shook her head. "I never had any intention of getting back with him. In fact, he's going to be proposing to Charlene—that's his girlfriend—over Christmas. He wanted me to meet her, which was why he'd called when I was in Juneau. But our schedules didn't line up until recently for him to tell me his good news. I met her, Gage, and I really like her. I'm so happy Ben found her."

"That day our phone call was cutting out . . . I thought . . . oh, geez," he groaned. "I've been going out of my mind at the thought of you reconsidering your decision not to marry Ben. And then, while you were at your family's Early Thanksgiving, I discovered the article you'd done for your magazine. The one about having left your heart with a mountain goat of a man on Conley Island." He smiled. "I also knew I had to put my heart out there before it was too late, and you married for something other than true love. So here I am."

Before Aurora could respond, Gage knelt before her, pulling a small, navy-blue satin ring box from his coat pocket.

She gasped.

Opening it, he held it up for Aurora to see. The ring nestled snugly inside the satin lining wasn't the traditional diamond-focused setting. Instead, there were two thin gold bands woven around each other to form one single band. Mounted at the top, surrounded by small, sparkling diamonds was a beautiful oval-shaped opal. One that held all the colors of the Northern Lights.

"Gage," she said, her gaze lifted to meet his.

"Marry me, Aurora. Let me be the man to love and support you as you travel around the world on assignments, living your dream. Together, we'll find a way to make this work."

"I'm not going to be traveling as often as I first expected to," she told him.

"You're not?"

Being able to tell him that filled her with so much joy. "I spoke to my editor while I was in Oregon, and we were able to come to an agreement about the amount of time I'm away on assignments. Better yet, they loved my Alaska photos. They have several articles coming up that they'd like me to cover there. One is on discovering wildlife on the move from a floatplane. But I'd need a pilot with a plane."

"You've got him."

"I was hoping you'd say that," she replied. "I was going to tell you all of this when I got to the retreat. I'm not about to give up on my heart's dream for the sake of my career dream. Not when I can have both."

"I love you, Aurora," he told her. "I would move mountains for you."

"Or climb them," she teased. "Being the mountain goat you are."

"Or climb them," he agreed with a chuckle. "If you're willing to relocate to Conley Island—"

"I am," she blurted out. "I can't think of anywhere else I'd rather live than where you are."

Gage smiled. "I was going to say I would move to Seattle if that's what it takes."

"No need," she said excitedly. "I happen to love everything about Conley Island. Especially this handsome float-plane pilot I met while staying there."

"He loves you too. So much so, I drew up plans to add an actual gift shop onto the lodge. One that I thought could carry some of your incredible prints. Maybe even some of Emmy's artwork, if she's interested."

Her heart was bursting with happiness and love. Aurora looked at the ring box Gage held in his hand.

"I know it's not the traditional diamond a man gives to a woman he's asking to marry him, but I knew this was the ring for you as soon as I saw it in the jeweler's display case. That opal in the middle carries all the breathtaking colors we saw swirling across the sky that last night."

"It's so perfect," she breathed. "I love it so much, Gage." Her tear-filled gaze lifted to meet his. "I love you so much."

"Then say yes!" The crowd's impatient chant echoed throughout the gallery. Aurora glanced around to find Emmy and every person in her art gallery standing there watching them. Heat flooded her cheeks.

"I like their way of thinking," Gage told her with a grin.

"I do too." Aurora's smile bloomed, and her heart threatened to burst with the happiness she felt inside. Just as her parents had done, she too had found true love under the Northern Lights. "Yes!" she told him. "I will marry you, Gage Weston."

Cheers rose up around them as he lifted the opal engagement ring from its velvety nest and slid it onto her finger.

It fit so perfectly, just like Gage did into her life.

He stood, drawing Aurora into his arms for a kiss that promised a lifetime of happiness and adventures, and, more importantly, love.

"You're back!" Glady exclaimed when Gage and Aurora stepped into the diner where they had first met, her happy gaze fixed on Aurora.

"I just couldn't stay away," she replied, glancing up lovingly at Gage.

"Is that a spark I see?" the older woman said in delight as she crossed the dining room to greet them.

Gage chuckled. "Nothing gets past you."

"We wanted to share our good news," Aurora said, beaming with happiness. Lifting her hand, she said, "Gage and I are getting married."

Glady gasped. She looked at Gage. "Does your mother know?"

He nodded. "She does."

"Constance never said a peep about it," she huffed.

"She was sworn to secrecy," Aurora told her. "We wanted to tell you in person. If you hadn't suggested that Gage take me to his family's retreat, I never would have found the love I'd dreamed about my whole life."

Tears filled Glady's eyes. "I'm so happy for the two of

you. Everyone deserves to find love. I'm so glad my little nudge helped the two of you to find it." Stepping forward, she gave them each a congratulatory hug.

"We know you've got a diner to run, but we'd love to have you join us for our wedding, if you can make it," Gage told her. "The ceremony is going to be at the lodge with our family and closest friends."

"Gage will be flying everyone to the island, and we've blocked off that weekend so our guests can stay over," Aurora added.

"Just give me the date," Glady told them. "I'll be there."

After exchanging information and saying their good-byes, Gage and Aurora headed outside. They had one more invite to extend before flying to the island.

They made their way through town, hand in hand.

"There he is," Aurora said excitedly, pointing to one of the benches across the street.

Crossing over, they headed along the sidewalk in that direction.

"Hello, Mr. Wilson," Aurora said when they arrived at the occupied bench.

The man, whose back had been to them as he leaned over to scratch his faithful companion behind her ear, paused to glance back over his shoulder. His eyes lit with recognition.

"Well, hello."

Bailey began wagging her tail excitedly.

"We were hoping to find you in town today," Gage told him.

"Unless the weather's poor, you'll find us out roaming about," Mr. Wilson answered. "Bailey needs her daily walks, and we like to people watch afterward." He looked at Aurora. "Glady said you'd gone back to Seattle."

"I did," Aurora replied. "But I'm going to be calling Conley Island my home very soon. Gage asked me to marry him." She held up her hand, giving her fingers a flutter.

"Well, I'll be." His gaze shifted to Gage. "Smart boy. Glady and I thought you let this pretty little thing slip through your fingers."

"I nearly did," Gage admitted, and then looked to Aurora. "Lucky for me, she's a patient woman."

"Congratulations," Mr. Wilson said with a widening smile.

Bailey barked as if in agreement.

"We'd like to invite you to our wedding," Aurora told him. "Bailey too. Gage will fly everyone to the island, and we'll have cabins available for all our guests."

"I'm honored." Mr. Wilson's eyes misted over.

"No," Gage said, "we'd be honored to have you join us."

Mr. Wilson looked at his dog. "What do you think, Bailey girl?"

Bailey barked several times and then nudged her nose under Aurora's hand.

"I'd say that's a yes," Aurora said with a giggle, her engagement ring sparkling under the afternoon sun as she petted the affectionate pup.

"Glady will be there too," Gage told him.

"We'll be sure to sit you next to her," Aurora said with a smile.

"I . . . uh . . . that would be nice," Mr. Wilson replied, his gaze drifting off in the direction of the diner.

"Glady has all the details for the wedding," Gage said. "But I'm sure we'll see you again before then. Enjoy the sunshine."

With a wave, Aurora and Gage walked away. She

glanced up at Gage. "Glady isn't the only one who thinks everyone deserves to find love."

He nodded. "Now it's our turn to repay the favor.

"Maybe the Northern Lights will be out on the night we get married," Aurora said hopefully. She knew firsthand the magic a Northern Lights sky had.

"For Glady and Mr. Wilson's sakes, I certainly hope so," Gage said with a conspiratorial wink.

Aurora laughed. "Life with you is going to be such an adventure."

His tender gaze sought her out. "I wouldn't have it any other way."

ACKNOWLEDGMENTS

I want to thank my wonderful agent, Michelle Grajkowski at Three Seas Literary Agency, for always believing in my ability to write a story that touches the heart in some way.

I want to thank Jenny Hale, founder of Harpeth Road Press, for getting my voice and offering me a place in the Harpeth author family. Your faith in my story means so much.

I want to thank my editorial staff at Harpeth Road Press, who helped polish and shine my story into so much more. Your work and suggestions were greatly appreciated.

I want to thank my family. My husband for his never-ending support. My daughters for their love and ability to bring me back to reality when needed. My grandson, Eston, for reminding me how much love a heart can hold. And my mom for always being there for me, and for proofreading my manuscripts before I send them off to my publisher.

I'd like to add a final heartfelt thank you to my besties (you know who you are). Thank you for sharing the laughter and tears that life brings our way.

Last, but not least, I'd like to give a special mention to 1820 House Co. Candle Company. The inspiration for my fictional candle store in *Under the Northern Lights*. The real-life store is run by Melissa Smith and her daughter, Sidney. These impressive women managed to keep their business thriving through not only COVID, but the nation-wide news-making, toxic train derailment in East Palestine,

Ohio, two years ago. I was so impressed by their persever-
ance, and by their wonderful candles, I was inspired to give
them a special place in my story. If you want to read more
about the 1820 House Co. Candle Company, you can go to
https://1820co.com/.

Hello readers!

I'm so happy you decided to pick up my novel, *Under The Northern Lights*. I hope you felt a part of Gage and Aurora's emotional journey to find love. Opening your heart can leave you vulnerable to heartache, but you'll never find true love without doing so. Gage and Aurora took the risk and found true happiness *Under The Northern Lights*.

If you'd like to know when my next book is out, you can sign up for Harpeth Road release alerts for my novels here:

www.harpethroad.com/lindsey-brookes-newsletter-signup

Your information won't be shared with anyone else. I'll only email you a brief message whenever I have new books come out or ones go on sale.

If you enjoyed reading Gage and Aurora's love story in *Under The Northern Lights*, I'd really appreciate it if you could write a review for it online. Feedback from my readers helps others who are considering picking up one of my books for the first time.

I look forward to sharing more heartwarming, happily-ever-afters with you in the future.

Happy reading!

Lindsey Brookes